Also by Ev Bishop

Bigger Things

A Sharla Brown Christmas

Wedding Bands (River's Sigh B & B, Book 1)

Hooked (River's Sigh B & B, Book 2)

Spoons (River's Sigh B & B, Book 3)

Hook, Line & Sinker (River's Sigh B & B, Book 4)

Silver Bells
(A River's Sigh B & B Christmas novella, Book 5)

Reeling (River's Sigh B & B, Book 6)

New Year's Resolution: One To Keep
(A River's Sigh B & B novella, Book 7)

The Catch (River's Sigh B & B, Book 8)

Writing as Toni Sheridan

The Present

Drummer Boy

EV BISHOP

The Catch

River's Sigh B & B, Book 8

THE CATCH
Book 8 in the River's Sigh B & B series
Copyright © 2020 Ev Bishop

Print Edition

Published by Winding Path Books

ISBN 978-1-77265-035-8

Cover image: Kimberly Killion / The Killion Group Inc.

The Catch is a work of fiction. Names, characters, places, and incidents are either the product of the author's imagination or are used fictitiously, and any resemblance to actual persons, living or dead, business establishments, events or locales is entirely coincidental.

To my mom, Susanne Marguerite Higginson, nee Forsyth

1953 – 1995

This isn't the first book I've dedicated to you and it won't be the last. I still miss you every day.

Love,
Ev

Chapter 1

MOTHER NATURE WAS AS BUSY revamping as the rest of the staff at River's Sigh B & B. Everywhere Aisha looked as she walked the trail to Minnow cabin, a lush green had replaced the dingy gray-brown of days earlier. Bursts of purple, white and yellow from crocuses, narcissi, and snowdrops popped everywhere—much to Mo's delight as she tromped alongside her mom. The sun had shed its wintery reserve and carried heat again, kissing every branch and bush with buds. Spring. It was usually a time of year Aisha loved, but today it kindled nostalgia and a strange longing, though for what exactly she couldn't say. (More like *won't admit*, her inner self snarked.)

She inhaled deeply. The cool, damp air smelled of fertile earth and the sharp sap of new growth. It should've been energizing and invigorating. Instead, it made her eyes tear.

Each sensory detail was as painful as catching yourself on a thorn in a blackberry patch, a reminder that just like the seasons did every year, whether you were prepared for them to or not, everything changed.

It was inevitable. And yet . . . could she seriously be considering leaving River's Sigh? Was she really willing to forsake tiny Minnow cabin, which had been her and baby Mo's refuge for all these impossibly sweet years? Then again, if someone had beaten her to the punch, was opening the very business she herself wanted to run, didn't she have to move? There wasn't room for two such similar shops in their small town.

Mo, Aisha's "baby," shuffled through a pile of twigs, smiling as they crunched under her boots and singing in the tinkly soprano of a little girl. *A little girl.* And that, in a nutshell, was why Aisha had the inevitability of change on her mind. As beloved as this place was and as much of a sanctuary as it had been for them, her "baby" was a *girl* now. And she, a kid when she'd birthed Mo, was a *woman*. River's Sigh was always supposed to be a temporary stay. A rock to rest on in the unexpected stream she'd found herself in. A safe spot to balance until she was ready to leap into the place she was actually supposed to be.

Four years ago, Aisha had been seventeen and facing an unplanned pregnancy under ugly circumstances, trying to decide if she should keep her baby or put her up for adoption like she herself had been, all while grieving the loss of her beloved mom. She never would've imagined that at twenty-one, she might feel just as confused as she had then.

She'd always considered twenty-anything, adult-*adult*, to be the age and stage of knowing . . . stuff.

Now she was hopeful that thirty would have more answers. It was a while to wait, of course, but it was good to have something to look forward to.

She'd expressed similar sentiments to her aunt the other day but hadn't exactly had them validated. Understatement. Jo was too kind to overtly squash her ideas about thirty, but Aisha caught a flash of suppressed laughter in her eyes. Knowing her luck, it meant Jo knew something she didn't—that she was fooling herself. Maybe you didn't know more at thirty than at twenty. Maybe all you learned, the older you got, was how much you still didn't know.

Mo's tiny hand clasped Aisha's. "Mom."

"Yes?"

But Mo's word wasn't a question. It was declarative. Like she wanted to inform Aisha, to remind her—or possibly to claim her, lest there was someone lurking around with any doubts—that Aisha was *her* mom. Or maybe she just wanted her cold little paws warmed up. Either way, it made Aisha smile, and she nodded at Mo. "Daughter."

Mo beamed and skipped along beside her, still holding her hand tightly.

As they continued down the trail, Aisha turned her thoughts to dinner. Something hearty and nourishing. Beef stew with roasted root vegetables, maybe? Mo especially loved turnips. Or Butternut squash lasagna? So creamy and good. As she'd learned so well from Jo, a home-cooked meal went a long way to soothing one's worries—and thinking about the task helped put her future in perspective, too.

Mo's hand in hers. Food to help her grow. A warm, snuggly bed. Clothes on her back. No matter how Aisha tended to obsess about things, what she had right now, in this moment, was all she really needed to know and focus on. She was a mom. A mother. It was a sacred gift and a calling, and she would live up to it.

She was grateful to Jo and Callum for letting them stay here, for enabling her to build a nest egg, for creating a sense of family and belonging, but it was time to figure out where she and Mo were supposed to put their own roots down long-term. Past time, actually.

Jo had hacked and coughed all last month. It was only a bad cold and she was mended now, plus Aisha was self-aware enough to realize the only reason it freaked her out was that since her mother died so young, she saw worst case scenarios everywhere. Still, it was a good nudge: being self-sufficient and reliant on no one had always been the goal, the plan. For the good of her child, she'd allowed herself to get waylaid, but it was time to make some tough decisions. To stay? To go? And either way, how to forge an independent life and permanent home for her and Mo, one that she was solely responsible for, one that no one but her had the power to build or tear down, one that was safe from all outside influences.

Chapter 2

THE GREYHOUND GROUND TO A halt and the bus driver's voice crackled over the speaker, announcing the stop. Greenridge. Jase was dozing and came to alertness slowly at first—then more quickly when he realized Colton no longer filled the seat beside him. One by one, the few people old-school enough, or broke enough, to still take a bus in this day and age filed off—but still no sign of Colton. Maybe he was in the john?

Jase unfolded his cramped limbs and lifted out of his seat, ducking his head to keep from knocking it on the overhead bins. A low voice purred behind him, "Offer still stands."

Rats. Becca. Still on the bus. He'd thought he was free and clear. He turned in the narrow aisle but didn't have to answer. Colton's grinning face appeared over Becca's shoulder, revealing where he'd disappeared to, though Jase should've known.

Colton spoke for Jase. "You're wasting your breath, sweetheart. Jase here is all work, no play."

Jase gave an apologetic one-shouldered shrug and

didn't disagree.

The diamond Monroe stud above the corner of Becca's heart-shaped mouth flashed in the dim overhead lights as she smiled. It was pretty if piercings were your thing, but they weren't his. Too impractical. Snagged on stuff. Ink was better. "If you change your mind, remember I put my number in your phone."

"Thanks." Jase smiled amiably, but thought, what kind of whack job grabs a random guy's phone and adds her name to his contacts? Ah, well, it took all sorts to make the world go around. Friendly Becca had boarded a few towns back and struck up conversation at a diner during a layover between bus transfers. She was fine but liked to party in ways he didn't. Colton, of course, had no such reservations.

Becca smoothed her short purple hair, waggled her fingers in farewell, then squeezed past him and swayed down the rubber-matted aisle, Colton stumbling behind her. Apparently, the party had already started.

Colton paused long enough to say, "I'll catch up with you tomorrow—meet you there, I mean."

Jase grimaced. All he needed was for Colton to show up for their first day of work hungover or worse, making them both look bad. Not a lot he could do about it though. His foster brother did what he wanted and only what he wanted and always had. Jase didn't fault him for it, but it wasn't how he was wired, no matter how often he wished it was.

He pulled his sweatshirt's hood up over his head,

hefted his backpack, which carried the full sum and total of his earthly belongings, including his steel-toed boots and climbers laced to one strap, then followed Colton and Becca's lead, hunching his shoulders to avoid hitting his head on the bus ceiling. When he stepped down onto the gravel shoulder, only a few of the other freshly debarked passengers openly stared, but all gave him a wide berth. It was the one perk of being freakishly large; strangers tended to be wary and steered clear. His shaved head, dark clothing, and heavy boots probably added to people's misconceptions, but he didn't cultivate an intimidating look on purpose. He was just practical. Long hair was hard to keep clean when you were on the road, and black clothes didn't show dirt.

Becca and Colton climbed into a jacked up truck sporting lots of chrome and a light bar that could probably be seen from Mars. The instant the passenger door slammed shut, the vehicle roared off in a belch of diesel fumes. Jase watched as one-by-one, other passengers disappeared into waiting vehicles—then surveyed his surroundings.

The stop was only saved from pitch-blackness by the glow of the strip lighting along the bus's side and a neon sign beaming "C-FFEE" from across the street.

Greenridge was new to Jase—well, new to both him and Colton, actually, but Colton hadn't discovered it, hadn't chosen it. He was just broke and decided, for practical reasons, to tag along when Jase came across the job listing online. It was more than that for Jase. It was an active decision. He was tired of city life and the constant partying Colton could never get enough of, and he liked small towns and had always wanted to explore the northwest. Admittedly though, this small and this far north might prove a bit much. The place seemed to have come together by accident, building up bit by bit alongside the highway and railway track that ran parallel to it.

Jase wondered if the town had once had a bus depot that closed down, a sign of changing times, or if Greenridge was so small it had never had an official one. Either way, being let off on the side of the highway in the middle of the night didn't do much to create a feeling of welcome.

"You're not here to be welcomed," he scoffed under his breath, since there was hardly anyone left to hear him. "You're here to make bank and take care of your responsibilities."

Tonight, however, alone in the dropping temperature, watching stranger after stranger take off with smiling friends and loved ones, Jase didn't feel as pragmatic as he tried to convince himself he was. He and Colton were only twenty-four, but he, at least, was starting to feel old—or like their lifestyle was.

Jase frowned. What was this mess in his head? He loved his nomadic life. Or found it the most comfortable way to live, anyway. If you're not attached to anything, you can't lose it and it can't be taken away.

He frowned deeper still.

He wasn't fooled by all the heartwarming greetings and tearful hugs of hello he'd just witnessed. For every happy reunion, somewhere nearby there was a huge fight brewing and a quick departure in the wings. For every mom or dad coming "home," there was another one leaving never to be seen again. And for every smiling lover, someone else was screaming and throwing things.

There were only two people left waiting now, a woman about his age with a small girl with pretty black braids. She reminded him so much of a picture he had of Emily from a few years back that he sucked in a breath. Did Emily still wear her hair like that or was it cut short or something? Familiar sadness and shame gut-punched him. What kind of loser didn't know that about his own kid? A beige Honda pulled up, slammed to a stop, and a man rushed out. "I'm so sorry I'm late, you guys."

"Daddy!" The little girl leaped into his arms. "I missed you!"

The adults laughed and as the guy hugged his daughter, the woman stepped into his embrace too.

The little scene was fresh salt in an old wound, re-minding Jase that recounting all the miseries some folks faced was no true consolation. Of course, there were genuinely happy reunions and truly close-knit families. What would it be like to have a home to come back to? To have people who missed you when you went away, who celebrated when you returned? Jase had no idea. Never had.

As if shoved into motion by his thoughts, the bus groaned and grumbled its way back onto the road again, swinging wide into the empty lane and rolling on into the night. Jase watched the hostile red-rimmed eyes of its taillights until they disappeared. Then he checked both ways and crossed the highway. Small as it was, at least Greenridge had a 24-hour coffee shop.

As he walked, Jase patted the chest pocket of the jean jacket he wore over his hoodie, feeling for the reassuring fold of paper on the inside pocket. He'd read the ad so many times, he had it memorized. River's Sigh B & B—a pretty name to go with what would hopefully prove to be a nice place to bunk down for a while. And he'd already touched base. They were expecting him and Colton. And sure, it had been a while since either of them had fallen a tree—but it was a *bed and breakfast.* How wild of terrain could it be? The owners were looking for glorified landscapers and with his and Colton's letters of reference, they were in. He just hoped Colton would control his wild side and not ruin this opportunity for them.

Chapter 3

A<small>ISHA WALKED ALONG THE TRAIL</small> from Silver cabin, carefully carrying the grungy bucket of mop water that she needed to dump, her mind wandering.

There'd been a slew of pre-arranged late checkouts today, so her cleaning schedule had been pushed back, but now, finally, each cabin was sparkling clean, perfectly restocked and prettily arranged again, ready for whoever its next guest might be.

She wasn't feeling the satisfaction she usually did at the end of a cleaning shift, however. The glow she got from a job well done had been dulled by time spent training two college students who were going to work for them April through August. The two girls were all right, she guessed, but they acted like every chore was drudgery or somehow beneath them—an attitude Aisha never understood. *No* job was beneath her.

It wasn't that she didn't feel frustration or annoyance when clients were slobs—and thankfully, most of their guests were awesome, so messes like today's were rare. It was that it was her job to clean it up and she took zealous pride in doing just that. Aisha had

expected similar enthusiasm, or at least similar dili-
gence, in the new hires and was disappointed. If they
didn't like scrubbing, didn't get a tiny thrill over a
gleaming toilet bowl, didn't derive a mild sense of
superiority from tidying other people's messes, why
did they even apply for housekeeping work? The north
was booming again. There were plenty of other places
hiring.

Then again, they were young. The thought triggered a wry smile because they were, no doubt, at least
her age if not older. Nevertheless, she'd take it as a
personal challenge to inspire them to be proud of their
work. And she'd try to stop taking it personally that Jo
and Callum were adding staff. It wasn't a sign they felt
Aisha couldn't handle everything. It was that River's
Sigh B & B was growing. It was exciting—and an
honor that she was in charge of new staff. She should
be celebrating.

Yes, *celebrating*. She was not a whiny, whinging
person. She didn't bitch and moan. She changed things
she was unhappy about. She would tackle—

Aisha's mini pep talk ended abruptly. Someone or
something was splashing ferociously in the creek
behind Rainbow cabin. There was a muffled grunt.
Then more splashing.

Her first thought was *bear*. Normally there was
enough action around the property—not to mention,
until recently, grizzled old Hoover barking his face off
at the slightest whiff of forest dwellers—that wildlife

stayed clear. But the season hadn't really started yet, and the grounds were extra quiet since Hoover passed, something Aisha tried to avoid thinking about because it filled her with so much sorrow for Jo who mourned him like the closest of personal friends, which, of course, he was.

And even in Hoover's day, barking maniac or not, it wasn't unheard of to have bear visitors this time of year. They always spotted at least a couple of black bears—and once a Kermode came through—in the spring, skinny and scrounging for easy food. Aisha wasn't scared exactly—no doubt it was just some hungry fella seeking dandelions and tender grass not available on the forest floor—but she wasn't an idiot either. A bear, if surprised, interrupted or made to feel threatened in any way, was a dangerous thing.

Moving more cautiously, she continued along the trail as it rounded the cabin—then slammed to a halt.

Two shirtless guys crowded the creek's scanty bank. One, incredibly massive with a shorn head and heavily tattooed back, was hunkered down, facing away from her. The other was ... seriously hot. Wearing nothing but a well-worn pair of work jeans with suspenders dangling around his narrow hips, as if purposefully showing off his well-defined pecs and deeply cut six-pack, hell, *eight-pack,* of golden brown abs, and gleaming with droplets of creek water, he looked like he was modelling for some calendar featuring working men or something—not like he actually *was* a working man.

Wait—working man. Working *men*. Right. Aisha gave herself a mental facepalm. Jo and Callum had mentioned something about hiring some guys to fall dangerous trees around the property, do some of the heavier landscaping, and maybe even cut wood for the following winter.

She plunked the heavy mop bucket down. Filthy water sloshed over the rim, splashing her yoga pants with chemicals and stink. Awesome. She didn't quite manage to hold back a disgusted groan. The two men visibly jolted and turned in her direction. Seeing her, the tall guy—he really was a monster height-wise— looked even more startled, not less. And she realized that Hot Guy had hotter guy competition. He looked like Jason Momoa, if Jason Momoa had a shaved head.

Hot Guy was first to recover from the surprise. He gave her a quick once over, which Aisha hated but figured was fair enough considering her own gawking. Then he grinned and winked. Ugh.

"Um, this is a work place," she said, then winced. She'd intended to sound stern, but the comment came out like she was asking him, not telling him. Why was she having such a hard time stringing words together? Talking was her forte. And good grief. She'd seen half naked men before—even a fully naked man. Mo wasn't an immaculate conception—no matter how much Aisha wished otherwise.

Still, it had been a long while . . . or, more honestly, *never* since she'd seen guys—*men*—this good looking. She especially liked how the big guy didn't seem as cocky as Hot Guy who was already annoying her. He seemed shy and kept his head ducked, his eyes averted. . . .

Shit! Her hormones were making her stupid. This was another shift within her in recent months—maybe the most unwelcome of them all. For years now, it had been a relief, how totally not into guys she was. She'd gone on a few dates, even attended a three-day music festival with someone really nice—but it was like her brain, her body, her whole being had hung up a "Closed" sign. She hadn't felt the slightest spark of romantic interest in forever—certainly nothing strong enough to make her willing to risk emotional roller-coasters, potential headaches, or pain.

Then Mo turned four, and the sign flipped back to "Open." Completely against her will, Aisha transformed into a version of herself she hardly could accept as being *her*. A guy-obsessed weirdo. She saw men everywhere and was hyper-conscious of their presence—especially when they were in the middle of her usually private and safe woods, apparently.

Hot Guy laughed out loud, seeming to know exactly why she was uncomfortable. He stepped forward casually, thumbs hooked in his belt loops.

Just to avoid his brazen eyes, Aisha honed in on a felt-lined denim jacket and black sweatshirt that lay stacked on top of a big backpack, near a pair of heavy boots perched on a flat rock—a pair of boots so big they had to belong to the giant, who was still kneeling by the creek.

Like Hot Guy, Giant wore only a scruffy pair of low-slung jeans, giving Aisha an interesting-if-unexpected—and unwanted, she reminded herself—eyeful of his boxers and half his muscular butt.

He lumbered to his feet, and she realized he was well-muscled too, just his height camouflaged it a bit—stretching the muscle out over bone and sinew. His nipples were dark as plums against his light brown flesh which looked as firm as a wood plank. Said nipples were hard and erect, showing they felt the icy temperature of the creek water glistening on his skin, even if the rest of him didn't. Scrolling text adorned his rib cage, but she couldn't make out what it said from where she stood.

Unlike Hot Guy, he seemed uncomfortable at being caught washing up in the creek. His obvious discomfort made Aisha embarrassingly aware that she was staring, though she felt powerless to stop—until she caught herself following the line of fur that ran from his naval and disappeared into his waistband—

She gave herself another sharp mental slap. What was she doing?

The giant shifted uneasily and finally spoke. "I'm sorry. I, uh, was told the season hadn't started yet, that the place was empty."

Aisha's brow furrowed and she arched an eyebrow.

Who had told him that? And even if the place was empty, how did that explain the ice-water bath?

The stranger must've read the confusion on her face. He shook his head. "I'm Jason—call me Jase—Scott."

Was he kidding? His name was actually *Jason*? Nerves made her earlier inner comparison of him to the famous actor seem extra hilarious and she snort-giggled.

Jason—Jase—took another step back. She tried to rein herself in.

"And this is . . . my brother. Colton Hislop." He motioned at Hot Guy with a huge hand. "We're going to be working here? We've been on the road a while, so we wanted to, uh, freshen up before presenting ourselves?"

So she wasn't the only one afflicted with the awkward tendency to make statements into questions when nervous. The thought mollified her. "Well, too late for that. Consider yourself . . . presented."

Jase the giant blushed—or else he was finally feeling the chill. Either way, his tan skin definitely went rosy.

"Um, you're not . . . Jo, are you?" There was a soft, shy note in Jase's voice, as if he was pleading that she wasn't, but Aisha was distracted by Colton. He was pulling a soft gray Henley shirt over his head with what seemed to her an unnecessary amount of stretching and pausing.

A thunder bolt of irritation crashed through Aisha, way too large for such a tiny trigger, and she knew it.

"No, I'm not *Jo*, thank God," she snapped.

Jase's body quaked in a shiver. She guessed it was nice that he didn't want to "present" himself to Jo and Callum without cleaning up first, but what an insane place to do it. He couldn't rent a hotel room or something?

Still struck almost mute by the view, stupidly, humiliatingly, Aisha's face started to burn. Jase's height and size really were jaw-dropping. To her shame, she couldn't think of one witty line or sharp comment to mitigate her discomfort.

"Follow your brother's example and put on some clothes," she finally managed through gritted teeth. "This is a family establishment. Geez."

It was absolutely no consolation that Jase looked as uncomfortable as she felt as he obediently stooped over his pack and rummaged for a towel and a clean T-shirt.

Like she hadn't sounded dopey or bossy enough, she added, "You guys'll catch your death of pneumonia scrubbing up in a creek that had chunks of ice in it a week ago!"

She snatched up the mop bucket again and stalked off, knowing she looked—and sounded—like a complete looney. Put on some clothes? It wasn't like the guy was naked. And "family establishment?" True enough, sure, but what was her point, exactly? Plus, he was right. There was no one around. She was being a freak—and not in her usual good-freak sort of way.

Still, it wouldn't have been the worst exit, all said and done—except her stupid foot caught a root and threw her off balance. She managed, barely, to keep from falling, but upended the bucket in the process, drenching herself with the rest of the gloopy mess.

Behind her came a surprised, slightly dismayed grunt—and a low whistle, followed by laughter. Aisha didn't have to turn around to know Giant Jase was the grunter and his brother was the hyena. She resumed a forward march, without a backward glance. She might have to listen to them laugh at her, but she didn't have to watch.

Chapter 4

JASE WAITED ALMOST A FULL minute, exchanged a glance with Colton, then knocked again, louder. Still no response. He shuffled back and glanced up at the carved cedar sign above his head, confirming they were at the right place.

Colton rolled his eyes. "Let's just walk in already."

"Nah, man. Give 'em another minute."

"What'd she say again?"

She. Jo Kendall-Archer. Their new employer. Jase had hung out in the coffee shop all night, while Colton was off . . . being Colton, waiting for a decent time to call Jo and let her know they'd arrived in Greenridge. When they spoke around 9:00 a.m. she'd said it was a busy day and to come in the evening and find her at the dining hall. She—or her husband Callum—would show them the grounds, outline what needed done, and then, if they still wanted the job, they'd finalize any last details and decide on a start date.

Jase glanced at the sign for a third time. Yep, definitely the dining hall. He hesitated another fraction of a beat, then smoothed his shirt down, and knocked again.

"Hello?" he called, opening the door. "Anybody home?"

Colton grunted and pushed past Jase—but stopped on the small rag rug inside the door, without going further.

The instant Jase crossed the threshold and shut the door behind them, he understood why his knock had gone unanswered. The beautiful solid wood door and walls were obviously well-insulated; not only had they kept him from being heard, they'd kept him from hearing the people inside. The music of clattering dishes and flatware, laughter and voices met his ears, and the tantalizing aroma of garlic and seafood made him extra aware of his hunger.

Colton shot him a wary look, all traces of his swagger momentarily gone. For a second, Jase couldn't see adult Colton anymore, just the scrawny eleven-year-old he'd been when they first got lumped together at Mike Trent's. He gave Colton a terse, understanding nod. For similar reasons, they were equally uncomfortable with big happy family groups—though their discomfort manifested differently.

Jase had mostly recovered from his encounter with the chambermaid who'd caught him and Colton cleaning up in the creek, but now he was hit with fresh apprehension. Still, he forced himself to move beyond the entrance and into the big communal eating area. His stomach growled audibly, just as a young girl's voice piped, "It's not funny!"

The roomful of faceless people, all backs turned to him, burst into laughter, and something inside Jase plummeted. Maybe this job wasn't going to work out after all. He needed it, for sure, and was trying to be firm with himself about taking it—but he'd done a brief tour on his own, while waiting for Colton to show up, and it gave him pause. The River's Sigh B & B advertisement hadn't exaggerated at all. The fanciness of the cabins he'd seen online when he did some investigating had fooled him, but now he knew better. It was a wild place situated in a legit *forest*. There were some deadly hang ups and widow makers. And now there was this . . . crowd. He'd obviously misunderstood Jo, or they had very different ideas about what constituted "not many people around." Yeah, probably the latter.

So why did he keep moving forward? He and Colton could leave. Jo and her husband would just write them off as deadbeats and find someone else. But even as the idea occurred to him, it was too late. A woman with copper curls and a pretty smile burst through a swinging door, coming from the kitchen. He was spotted.

"Oh, hello! You must be Jason-goes-by-Jase." She crossed the room to him, wiping her hands on her apron, which was decorated with the words, "I love to cook with wine. Sometimes I even put it in the food."

As she beamed with welcome, he cursed himself for not splitting when he had the chance. He bowed his head, unused to such intense attention.

"I'd heard you arrived, that you were out . . . getting acquainted with the property, and I would've joined you, but," she motioned in the direction of a swinging kitchen door, "I was cooking. Anyway, you're just in time. I've already set you a plate."

Hiraeth. The word appeared in Jase's brain with no rhyme or reason, kicking like an angry goat. He could no longer remember where he'd first come across the Welsh word, though it was definitely in a book, probably a novel, but it had instantly resonated with him. He often got hit with this sort of useless longing, almost like homesickness, for some version of home that no longer existed for him, or that maybe never had. He didn't trust rare flashes of early childhood memories that a certain scent or sound or some other intangible thing sometimes triggered. Wishful thinking just made you . . . wishful.

And that was the real reason he didn't want to be here. Big, seemingly happy, noisy family gatherings, if that's what this was, always threw a hard punch, reminding him of a truth he'd internalized long ago. They were something other people got to enjoy. They were not for him.

"Jase?" Jo's voice had a concerned lilt. He started and Colton tensed behind him. Right. Colton. He'd forgot all about him for a second—and shoot, Jo had said something else while he'd been zoned out.

He shook his head. "Sorry, long day. I didn't catch

what you said."

Jo studied him for a moment and her eyes stopped smiling. Or was he being paranoid? "I just asked if this is your brother. Colton, right?"

Colton came to life finally, sticking out his hand and laying on the charm. "Yes, ma'am. Colton Hislop, at your service." He raved about how whatever she was making smelled delicious, effusively complimented what he'd seen of River's Sigh B & B so far, and finished with a wink and a comment about how pretty everything was, especially the proprietor.

To Jase's relief, Jo rolled her eyes slightly, but didn't seem offended—and she definitely didn't seem overly flattered or become flirtatious in return. Either extreme could lead to potential headaches with Colton. As Jo and Colton continued to small talk, Jase relaxed. Usually the charm Colton put on or discarded with the ease that other people slid jackets on or off annoyed Jase, but tonight he was grateful for it. It wouldn't hurt for them to appear to have some semblance of social skills.

"Okay," Jo continued, after she'd smiled and laughed at a few more Colton-isms, "we'll discuss the nitty-gritty later. Let's get you guys something to eat."

"Thanks, that'd be great." Jase meant it but was concerned that she hadn't brought up the other important order of business. He should tackle it now. This place was in the sticks, and people were reluctant to pick up hitchhikers nowadays, especially big lugs like him. He'd managed to hitch a ride part of the way, then walked the rest, including the long driveway, but it had taken forever. He didn't like his chances of having the same luck on the way out if they weren't on the same page. And he didn't fancy the idea of putting himself at the mercy of whoever Colton's new friends were, when it came to getting back for work on time.

"Dinner sounds great," he said, nearly repeating himself. "But just confirming . . . Callum, your husband, right?"

Jo nodded.

"He said lodging was included with this job, right? Or did I get my wires crossed?"

"Yeah—no," Jo said, as if noticing his large backpack for the first time. She shook her head, then nodded, making her curls bounce—and Jase was suddenly reminded of the angry chambermaid from earlier. Her hair was a lot lighter than Jo's, a stunning white blond, but it was the same riot of curls. And their faces were very similar. Jo's younger sister maybe? Too old to be a daughter.

"I'm sorry," Jo interrupted his thoughts. "Either Callum forgot to mention it, or it totally slipped my mind, but I wasn't aware you were expecting to room here. It's not a problem, though. We'll hammer out the details after dinner."

So apparently, he'd made the decision to stay, Jase mused as Jo led him and Colton to a massive cedar table, filled with enough food to feed an army. He hated the relief flooding through him, but at the same time, he couldn't help it. Hopefully the job would last for a while. He'd never stretch things out or rip off an employer, but maybe when they saw how he put his back into things, they'd like his work ethic and find other stuff for him to do.

Okay, enough, he commanded inwardly as he caught Jo glancing curiously at him again. You spend too much time alone in your own head. You're with people now. Quit the incessant introspection.

He hung his head. Oh, yeah, he was nailing the stop-talking-to-himself thing. Totally.

"Everybody," Jo announced, "I'd like you to meet Jase and Colton." She made a sweeping motion in their direction as she said their names. "They'll be doing some tree removal and other work around the place. Jase, Colton . . . everybody."

There was a cheery rumble of hellos and nice to meet you's.

Jase nodded and tried to look friendly, to not feel on the spot—but only felt more uncomfortable.

The blond chambermaid was seated across from him, wearing what could only be described as a scowl.

Colton didn't notice her expression, didn't realize it was targeted at them, or didn't care—one of the three. He slid into a seat with confident cheer, his smile only deepening as her scowl did the same.

Jase lowered himself into the chair beside Colton, figuring it would be weird to sit apart from him. He wanted to tell the girl they weren't intentionally trying to piss her off—or he wasn't anyway.

"I won't overwhelm you with names right away. You'll meet everyone individually soon enough, but let me introduce Aisha." Jo motioned at the scowling chambermaid. "She's pretty much in charge of everything cleaning and maintenance related these days, so if you have any questions, go to her. Ditto if you need help with anything."

Aisha looked less than impressed by this arrangement. In fact, she looked positively furious. Jase felt the stirrings of emotions he'd been sorely missing as of late: curiosity, intrigue. What was her glitch? Why did she appear to hate him so much? There was no way they knew each other because he never would've forgotten someone as striking as she was.

Colton leaned across the table and extended his hand. "Nice to meet you . . . officially." Jase couldn't see Colton's face, but he was sure Colton gave one of his douchie winks.

Aisha stared like Colton was offering her a poisonous snake, and Jase noticed that she had incredible jade-green eyes. Were they natural or were they colored contacts? He was also surprised to realize he was holding back laughter. He was used to any girl Colton turned his attention to practically melting on the spot. This was Aisha's second encounter with him, and she was melting all right—in a volcanic temper-like-lava sort of way.

Colton didn't withdraw his hand in embarrassment like Jase would've, however. After a long moment, she finally met Colton's hand with her own. Jase was strangely disappointed that she caved—then felt like a traitor. He should be siding with Colton, not rooting against him.

"Don't let your food get cold," she commanded, pulling out of Colton's grip. "It's delicious." Even the last bit, which should've been a complimentary observation, sounded confrontational—like the food better be delicious *or else*.

Jase obediently dished up a heaping serving of the food that had sent his senses into drool mode earlier: a garlicky prawn and scallop dish in a mouth-watering cream sauce.

Noticing that Aisha's intense glare was now fixed on him, Jase fumbled for something to say and finally mumbled, "I'm looking forward to working together."

She practically threw a bowl of crusty bread at him.

Chapter 5

AISHA WHISKED ANOTHER RACK OF mugs from the counter and lowered them into the steaming bleach solution in the big double sink. Late afternoon sunshine filtered through the dining hall's kitchen windows, dappling the counters, making the pine cabinets shine, and turning a bowl of apples on Jo's bright yellow vintage table into a glowing work of art. How much she loved this place was really getting on her nerves. She let out a small huff of annoyance.

Jo misunderstood the sound. "You've been working all day. You're clocked out. Why don't you let me do this?"

"I like to help. You know that. Besides, what else would I do? Mo's having a tea party or something with Sam."

If it struck Jo as odd that Aisha only referred to Sam as being Mo's grandmother when Mo was around, she didn't let on. Instead she made a hard to interpret "Hmm" sound, then asked, "Everything okay?"

Leaving the new tray to soak, Aisha had grabbed tongs and started to remove the first batch of freshly whitened and brightened mugs from the scalding rinse water. Now she stopped mid-motion to glance at her aunt.

"Yep, all's fine."

"There's nothing wrong? You're sure?" Jo hefted another tray, teacups this time, onto the counter beside Aisha.

"I'm sure. Nothing's wrong. Or nothing real anyway—and definitely nothing that has anything to do with you and Callum. You guys are great."

Jo hesitated for a breath, then pressed on like the straight shooter she was. Just one of the many qualities Aisha loved about her aunt. "How are things with Sam?"

Okay, on second thought, sometimes she wished Jo would just avoid uncomfortable, awkward conversations like a normal person. Not that she was any better than Jo usually, but she fully embraced her double standard. Being direct was far more of a plus when you were the one being direct, not the one being targeted by the direct person.

"So, it *is* something to do with Sam?" Jo pressed when she didn't answer right away.

"No, it's not *Sam*. She's fine. We're fine."

And that was generally true—but their relationship was still strained for Aisha, even after nearly four years. Maybe it always would be. She had all the issues you'd expect someone to have when they had unresolved grief over the loss of their mom and then their dad got remarried too soon. Okay, the "too soon" was unfair. It hadn't been that soon—just Aisha couldn't seem to stop hating the fact her mom had to be replaced at all. And that the new wife, the *replacement*, also happened to be Aisha's biological mother was just, well, *ugh*.

Yet she was the one who'd sought Sam out—for advice on what to do when she found herself in her birth mom's shoes, pregnant at seventeen—so it was a bit stupid to resent her presence. Of course, she hadn't foreseen Sam falling for her dad or becoming a permanent part of her life as her *stepmother,* or she might've reconsidered the whole bio-mom search. Except that . . . it was also great to have Sam around. She genuinely liked her. Most of the time. And admired her. Often enough, anyway. Plus, Mo deserved every crazy-in-love-with-her adult that Aisha could provide her with. If she ended up dying young too, she wanted her daughter surrounded—absolutely surrounded!—by strong women and a big supportive family. And speaking of which, last but not least, searching for Sam had gotten Aisha Jo. And River's Sigh. And even, in a roundabout way, Mo herself.

Jo was patiently scrubbing away at a particularly tough tea stain ringing one mug. Aisha sighed. "Don't worry about me. I'm just a loser these days. I'll get myself figured out."

"That's it!" Jo's rubber dishwashing gloves made sharp sucking sounds as she snapped them off. "I'll finish these later. We're having a coffee break and then you're out of here. Go work in your shop, visit Katelyn and brainstorm new upcycling ideas, draft floor plans, or have a nap until Mo returns, I don't care—but I won't listen to nonsense. You are the furthest thing from a loser. The *furthest* thing."

Aisha removed her gloves too, let herself be pushed onto a vinyl-seated, chrome-legged chair, then accepted the steaming coffee mug Jo shoved at her. Her docile acquiescence made Jo's big amber eyes narrow with even deeper concern and suspicion.

Before Jo could say another word, Aisha raised a hand. Her short fingernails, painted with shiny black polish, caught the sun and gleamed with a maniacal cheer that Aisha wished she could feel again. "Just stop. Please. You're right. I am kind of going through some stuff. I'm worried that maybe I'm stagnating here. I love it—but is that healthy? I'm twenty-one, and I live like a sixty-year-old."

Jo gave Aisha's vintage rock T-shirt and neon blue skinny jeans a pointedly dubious look.

"I didn't say I *dressed* like a sixty-year-old. I said I *felt* like one."

The gentle teasing in Jo's expression fell away immediately. She sipped her coffee and waited for Aisha to continue.

"No, that's not it either, not really—or it's just part of it." Aisha scrunched her face and rubbed her temples. "Fine," she said resignedly. "It's not going away on its own, so I might as well tell you. It's two-fold, I think. Maybe three. I don't know."

Jo nodded like Aisha wasn't a totally annoying drama queen—a kindness Aisha appreciated, but didn't extend to herself.

"First, yes, as you guessed, it's Sam. I know it's pathetic, but I'm still confused about who we are to each other, really—who she is to *me*. She's Mo's grandmother, sure, but everyone acts like she's my mom and . . . I don't need that. I had a mother, a really great one." Aisha broke off, trying to figure out exactly what she was trying to say, but, as ever it seemed, failing epically. She exhaled a blast of frustration and cracked her knuckles. What did she owe Sam? Anything? What did she owe her deceased mother, except everything?

Jo cleared her throat as if to speak but didn't, so Aisha continued. "Second, I thought I'd be doing something important by now—making a difference of some kind, running my own business, helping reduce the amount of stuff that goes into landfills. . . . Instead I'm living this cushy, pampered life—and ugh . . . I don't know!"

Jo winced and her eyes grew shiny. "And the *maybe three*?"

Aisha looked down at her hands which were folded—more like clenched—in her lap.

"I'm lonely," she wanted to say, but didn't. How could she without sounding, without *being*, ungrateful?

She had Mo. She had Katelyn, her best friend and a true kindred spirit. She had her dad, and Jo and Callum, and yes, even Sam—plus a myriad other friends and acquaintances of varying degrees of closeness. Besides, she worried enough about prematurely losing people she loved, as it was. The last thing she needed was someone else to be concerned about. "Nothing," she said finally. "I'm just being dumb about a non-issue."

Jo waited a beat, a question on her face, but finally let it go. "Well, you know my advice about Sam, but I'll say it again in short form—and I'll repeat it as long and as often as you need me to."

Aisha nodded.

"Don't stress out trying to define your roles with each other. Let her be her, and let you be you. It's enough. You don't have to label it."

Aisha nodded again, but it was easier said than done. Sam, as Aisha's father's wife and Mo's grandma, was set up in a specific spot in Aisha's life, no matter how Aisha fought it, or how much it chaffed. None of that meant Jo's advice wasn't good though; it just didn't fit Aisha. She wasn't as chill as Jo. She wanted concrete lines.

"And about the rest. You're being insanely hard on yourself—"

"No!" Aisha inserted, ready to argue—and only didn't because Jo held up her hand. Apparently stop sign hands were another genetic trait. Who knew?

"Hear me out. Your goals are intense, inspiringly so, and I'm positive you'll meet or beat every one, but here's the thing, Aish. You're young. You may not feel like it, but you really are. And you have an amazing child who you're doing a fantastic job raising."

Aisha shrugged off the compliment.

"And you work your butt off here, so I'm not sure what your idea of pampered and cushy is, but dude, it's sure not mine—and it's definitely the furthest thing from your birth mama's."

Aisha shook her head and smiled despite her crappy mood. Whenever Jo tried to talk "hip" it was hilarious.

"And," Jo emphasized, "I'm also sure that if what you really want is to have your own shop, you will. Look how much work you've done toward it already."

Aisha thought of the bank account she'd managed to grow over the last three years—not huge, but not nothing, either—and in her mind's eye, she saw her increasingly packed workshop, stuffed with secondhand goods and eclectic furniture pieces of all sorts, restyled or refurbished by her. And then she replayed the rumors of a new store opening downtown, and something inside her withered.

Yet didn't the fact that she'd dropped the ball, hadn't opened her business sooner and lost her chance, say something important that she needed to consider? Maybe she hadn't merely been focussing on having enough stuff to sell and making sure she had enough money to support a year or two that might not see a profit. Maybe she'd been procrastinating for another reason. Maybe she wasn't supposed to be *here*.

"I'm not sure about my shop idea anymore. You've heard the rumors too, I'm sure."

Jo nodded pensively.

"So, what do I do? Move somewhere else?"

"Selfishly, I hope not."

"Me too. I wish there was a way I could stay here forever without being a lame squatter."

Jo's eyebrows shot up. "You totally *can* stay here forever, and you earn your keep and pay and then some. If anything, I worry we're taking advantage of you."

Aisha laughed, and an idea flashed—then disappeared as Jo continued, "Don't make any rash decisions, Aish. You were right, *are right,* when you said you'll figure it out. And regardless of what you end up doing or not doing down the line, right now you're already doing something important, something that makes a difference—raising Mo, helping me and Callum, just being *you*."

Aisha snorted.

"I'm serious," Jo said softly. "You don't know how much I appreciate you, or how much having you as my niece means. I always longed for family and for connection . . . and now I have both. I'm sorry for the sappy word, but seriously, you really are a blessing."

"Gross," Aisha muttered.

Jo's eyes crinkled with silent laughter. "I knew you'd like that."

And that was the thing . . . Aisha *did* like it. She liked everything about her coddling big-sister-like aunt. It was the hugest part of her problem, the part she couldn't bear to tell Jo: how deeply she loved being an integral part of River's Sigh's operations, how much she too enjoyed and benefited from this new-to-her extended family—with her dad and Sam on neighboring property and Callum's brother Brian and Katelyn, her best friend and fellow maker-of-unique-things, on an acreage just north of them. How good she had it was making her apathetic, complacent and comfortable. The idea of moving on and being self-sufficient was terrifying—and that she felt that way was even *more* terrifying.

She'd always viewed herself as independent, spontaneous and willing to take risks. If she wasn't those things, who was she? Confronting this scaredy-cat version of herself was—

Jo interrupted Aisha's thoughts. "Also, give yourself a break. Angst is normal. You're on the cusp of big changes. You never used to have a moment to yourself, between all your work here to support you and Mo, and her needing you every second you weren't working."

"But I loved that. I never resented—"

"I know that." Jo's eyes crinkled once more, and Aisha was struck yet again by how looking at her aunt—and definitely at Sam—was surreal sometimes. It was like gazing into a mirror that showed exactly what she would look like in another fifteen years or so. As a kid, she'd never felt deprived not seeing her features in someone else, but now that she did, she was continually floored by how weird and cool it was.

"And I'm not saying it wasn't wonderful," Jo continued, "and I know you miss Mo's baby days in a lot of ways, but she gets more independent every second—and gee, who does she get that from, I wonder? When she's in regular school, you'll have even more wide-open days like this. You're going to be able to move from dreaming and planning to *doing*. I know how terrifying that is."

Aisha nodded. Jo really *did* know what it was like to want something desperately and to wonder if she could ever pull it off. Yet here she was, making a go of it. Plus, as skeptical as Aisha sometimes was about the notion of love-true-love, at least for herself, Jo was another unique soul—yet she'd found a true partner who shared the same passions. These days especially, Aisha felt there were things she was missing out on by being single. Her traitorous brain flashed an image of giant Jase scrubbing up in the creek.

"Aisha?" Jo sounded mildly alarmed.

"What?"

"Your face is bright red. What did I say?"

Aisha's cheeks burned hotter still, no doubt giving the bowl of apples in front of her some competition.

"Nothing. I appreciate your input. Thank you."

Jo's eyebrows raised. "Umm, you're welcome?"

Aisha shook her head but smiled a little.

"Okay, quick subject change before I forget—"

Whatever Jo was going to say got cut off. The kitchen's swinging door banged open and Sam appeared with her usual combo of dramatic flair and terrible timing.

"I have to say, Jo, the new landscaping guys are very, well, just *very*. Have you noticed?"

"No comment."

"So you did!" Sam exclaimed triumphantly, then added conspiratorially, "I'm afraid I stared at the big one—but I'm sure he's used to it. He must be. What is he, do you think? Seven-three? Four? Taller even? He's . . . striking."

"They're employees, Sam. *Young* employees."

Sam ignored her. "And the one who looks like he's constantly in the middle of some photo shoot?" Sam waggled her eyebrows at Aisha. "*Whew*. Am I right?"

Aisha didn't respond, so Sam turned back to Jo. "Seriously, we could do a hot guys of River's Sigh B & B calendar as a fundraiser, starring those boys."

Aisha bit back a grouchy sigh. It was an all too common, very annoying phenomenon: Sam muttering something out of the blue that closely echoed something Aisha herself had thought.

Sam grinned again. "They look like they're around your age, Aish."

Ugh. So *not* going to talk men with my birth mom a.k.a. my father's wife, Aisha thought. She stuck her fingers in her ears. "Can't hear you—and also you do know you're *married* to my dad, right?"

"Oh, your dad won't mind me ogling. I'm only human. Besides, he'd ogle them too, if he wasn't such a prude." Sam winked. "Not to mention, he'd make a super-hot addition to the calendar himself."

Barf! Aisha was saved from having to respond, however, because the kitchen's swinging door banged again.

"Mom!" Mo hollered, running in—and Aisha was more overjoyed than usual to see her daughter.

Mo twirled her hands in Aisha's direction. "Grandma and I had mani-pedis. Aren't they *gorgeous*?"

Aisha sighed. It wasn't that she had an issue with nail polish. That would be hypocritical, obviously . . . just she liked it best when Mo spent her time doing kid things. She was only *four*, after all.

"And then we made mud pies in her real kitchen! Real mud pies out of real mud! In her *real* kitchen! It was hilarious! And then I hammered her door with a real hammer—well, not her door. A real nail was sticking out on the frame-thingy and we fixed it ourselves."

Aisha blinked. Then laughed—though at what exactly, she wasn't sure. True, Mo's overuse of the word "real" always killed her. The kid was obsessed with the concept lately, ever since she'd realized that some things were pretend or imaginary and others were, as she noted again and again: *real*. But she could've just as easily been laughing because . . . *Sam*. She didn't think she'd ever get used to the complete contradiction the woman was. Her mother. Stepmom. Bio parent. Whatever she was.

"I'm gonna head out," Aisha said, getting to her feet. "Mo and I are hitting the public swim in town with Katelyn and the kids."

"For real? Yay!" Mo jumped up and down, making the three primary women in her life grin widely.

"Oh, wait, I just remembered. What were you going to ask me before Sam"—Aisha caught herself just before she said *interrupted*—"arrived?"

"Right! Thanks for reminding me. We have lots of advance warning, but apparently Callum's mom is moving forward with the gallery show."

"Really?" It was hard not to sound downright disbelieving let alone skeptical. How many times had Caren postponed the show? Like at least three times in two years. Aisha was almost surprised the gallery would still work with her, but then again, she was an amazing talent. . . .

Jo shrugged. "That's what she says, anyway. Are you interested in making a few bucks running the bar?"

"Absolutely."

"Great. It's a couple months out, and I'll let you know when—if—I know more. I just wanted to get a sense of whether you wanted the work or if I should ask someone else."

"No, I'm in. Definitely. Thanks." Aisha herded Mo toward the door, then turned back. "Thanks for watching, Mo, Sam. I know she had a blast."

"Anytime. I mean it."

Aisha knew Sam was sincere and wished she didn't feel a flash of irritation. Also, was it her imagination or did Sam look a little sad?

Mo rushed back from the door and threw her arms around Sam's legs. "Good-bye Grandma! I love you!"

"I love you too, sweetheart." Any sadness in Sam's face, imagined or *real*, dissipated as she bent down and pressed exaggerated kisses—"Mwah! Mwah!"—on each of Mo's chubby cheeks, making Mo giggle madly.

The tiny awkwardness of the previous moment was instantly smoothed over, thanks to Mo—so why did Aisha feel so out of sorts?

"Come on, my girl," she called and Mo, ever enthusiastic—and so endearingly free of reservations about any of the women in her life—skipped over and followed her out the door.

Chapter 6

JASE PAUSED ON MINNOW CABIN'S porch steps. Like every building at River's Sigh B & B, the aptly named cabin was picture perfect. Set in the shelter of three massive cedars, Minnow was sided with warm wood, trimmed in deep scarlet, and featured a wall that was mostly windows. With its tiny porch, huge black rocking chair—replete with a comfy-looking quilt—and the gleaming burl platform that served as a table attached to the railing beside the chair, it was like something that should be on a cabin life Pinterest board or something. (It killed Jase that he even knew what Pinterest was, but he had no good defense. His last employer was addicted and passed the pleasure of daydreaming through various boards onto him—much to Colton's glee and harassment.)

The only detail about River's Sigh that stood out as not quite right was the absence of a dog. A place like this should have at least one friendly mutt to hold down the fort—and if it was his place? He'd have three. Or two, at the very least.

He was bending to check out the titles of the small

stack of books on the table when the door flew open.

"Hello?" Aisha's voice was friendly and seemed on the verge of adding something else—and then she appeared in the doorway and her tone cooled. "Oh, it's you."

Jase flushed, realizing what it looked like—like he'd been lurking on her deck, scoping out her stuff. Which, of course, was exactly what he had been doing. "Sorry, I was about to knock. I got distracted."

Aisha smiled wryly and glanced down at her reading material. "Oh, yeah?"

"Um, I'm sorry, but we seem to have gotten off on the wrong foot, or—"

"No, I'm sorry," Aisha said firmly. The blushing, awkward girl he'd first met in the bushes seemed to have taken a hike. "I've been rude to you."

Yes, she had been. Multiple times. Jase didn't really care, but he was curious about *why*. What was it about him that set her off? She didn't elaborate further, and he shifted his weight from foot to foot. There was no way she'd appreciate what he'd come to say.

Her eyebrows—perfectly arched and penciled to be darker than her fair hair—shot up. "So, going to share why you're here, or do I have to guess?"

Jase considered the question and her snippiness in general, and wished he was one of those guys who had "game." Colton would've given an *aw, shucks* grin and said something like, "Do I need a reason to chat up a pretty girl?" and she would've lit up and just like that they'd be friends or more. But if Colton's skills hadn't rubbed off on him by now, it was pretty obvious they never would. Also, he never wanted to say or do anything that could be construed as creepy or threatening, so he just slouched there like an idiot, hands in his pockets.

"Seriously," Aisha said, "*what*?"

Feeling more foolish than ever, he stood a bit straighter. Tried to tell himself it was a coincidence when she took a step back. "I told him it wasn't a big deal, but Callum's pretty firm."

"About?"

"That I have a spotter when I'm falling some of the bigger stuff. Colton's . . . not here, and Callum's in town all day. Said I should ask you."

"Yeah, okay. Is there something else you can do for an hour, though?"

The gauzy curtain covering the big window overlooking the porch moved. The little girl from the dining room popped into view and pressed her face against the glass, her glossy curls a mop, her huge brown eyes full of curiosity.

"Oh, you're babysitting—or is that your kid sister? No problem. When does she get picked up?"

A funny, almost shy expression softened Aisha's face, and Jase realized something. Even when she'd been blushing like crazy the other day, she hadn't appeared anything less than one hundred percent confident. She crossed her arms over her chest. "Not babysitting. No siblings. *Parenting*. My daughter. But she has a play date at 10:30."

Aisha had a daughter? She must've been a kid herself when she had her. Jase's stomach did the weird twisting, tightening thing it always did about some subjects.

"Should've clued in," he said, motioning at Aisha's captivating white-blond hair. "The curls. Different color, but they're yours."

Aisha nodded and wrapped her arms around herself even more tightly.

"No worries. I have lots to do. Just come find me whenever you're ready."

Chapter 7

AISHA STARED UP THE TREE—WAY, way up—and despite not normally having any fear of heights, the backs of her knees wobbled, and her stomach turned to jelly. Jase had already removed as many of the branches as he could reach from the ground—which explained the mountains of sap-dripping limbs she'd had to maneuver around to find him. Missing its lower branches did nothing to make the tree look less formidable, however. If anything, the rough knobs and patches of angry pink flesh showing where bark had been sliced away only made the monster seem taller and scarier. Jase wasn't really going to climb to the top of that. Was he?

She turned back to Jase, so thoroughly shocked that she forgot to be guarded and on the offensive. "You're kidding me, right?"

He glanced up from where he was sitting on the fresh stump of a much smaller tree, fastening wicked-looking spikes to his boots with a series of straps and buckles. "What's to kid about? It's gotta come down."

"And so you're going to climb it, just like that—

with a chainsaw?"

Jase nodded like it was perfectly normal behavior. He stood, flexed his feet, then stooped to readjust his boots. "Yeah. It's too close to Chinook cabin, and too tall to fall in one swoop. It needs to come down in pieces, so it won't take out the building—or snag any nearby trees and knock them onto other cabins or what have you."

"And I'm . . . spotting for you. Which basically means . . . watching in case you fall from a huge tree, armed with a running chainsaw."

Jase gave each strap another firm tug, rocked back and forth a bit, and finally seemed satisfied by how they felt. Maybe for the first time since they met, he didn't look slightly past her or away when he talked to her. He met her gaze directly and Aisha was unhappily hit with a zinging sensation. He had the most beautiful eyes she'd ever seen, though sexy was also an incredibly fitting adjective. Heavy lidded with lovely long lashes and the most interesting irises—cool gray-blue, with brown rings at their outer edge. He seemed surprised by the eye contact too but didn't break it. Just gave a slow smile.

"Well, hopefully, I'll manage to toss the saw if I start coming down—so it won't land on top of me. If I yell 'heads up,' run."

"You've got to be—"

"Yeah," he agreed quickly, ducking his head and averting his eyes again with the shyness she was more used to from him. "I'm kidding. I'll be fine. Don't worry. I've done this a lot. You're really just here for Callum's peace of mind—but if I do happen to fall, don't bother with the ambulance. Just call the coroner right off the bat."

"Not funny."

But it kind of was. They both smiled a little and Aisha felt . . . weird.

As Jase harnessed himself to the tree, sunk his spikes into the trunk, and started to climb, any humor about how nuts he was disappeared. "Please be careful," she called earnestly.

He looked over his shoulder and for half a second seemed touched by her concern. Then he grinned in a surprisingly cocky way. "Careful's for pussies."

So he was just your typical arrogant guy after all. His obliviousness to the dangers of his work, and his casual use of a word she hated made Aisha irritable again—a state she was far more comfortable with, regarding him. It was a bit ironic though, to find herself on firm ground once more, as he moved steadily away from it.

She traversed the distance they'd agreed on, about two hundred feet or so, far out of the range of where any of the sections might fall, or so they hoped. Then turned and watched him scurry up the tree, like he wasn't carrying a saw that was probably a third of his bodyweight, while wearing the world's heaviest steel-toed boots, and cumbersome leather pants.

That first time she'd laid eyes on Jase, she'd been awestruck by his height and his superhero physique, but now she got it. He wasn't born with it, or not all of it, at least. He was built from the crazy amount of physical work he did for his living—so fit that he made even the most strenuous tasks look effortless.

The heavy metal buzz of the saw pulsed in her blood, and the crash of newly shorn tree branches hitting the ground reverberated through her. Every five or ten branches, depending on the size, Jase climbed down and bucked the limbs into more manageable pieces. Then they worked together to move the sections that would be cut for firewood into a growing pile and threw the bushy needled boughs into huge stacks that would eventually be burned.

"You don't have to help—" Jase started to say before they moved the first batch, but she'd just rolled her eyes and put on her leather work gloves.

"Don't be dumb. It's going to be a long day as it is. I'm not getting paid to sit and watch you." But she sort of was.

It was heavy work and Jase wanted the tree down well before the afternoon light started to fade, so they didn't chat much. Aisha wasn't sure what she'd have said in terms of small talk, anyway. She was impressed by how hard he worked, and there was no way it was just because he was being chaperoned by the boss's niece. A person couldn't fake the kind of effort he was putting in and wouldn't have the ability and stamina he had if today was a one off, for show.

At one point, he paused to take a long drink from a water bottle, then offered it to her. As she took a greedy slurp, he wiped his brow with his forearm and said, with admiration that seemed sincere—and was unwittingly exactly the kind of compliment, maybe the *only* kind of compliment, that made Aisha go weak in the knees—"You're a friggen machine, hey?"

"Not like you though." She meant it. He nodded like he appreciated the returned compliment as much as she'd appreciated his original one.

Finally, after a great deal of effort, there it was: two-hundred and fifty feet of branchless tree, waving like a blade of long grass in the light breeze now that its limbs weren't holding it steady. It looked impossibly skinny at the top.

"Here goes nothing. Should be no problem, but make sure you stay back like we talked about."

Aisha looked up at the sky—or, rather, at the extremely thick cloud cover, moody and wearing a dozen shades of gray. "Do you have time? It still gets dark pretty early these days." Jase glanced at his watch. "Plenty of time. This is the fun—and fast—part."

Aisha had to remind herself to breathe as she watched Jase make his final ascent. The tree bounced and swayed with his weight, especially as he neared the top, and her insides did similar.

And then, with a terrifically loud crack, the first segment thwomped to the ground. Jase descended part way and cut again. And repeat, repeat, repeat—until Aisha lost count of how many sections he'd cut. It was crazy how quickly the massive tree came down. Soon there was nothing left but a pile of logs in eight to ten foot lengths, and Jase was back on the ground, setting his saw down, and pulling off his hard hat. His shaved head gleamed with sweat and he pressed his fists into his lower lumbar and leaned back, stretching his overworked spine.

"I'm hungry from the feet up—but I'm also so beat that skipping food and going straight to bed is equally tempting."

"Flattering," Aisha quipped before she could stop herself, "but I hardly know you."

Jase's eyes dropped and his skin deepened to a rosy-plum hue that was already growing familiar to Aisha. She instantly felt bad for teasing him. Sometimes she definitely had too much of Sam in her for her own liking. Also, she'd changed her mind about her earlier snide observation that he was "your typical arrogant guy." The only thing he seemed confident about was his ability to work—and fair enough. His high opinion there was obviously well-deserved. In every other aspect of life, he seemed almost painfully shy—though looking the way he did, she couldn't understand why. He must be used to having women all over him in droves.

"I'm so sorry. I was only joking. I'm not—" She stalled mid-apology when Jase shrugged, and his slow grin appeared again.

"So not bed, perhaps, but maybe want to meet up in the dining hall later?"

A stupid tingle went through Aisha at the possibility the word "perhaps" suggested. This was how bad she was at flirting now. A man could cringe at her joke and kindly but firmly turn her down and she'd still be titillated.

"I don't think so. I want to have a quiet night in with Mo."

"Sounds nice." Jase sounded like he meant it, which was refreshing. So often people her age said stupid stuff about her being tied down. He started gathering his gear. Aisha, for reasons she didn't want to overthink, lingered too, reluctant to see the productive day come to an end. Someone in one of the nearby cabins must've started a fire in their woodstove because the cozy scent of burning cedar filled the chilling air, mingling with the sharp piney scent of their labor. The sun was just starting to set, and Aisha wished she had a thermos of hot chocolate or something to offer Jase and help tide him over until Jo served dinner.

Jase tossed his boots and the metal spikes he called "climbers" into the back of Jo's pickup, which she'd volunteered for their use. Next, he hefted the chainsaw and situated it carefully in the truck box. When he finished, he glanced over at Aisha, as if surprised she was still there. She didn't blame him. She was surprised too.

She started coiling a large piece of heavy chain that they'd thought they might need for moving some of the larger branches but hadn't actually used. "I don't know. Mo and I might come to the dining hall for dinner, after all. Whatever Jo's making will be way better than anything I can scrounge up."

Jase smiled. "Oh, I see how it is. She'll deign to grace us with her company if the food is good enough, hey?"

Aisha shook her head at him and walked off without saying good-bye. She wanted a shower. And to stop making an ass of herself.

An hour later, Aisha entered the dining hall and the scent of Jo's delicious lamb curry and Callum's homemade naan lit up every happy sensor in her brain. The cheerful roar of the small crowd, which included two cabins' guests, the new kitchen staff, and the other two chambermaids that Jo had brought in for some extra hours to do other clean-up, suggested everyone was looking forward to dinner as much as she was.

Aisha said her hellos, then settled herself and Mo in chairs near—but not right beside—Jase's. It was a silly attempt on her behalf to make it seem like they weren't sitting together when they obviously were, and after a few minutes, he changed seats to one right next to hers, so they wouldn't have to small talk as loudly. Then he proceeded to eat so much that even ever-ravenous Mo noticed.

"Wow, you eat *a lot*," she said, raising her eyebrows and widening her eyes to emphasize her point.

"Thank you," Jase said humbly, as if Mo had meant it as high praise and wasn't just voicing a typically tactless four-year-old's observation. And who knew, maybe it was a compliment. She did seem impressed.

Aisha ate with a voracity that matched Jase's, though she didn't come close to competing with the volume he consumed. When she'd taken the sharpest edge off her hunger, and Mo was finished and had asked if she could go play with Lego in the corner of the big room, Aisha finally caved to her desire—at least partially—and struck up a real conversation. "When you first showed me the tree you were going to climb, I thought I'd have a heart attack."

Jase broke a piece of naan in half and dipped it in his third bowl of curry. "Me too."

"Really? You didn't look like it fazed you at all."

"It's why I don't eat lunch on days I'm climbing. I'm afraid my nerves will make me hurl—and today it was extra bad."

"Why?"

"Well, who wants to puke in front of a pretty girl?" His smile showed again, along with maybe the tiniest twinkle in his eye? He was getting used to her. And he thought she was pretty. Both ideas were frighteningly pleasing.

"You're seriously scared when you take down trees

like that?"

"Only an idiot wouldn't be wary of climbing a tree that tall or bringing down a snag."

"So, why do it then?"

Jase squinted like the question didn't make sense, then shrugged. "It has to be done, right? I was a little intimidated when I saw the scope of what Jo and Callum need done, but I signed on for the job, so I'll see it through."

Aisha was impressed against her will—and also skeptical, something she was much more comfortable with. "So if you 'sign on' for something, you always see it through, even if it's not what you expected or it's harder than you think it will be?"

His bowl scraped clean and apparently finally satiated, Jase stirred cane sugar into his mug of chai and considered her question. Or, at least, Aisha thought he was considering it because he didn't answer right off.

He didn't sip the tea, however, just kept stirring. When he eventually looked up, he didn't seem surprised to find Aisha staring at him, though she was embarrassed to be caught at it—again. In fact, he nodded like her scrutiny was part of their conversation and added in a soft, serious voice, "I try to."

That was the moment Aisha realized she was in trouble. She didn't just find Jason-call-me-Jase attractive. That, as annoying and potentially problematic as it was, she could deal with. But she actually *liked* him. Found him interesting. Admired the work he could do in a day. He wasn't just a pretty face, and that made him much, much more dangerous.

"Where is Colton anyway?" she blurted to change the subject, not because she really cared.

A shadow passed behind Jase's eyes, and again he seemed to weigh his words before answering. "In town, had some prior commitment. He should be here for work tomorrow . . . I hope."

Something in the length of the pause before Jase said "I hope" suggested there was more he wanted to say. Aisha tilted her head, waiting, but he offered no follow up, just turned his attention to his chai again. And Aisha, never one to spurn a good cup of tea, sipped hers too. It was kind of nice, just sitting, sipping tea . . . with a man. Jase looked over and caught her gaze. The shadow was gone, his eyes were smiling again—and it seemed to her that he was enjoying himself too.

Chapter 8

JASE SET HIS TABLET AND digital pen down on the little table beside his bed, happy he'd switched to this journaling method a few months ago. It felt like writing on paper but was instantly transformed to text via an app he'd discovered, and easily saved. For so many years, he'd filled notebooks, only to discard them. He liked the permanence of this, an online collection of his own work, and was pleased with the lines he'd jotted today.

He sighed contentedly and stared up at the glowing pine ceiling of "his" cabin—a little A-frame with all the primary living space on the main floor and a beautiful loft, accessed by a wide ladder, containing a spacious bedroom with the most luxurious bed he'd ever slept on and a much smaller room with a cot. That's where Colton could stay if he burned his bridges with his new-found friends or whatever they were in town, although what Jase would really love to do with the room—what he *would* do, in fact, if this cabin really were his—was make it into a mini library. Yep, line the walls with books, put in a good lamp and just one big comfy chair. He thought of Aisha. Okay, since he was dreaming, might as well make it utter fantasy—*two* big comfy chairs. Oh, and two little comfy ones, as well. One for Mo, of course. And one for Emily, like symbolically. . . . He hoped Bonnie read to her at bedtime. He'd never had someone to read with at night, but he imagined it would be nice. And, once the little chair's occupant had trundled off to bed and was soundly asleep, some other nighttime activities would also be nice, but those were less original fantasies.

He stopped his thoughts there, berating himself. You work with her, as in she *literally* only spends time with you because she's paid to. You exchange a few words once in a while over dinner, and you drink the odd mug of tea together. From those things you develop the mother of all crushes? Colton was right. He really was a loser. The insult came quickly, was at the top of his mind, which he guessed made sense seeing as Colton had finally responded to his last batch of texts, with a barrage of three:

The first: Not working today. Probably Monday.

The second: Jo and Callum are chill. Why not you?

The third: Stop being such a loser, bro.

Jase sighed. Colton was right. Jo and Callum were "chill." They didn't seem to mind that in the past two and a half weeks, Colton had only worked six days— and that now it was a Saturday again, thus a "week-end," which, of course, meant he'd want another string of days off. Miraculously, they didn't appear to hold his unreliability against Jase, even though he'd been the one to put himself out on a limb, at Colton's insistence, and ask if they had work for two guys, not just one like the ad asked for. He'd even warned Colton not to blow this gig for him, but he couldn't blame Colton for being himself. He was the one who should've known better.

Still, Jase couldn't get too seriously down on himself for being duped by Colton yet again, or depressed by his other issues, not here, not in this space. Had he lucked out or what? Imagine getting to live here year-round! It would be amazing. He had assumed, when Callum originally mentioned that room and board could be part of the compensation, he was referring to a bunkhouse of some kind, or maybe an empty room or two off the dining hall for extra staff in the busy season. He never imagined in a million years they'd put him up in one of their guest cabins—and one so brand spanking new it hadn't been named yet. He bounced lightly on the king mattress. He was the first person to ever sleep on this bed! Considering some of the seriously nasty places he'd bunked down, it was . . . surreal.

When Jo first took him over to the cabin, he thought they were making a stop for her to point out another snag or branch that needed taken care of. But then she'd handed him a key and waited expectantly. When it finally sunk in that he was meant to stay there, he was speechless—though that wasn't exactly new. Then he broke into a huge grin that he couldn't control.

Jo seemed to think his response was perfectly fine, however, and after a few minutes, when he finally found his voice and said he was really grateful and that he'd take good care of it, she had beamed, then asked, hesitating a second, if he needed an extra key for Colton.

Jase hadn't needed to pause for even a moment. "Naw, he's got other sleeping arrangements. If that changes, I'll let you know—but I'll still be the one in charge of the cabin and one key will be all we need."

She'd nodded and left him to wander about the place, feeling like he'd won a lottery he hadn't even known he'd entered. All these weeks later, he was still blown away.

Smiling, he climbed out of bed and practically slid down the ladder to the main floor, happy as an eight-year-old given his own pirate ship. Come to think of it, having a ladder to go up to the loft and a fire pole to slide down would be totally sweet.

He put coffee on—he'd never ground his own beans until staying here and it felt very fancy—something that made him both blush and feel weirdly pleased—then had a shower. He wanted to shower three times a day, and refrained—but man, the shower was . . . amazing. Instantly hot. Fantastic pressure. A panel of massaging body jets that he could turn off or set with varying levels of intensity and an adjustable shower head—that actually slid high enough that he didn't have to stoop. Being paid a wage on top of his meals and accommodation here was sort of like stealing—and on that note, he decided he'd better stop daydreaming and get a move on. He threw on his clothes, made quick work of his breakfast—oatmeal, three eggs, and some fruit—and equally quick work of the dishes, then headed outside.

As he took the trail toward the area he planned to focus on for the rest of the week, it was like each of his senses was set to hyperdrive. He was even conscious of the air, practically feeling it move in and out of his lungs. Fresh and piney and so . . . clean and simple. Unburdened. It was a weird way to think about air—but whatever.

In a few minutes he passed the small bend that led to quirky Minnow cabin and disappointment smacked him. There was no sign of Aisha. They'd planned to cut and stack firewood together, creating enough room to fall the next set of trees. But it wasn't like she didn't have enough other chores to keep her busy. Maybe she wasn't going to help him after all.

The disappointment was followed by an equally unsettling niggle of warning. It was fine to enjoy working with her. Who wouldn't? But he'd better not be entertaining notions of anything more except as the stuff of daydreams. There was no way a girl like Aisha, someone with roots and family and firm ideas about where she wanted to go in life, would have any real, sustainable interest in someone like him. She might flirt occasionally or make a joke, but that was just her friendly way. It meant nothing and he'd never be stupid enough to think he had something to offer someone like her.

Still, there was something beyond special about this place, about Jo and Callum—and definitely about Aisha. The combo intensified the strange feelings he'd been fighting the few months before ending up here, and that was no good. No good at all.

The plan, he reminded himself. Stick with the plan, and don't risk your luck by going gaga over the boss's niece. There are rules in life and number one is, people like you are not for people like them.

But damn—he glanced down the still-empty trail again—he did . . . like her. It wasn't just that she was cute as hell, though she was. She had a strange old-school goth meets Sailor Moon meets Downton Abbey meets farmer-slob vibe going on—not all at the same time, obviously. He had no idea where on earth she got her extremely varied wardrobe, but he liked her style. A lot. In the short time he'd been working at River's Sigh, he'd already gotten used to the fact that he'd never be prepared for—or able to predict—what she'd show up looking like. She changed her hairstyle regularly, wearing it in braids or pigtails or tiny buns on either side of her head—or straightening it so it swung in a flat, shiny sheet. His favorite was her natural riotous curls, though.

Her fashion whims weren't affected in the slightest by the work they were doing, however labor intensive or dirty. If she was wearing something delicate, she'd just pull on bulky coveralls and get to it. Her one concession to practicality was footwear. Indoors anything went. He'd seen her in stilettos at breakfast, every style of flat from converse sneakers to silver-glitter things decorated with rhinestones he suspected she'd glued on herself. Outdoors, however, her shoes of choice were always heavy duty and looked like they could kick your ass if need arose. She favoured steel-toed hiking boots—and yes, it did strike him as weird to have noticed. Why did he mentally record every single thing she wore?

He knew the answer, of course. Because she wore things very well. And every outfit was original and unique, which summed her up perfectly. He hadn't met anyone like her before, so disciplined and rigid and extremely capable. There didn't seem to be a job she couldn't do and do well. It should be intimidating. But the flipside of her seemingly endless dependability and intense seriousness was a sense of humor that ranged all over the place, from silly to surprisingly dry and witty, an offbeat, cool way of viewing the world, and a transparent, obviously limitless love for her daughter.

Mike Trent, the best guy Jase had ever lived with, who ran the group home where he'd met Colton and taught them arborist and landscaping skills, as well as general construction, would've called Aisha a "force."

Jase never understood the old-fashioned phrase until now. It seemed made for Aisha. She *was* a force. Someone to be reckoned with.

He was smack dab in front of her cabin now and he paused. He could knock on the door, just in case she was there. Or he could wait for her on the porch, or—

"Hey, stalker. What's up?" Aisha's voice behind him made him jump.

He turned and Aisha gave him a huge, happy smile. Jase's insides danced. Oh, yeah, he was doing a great job of not falling for her. He knew she gave that big warm smile to lots of people. It flashed numerous times a day. She was like that, generous and welcoming of everyone—even with him now that she'd let go of whatever she'd held against him the first few days.

She fell into step with him. "We still on for today?"

"Yep, firewood duty."

"Fun!"

He laughed out loud, and she shot him a look. "What?"

"Nothing." He shrugged self-consciously. "Just most people would've been saying that sarcastically and you weren't."

She beamed. "Thanks for noticing—and as for most people, they're idiots, right?"

He couldn't disagree.

"Besides, what's not to love? Working outside in the fresh air, seeing what you accomplish stack up— literally. Not to mention, it sure beats cleaning toilets."

"Whatever. You like cleaning toilets too."

Aisha rolled her eyes, but Jase knew it was for show. Her real response was written all over her face, and finally she admitted it. "There's just something satisfying in a job well done, you know? It almost doesn't matter what kind of job. My mom always said, 'Anything worth doing is worth doing well,' and she wasn't only referring to big things. She approached every task, no matter how mundane, with the same attitude. It drove me crazy. Dishes suck, right? Why are they worth doing well? I should be able to keep my room a pigsty or any other way I want. It's my room! But then . . . I don't know. I started to see how few people really give a damn—and how much could be changed in our world if everyone cared just a little more, in pretty much every respect, and I kind of . . . well, got what she meant, I guess. Plus, if you're not responsible with small stuff, you won't be with big stuff either."

It was the longest thing she'd ever said to him in one shot and Jase wanted her to keep talking, but she didn't. Her expression changed; angry Aisha was back. She picked up her pace and practically jogged to the worksite.

Jase followed slowly, giving her space. The admiration Aisha had for her mother was loud and clear in every word of her short anecdote. He wondered what it was like to have a parent you respected so much, and how it felt to know, whether you always agreed with them or not, that they were doing their best to raise you well. A woman with the kind of attitude Aisha described would have taken raising her child seriously too, would've tried to do right by her. So why, when they were so clearly close, did Aisha stop sharing about her mom so abruptly and bolt like a horse stung by a bee?

Jase had driven Jo's old pickup down to his current work spot earlier in the day, so they'd be able to relocate the wood as they chopped it, and by the time he caught up with Aisha, she had already grabbed a splitting maul from the truck box and gotten to work. Some of the logs that Jase had bucked into lengths were winter blowdowns, not as green as the fresh trees he'd fallen, but regardless, none of the pieces were truly seasoned and that made for tough splitting. Not that anyone would guess it, looking at Aisha.

She had obviously chopped a lot of wood in her day because she had great form and rhythm. Time and again, she quartered each piece with three well-aimed blows—the first cleaving the log into halves, then a quick chop for each of those two pieces, halving them again. No sinking the blade then having to thump it again and again, fighting to either free the blade and try again or to wrestle the piece in half.

The methodic crack of her axe, the snap of wood as it gave, and the thunk and thud of piece after piece hitting the ground created a cheery soundtrack to accompany the pile rapidly growing around her chopping block. He was pretty sure there was no way she'd be able to maintain the pace she was setting for long, but her speed and strength were impressive. And man, her ass in yoga pants . . . He got a stellar view every time she bent over and reached for another piece of wood. It was impressive too.

Wishing he could watch her all day but knowing that was a bad plan for a lot of reasons—not to mention, it was dangerous to be distracted when using saws and splitting mauls—he tore his eyes away and got to work.

He'd loaded a full row in the truck's box, stacked past the top of the cab, when Aisha approached, splitting maul in hand, sweating lightly. "My mom's dead," she said.

"What?" Jase asked, reeling. He'd seen her that morning with Mo. It didn't make sense. If something had happened to Sam, why the hell was Aisha out here?

She registered his confusion at once and shook her head. "Not Sam. My real mom. Her name was Maureen—Mo for short. My Mo is named after her."

Jase was still baffled. Mo called Sam "Grandma"—he'd heard her with his own ears—and Sam and Aisha were spitting images of each other. "Sam is my *biological* mother." Aisha sighed heavily. "It's a long story. My mom died of cancer. I went off the rails for a few years. Then I got pregnant. While I was trying to figure out what I should do, I decided to look for my birth mother. I'd never really cared about finding her until . . . well, until I did. Anyway, my search brought me here . . . To Jo first, actually, then to Sam."

"But isn't Charlie your dad?" Jase wasn't one for doing a lot of talking himself in the dining hall, but he did listen. Whenever Aisha talked about Charlie, they seemed really tight, which was weird if Charlie was only her newly discovered birth mom's husband.

Aisha huffed dramatically—but it seemed directed at the situation in general, not at him for being slow on the uptake.

"Mo and Charlie adopted me when I was only a few days' old; they're my real parents. My mom, Mo, *Maureen*, passed away—and I wasn't the only one to lose my shit for a long time. My dad fell apart too. He was starting to piece himself together again, a bit anyway, when I got pregnant. He was super resistant to me searching for my birth mom or coming out here by myself when I did find her, so he came with me to meet Sam."

"And they got together? They *are* together? That must've been . . . weird at the time."

Aisha's nose scrunched. She really was cute. Jase looked away.

"At the time? Are you kidding me? It's *still* super weird."

"Yeah, no doubt." He hated how he was always tongue-tied. What he wouldn't give to know what to say at critical moments.

Aisha was looking at him expectantly, which only made him feel more convinced that there was something else to be said that he was missing. "So, um," he tried, "I'm not exactly sure . . . why are you telling me this?"

He cringed and could've kicked himself. He didn't want her to think she couldn't talk to him. The absolute reverse was true. He wanted her to feel free to talk about anything with him, even if he'd never have the same luxury.

Aisha shrugged. "I just wanted to explain why I went off on that corny tangent about my mom—Rah, rah! My mom was amazing!—and then ran off like a crazy person."

"It wasn't corny," Jase said. She was open and direct with him. He would try, as much as possible, to be the same with her. "It's awesome you had a parent who was that inspiring and worth looking up to. You're lucky."

Aisha blinked and her eyes grew extra shiny.

Shit, Jase thought. He was a moron. "I mean, I'm sorry she died. Lucky is the wrong word."

"No, you're right. I was. I *am*. Just most of the time, as soon as people learn she died when I was a kid, that's all they hear. They go into condolence mode."

Jase suddenly realized he'd left Aisha holding the axe that she'd wanted to pass off to him. He caught her eye as he took it, then, not knowing what more to say, strode over to the chopping block and positioned a piece of wood. It was one thing to take a quick break here and there, but he wasn't being paid to talk and he needed to remember that.

Aisha followed him but stayed far enough away to be safe from flying debris or a chunk of wood if it went wild. "So what's *your* story?"

He could tell by her tone that the question wasn't just filler, like the way people greeted each other with phrases like, "How's it going?" or "How are you doing?" only to walk off before you even answered. The big axe was already in motion, however, like it was an extension of his arm, windmilling behind him, arcing high, slamming down. The piece split into three.

"Well, it's not like yours," he said, reaching for another log.

"Kinda figured."

"I mean I didn't end up in a place like this, or with some big loving family."

Aisha nodded, and Jase wanted to tell her about himself, but the words, how to start, wouldn't come. Though she'd only touched on how hard losing her mom had been on her and her dad, Jase knew what "going off the rails" looked like and how it was to live with someone as they went to pieces. Maybe in some ways Aisha's story was even harder than his own because she'd had something solid to begin with and had to watch it come apart. Even in the "good" years with his mom, he'd lived with the sensation that he was on a sandbar, one that was slowly but inevitably washing away in the tide. He hadn't been able to articulate it that way then, could only feel the creeping loss as her drug use took more and more ground.

Aisha waited without impatience, squatting and loading her arms with nearby pieces. When he remained silent and positioned another piece of wood on the block, she nodded again, as if his inability to converse like a normal person was no big deal. "Maybe you'll tell me another time?" She moved toward the truck with her large armful of wood.

He grunted, relieved. "Yeah, maybe." The big axe was already in motion again.

They got down to work in earnest, falling instantly and easily into a good rhythm. Jase had bucked everything in this location the past two days, so there was no loud, intrusive whine of the chain saw, just the repetitive crack of the axe, the clatter of wood hitting wood as they loaded Jo's pickup, and the quiet shhh of their slightly labored breathing. The piney air was the perfect temperature for hard physical labor, brisk and refreshing but not cold. Above their heads, birds chattered and called, once they realized they weren't at risk, and squirrels scolded them non-stop. Every so often he and Aisha exchanged conspiratorial smiles, wordlessly sharing pride in their work.

And Jase surprised himself by not missing Colton's "help" one whit. In fact, he wished he'd bugger off for good because when he showed up, Aisha did other work around River's Sigh. It was only when Colton was absent that she was his partner—and Jase didn't bother lying to himself. The more time they spent together, the more he craved it.

Chapter 9

IT RAINED FOR THREE DAYS straight, a heavy, relentless downpour that flooded the low areas of River's Sigh, creating massive puddles in odd places and filling the creek to the brim. It also sent a strong warning: no matter how nice and mild it could be, weather in the north was unpredictable, regardless of the season. Now, although the deluge had ceased for the time being, the sky was a lumpy porridge of dark clouds, which suggested it was merely taking a break and was nowhere near done pouring on them. Aisha hoped it didn't mean that yet another one of her and Jase's workdays would get cut short. It was literally the calm before the storm. There was so much to do! When she'd dropped Mo off to Sam in the office, Jo mentioned they had a couple of full weeks coming up—some artists' retreat.

Aisha was used to the busyness of running at full capacity in the summer; they all were. But to have max numbers this early in the spring? Before high season even kicked in? She'd be so knee-deep in housekeeping, it would be tough to find time for all the extra work that preparing for a busy summer required. And it meant she wouldn't be as available to Jase's beck and call. She didn't like how much that disappointed her, and she sucked in a deep, steadying breath. Maybe it wasn't about the boy. Maybe it was about the physical exertion. She loved outdoor work!

Jase's shy smile filled her mind. Oh, yeah, she thought. That's what you're enjoying. The "outdoor work." She rolled her eyes at herself but couldn't help but notice she'd started walking faster the moment he entered her head.

Come find me when you're ready. Jase's words all those weeks ago still played through Aisha's head occasionally. She was sure he hadn't intended any double meaning, so why did she keep torturing herself with the idea that maybe there was one, or that the universe was prodding her or something? She was not interested in Jase. He was not interested in her. They were just working together—and surprisingly efficiently and well, at that. If her extreme bizarreness when they first met had registered with him, the time they'd spent together since had made him forget about it. Thank God.

And think of the devil. Jase's voice came from some hidden vantage point beyond a massive brush pile, though he could obviously see her. "So she decided to finally show up today? How lovely of her."

Aisha covered her mouth with her hand, feigning a cough, so she wouldn't give him the satisfaction of seeing her laugh. Teasing her by talking about her in the third person had become a habit for Jase. It was super weird. And silly. And somehow, maybe because as far as she could tell, he only did it with her, sort of sexy. (Something she wouldn't admit aloud to another living person even under torture!) Silly and sexy. Who even knew that could be a combo?

"Well, somebody has to work," she retorted, "and since that somebody never appears to be you, I guess it only leaves me."

Jase literally jumped out of a tree just beyond the brush pile she'd now reached, and landed right beside her, grinning at her insult.

She tried not to think about the wiry strength of him or what it might feel like to—

"What are you smiling and looking so cheerful about?" Jase asked, just as a breeze kicked up and sent a tangle of hair into her face. He reached out and for half a second, she thought he was going to smooth it aside. Her stomach leaped.

Equally quickly, looking abashed, he dropped his hand.

A rush of disappointment warmed her cheeks and confused her. She hid her discomfort by looking down and fiddling in her pocket for a hair elastic. She bundled her mop into a tight topknot. "No sign of Colton yet again?"

Jase kicked at a chunk of wood on the path, catapulting it out of the way. "No. Sorry. I really thought he'd be here today."

Aisha looked up again and knew she was grinning. "No apology necessary." The day, which she'd already been looking forward to, was instantly even better. There was something about Colton that still made her edgy. She preferred having Jase to herself. The thought made her redden and Jase must've noticed because he gave her a searching look.

"Let's get to work."

He agreed silently, moving immediately into motion—but his work was curtailed as quickly as it started by the roar of a four-wheeler. Callum.

Callum got off the quad, pulled off his helmet, and nodded at Jase. "Hey, how's it going?"

"Good, good," Jase mumbled, but didn't quite meet Callum's eye. Aisha wished he would. And that he'd stand straight and be still, instead of hunching his shoulders and shifting foot to foot like he was up to something dodgy. She knew Jase was a trustworthy person and a hard worker. They'd spent enough time alone that if he had a sleazy side it would've shown by now, but she worried that everyone else at River's Sigh wasn't as convinced as she was. Sam and her dad, especially, seemed bizarrely curious and unfairly critical.

Callum looked around, nodded once more, and put some of Aisha's concerns to rest. "I have to say Jo and I are impressed with your progress. You're way ahead of where we thought you'd be by now, even if your brother had been helping."

Aisha exhaled and felt misty-eyed—a freaky over-the-top response to say the very least. She must be pre-menstrual.

Jase darted the quickest of direct glances at Callum, and his head bobbed in acknowledgement of the compliment. "Thank you, sir. I'm glad."

"Call me Callum, Jase," Callum said, his voice kind but carrying a slightly exasperated note like he'd made similar requests more than once. "When you're done for the day, can you come to the office? Jo and I want to talk to you about something."

"Yeah, sure." Jase shot a questioning look at Aisha, but she raised her shoulders in reply. She knew nothing. His gaze returned to Callum's general whereabouts but not his face. "I'll be there. Definitely."

Aisha shared Jase's unease, although nothing in Callum's tone sounded ominous.

Callum looked around again, but when neither Jase nor Aisha said anything else, he gave them each a weird look and shrugged. "Okay, well . . . I'll leave you to it."

Jase nodded and Callum retreated along the trail, the roar of the quad's engine going with him.

"Where's Mo today?" Jase asked as he stooped and got down to work.

"With my dad and Sam."

It seemed like something was weighing on Jase's

mind, but he didn't say what. Just lifted what were obviously the heaviest pieces of wood so she wouldn't have to and started a new row in the back of Jo's pickup.

They worked in companionable silence, Aisha growing ever more aware of her growling stomach. She should've eaten more for breakfast. Plus, despite the physical work, she was feeling chilly. Suckered by the mild temperature of the past few weeks, she hadn't dressed warmly enough.

"I'm sorry," she finally said. "I've got to break for lunch."

Jase looked up at the sky, which was considerably darker than it had been even half an hour earlier. "I think I'm going to need rain gear anyway, so I'll join you—I mean I'll get something to eat too, not that I'm forcing my company on you."

"It won't be fancy, but if you're into soup, you actually are welcome to join me."

"Really? That'd be great. I've been living off Jo's cooking, which is awesome, but I should hit a store soon and grab some staples."

Aisha hesitated, but only for a second. "I've got plans in the morning, but I'm going into town tomorrow afternoon, if you want to come with."

Jase wavered too—but also for hardly a breath. "Sounds good. Thank you."

They were halfway back to Aisha's when the clouds opened up like someone was emptying buckets on the earth. She and Jase shrieked like kids and tried to outrun the worst of it—but of course they couldn't. It was kind of hilarious until Aisha slipped on some muddy leaves. Her feet flew out from under her and she went down hard, landing flat on her butt with a big sploosh in a low boggy spot. She gasped as icy fingers of water went right through her jeans.

Laughing, Jase reached to help her up. "I'm sorry." He laughed again. "Are you all right?"

Aisha took his offered hand and shivered. The contrast between the temperature of her cold fingers and his, which radiated heat like his heart was beating in the palm of his hand, made her insides squeeze in pleasure. She'd been about to make some crack like, "Oh sure, you seem really sorry," but all she could manage was a hoarse, "Yeah."

Jase stared down at their linked hands as he pulled her up. His eyes locked with hers and her stomach squeezed again.

She didn't want to drop his hand, but to keep holding it as they walked would suggest something she wasn't ready for. Something she wasn't sure was actually on the table or being offered. It could be all in her head. Something she didn't even know if she really wanted.

Chapter 10

JASE'S MIND SKIDDED, TRYING TO organize and control the conflicting emotions and sensations flooding through him. Aisha's hand in his, smooth and cold—a perfect companion for his always-running-hot body temperature. Would the rest of her feel cool to his touch too? Well, the soaked part of her definitely—he quelled the thought, hoping his face didn't reveal where his thoughts immediately ran at this smallest bit of physical contact.

Her cartoon-worthy fall and splash had made him laugh, and for a second her face registered annoyance. But the minute he gripped her hand, her expression changed. Now she was biting her lip, looking up at him, and he was hit with the kind of surging desire that made rational thought difficult. He wasn't a kid anymore, so it wasn't impossible to control, but it was . . . surprising. And uncomfortable. And . . . awesome. It had been a long time since he'd felt anything like this, this sense of possibility. This rush of pure physical want. This welcome awareness that it was mutual.

Aisha dropped his hand like it burned her, and that made sense to Jase. He felt like he'd been branded.

They inhaled sharply at the exact same time, then simultaneously jammed their hands into their jacket pockets, and turned away from each other. Anyone watching would know something was up with them, but not what exactly.

Join the club, Jase thought.

They didn't exchange another word until they were at Aisha's door. Jase was suddenly uneasy. He'd made her uncomfortable. Maybe she would change her mind about feeding him lunch.

But Aisha smiled up at him and inclined her head toward the door in obvious invitation. "Pumpkin or tomato?"

Jase had read about pumpkin soup, but it wasn't something his circle of acquaintances ever cooked up. "I'd love to try pumpkin," he said.

Aisha's beautiful eyes crinkled, and Jase was lost. "My favorite."

My favorite, thought Jase.

Minnow cabin smelled like what Jase imagined Aisha's skin would if he pressed his lips to it, the lightest essence of patchouli, cedar and coffee. Sexy, earthy, hot.

"What?" she asked and Jase, afraid his face revealed his hunger, pretended not to hear. He wanted to study everything in the snug, unpretentious room that was so uniquely Aisha. The first thing that grabbed him was a large collection of rocks—quite nondescript ones, actually, which made him smile for some reason—and equally plain scraps of wood and branches on the large picture window's wide cedar sill.

"Mo's," Aisha said from behind him, a smile in her voice.

He turned. "Sorry, what?"

"The 'most precious treasures' collection." Aisha motioned at the pile closest to him. "Friends of ours, Gray and Mia, collect interesting things while they walk, much to Mo's fascination. She latched onto the idea and now there's not an unloved bit of gravel or plain-as-dirt stone around the place. Every one's a priceless treasure. I finally had to make a rule that in order to add a new one, she has to part with an old one."

Jase chuckled. He'd seen and heard enough of Mo in action at the dining hall to know she'd resist that.

Aisha nodded like he'd spoken his thoughts out loud. "You laugh, but I'm a serious cramp in her style. Sometimes there are actual tears—not real ones. Just ones to make Mom feel bad."

Jase laughed again. "How old were you when you had her?"

Aisha's jaw tightened—almost imperceptibly. If he wasn't always studying her so intently, he might not have even noticed. "Seventeen, but it didn't keep me from graduating from high school. With honors."

The response came instantly to his mind, heavy and

hard to contain. I have a ten-year-old daughter, he desperately wanted to reply, but I never see her. I really admire you. You're amazing. He didn't let himself say any of that, of course. He was shocked and alarmed he even wanted to. He kept his jagged-edge fatherhood status well-buried and tried to avoid thinking of it directly, let alone sharing it.

"Cool," he said eventually. "I didn't graduate from high school, but I read everything I can get my hands on."

Aisha looked at him oddly. Did she think less of him because of the school thing? "I'm going to get out of my wet clothes, and then I'll put the soup on. Will you watch it for me so I can go grab Mo? I'm calling it quits for the day."

The rain was falling in sheets beyond the big window, so Jase understood the decision, but was still unreasonably disappointed. At least he still had lunch to look forward to. He'd focus on enjoying that. "Sure—and yeah, makes sense."

Aisha disappeared through an arched door off the kitchen. Jase sat on the floor to stretch out his back and tried not to think of her stripping down to skin just beyond the wall closest to him.

She reappeared a second later in nothing but an oversized gray sweater that hung almost to her knees. Her bare legs and feet were bright pink. "The leggings I want are in the dryer." She caught him looking at her legs and lifted one, waggling her foot. "I am freeeezing."

Minnow, as its name suggested, was a very small space and her foot was right there. Jase caught it without thinking. "It's like ice," he agreed. He was about to release her, but the heat in her eyes stopped him.

"Your hands are so warm," she said breathlessly.

Resting her foot on his outstretched leg, Jase smoothed his hand over her cold skin, rubbing her calf and shin, then her knee and thigh. Her flesh started to warm with his heat. All the while, her eyes were locked on his. She didn't stop him, and she was biting her lower lip in that familiar, sexy way of hers.

Jase was sure he would've stopped before he got much higher. Or he hoped he would've. If they were going to start something, this wasn't how he wanted it to begin—though, on second thought, he could think of worse ways.

A loud rap on the door, followed immediately by the rattle of a latch and the turning of the doorknob almost stopped Jase's heart. He practically shoved Aisha's leg away, then bolted to his feet. She, equally startled, leapt back from him as if scalded.

"Mom!" Mo exploded into the room, then stopped and stared at Jase, open mouthed.

Sam entered on Mo's heels, but walking slightly backwards, holding the door with her skinny butt and maneuvering inside with a large box in her arms, speaking over her shoulder as she did. "I thought you

might be taking a break on account of the rain and—"
She turned, caught sight of Jase, and almost dropped
the box. She didn't stare quite so literally gape-
mouthed as Mo, but close.

Jase saw the room, saw Aisha, as if he were removed from the scene and knew how it looked. Her,
half dressed, rosy-skinned, hair damp, like she'd just
come out of the shower. Him—a big awkward dope,
definitely looking guilty of something because he *felt*
guilty.

Sam looked at Aisha, looked at Jase, then looked
back at Aisha. She was obviously thinking something,
but her face gave no clue as to what.

"I'm sorry. I didn't realize you had company."

Mo pinned her mom with a bossily inquisitive
look—an expression Jase didn't know existed until
seeing it on her. "Why is the man who eats so much in
our house?"

Unlike Jase, Aisha was, thankfully, capable of not
being a complete dimwit in social situations. "Funnily
enough, he's here to eat lunch, Mo-Mo. Your grandma
is right. We got rained out." She glanced at Sam who
rested the big box she was carrying down on the small
two-person dining table. "Good timing. I was going to
put soup on, then come to grab her. What's that?"

"A bunch of junk I thought you'd love."

"Ooooh, very intriguing!" Aisha seemed genuinely
thrilled, which made Jase wonder what their idea of
junk was.

"Do you need me this afternoon? I'm available till you name it."

Aisha rested her palm on Mo's crown of curls. "I'm actually taking the rest of the day off, and tomorrow too. Me and the monkey have serious play plans."

"Goody!"

"Do you want company?"

"No, we're good. Thanks though."

Sam nodded and Jase saw a flicker of something he thought he recognized in her face. Before he could nail down what it was, however, her smooth, give-nothing-away smile was back in place.

Aisha had been looking at the box, now she glanced back at Sam. "Dad flew out to that writing conference in Florida yesterday?"

Sam nodded.

"When does he get back again?"

"Not for a month! He's doing the con, then having some down time, then meeting with some writing friends, then presenting at a retreat. I was thinking of flying to join him, but I know it's a busy time for you. I want to be available, in case you need me."

"Oh, don't postpone on my behalf. I can figure out other childcare, no problem. I don't want to put you out."

This time, the flicker was more pronounced. Sadness, Jase thought. No, that wasn't quite right. *Longing*. He thought about his first impressions of Sam and Aisha—well, of the whole family, actually—

watching them in the dining hall, hearing them discuss various bits of work and personal life. He'd viewed them as this perfectly in sync unit and been struck by how much he'd missed. Now that he knew Aisha's story, though—or a tiny part of it anyway—the gulf between her and her biological mom was crystal clear.

"You could never put me out," Sam said brightly, "but I'll let you know what I decide in the next few days." She kissed Mo and Mo put her through a complicated "secret" handshake that Jase was pretty sure she was making up as she went along.

When the door closed behind Sam, Aisha took a deep breath and put her hands on her hips. "Okay, let's get this party started, shall we?"

"Yay!" cheered Mo.

Jase wasn't sure how pumpkin soup would equal "party," but he was almost as excited as Mo to find out.

And he wasn't disappointed. Lunch did seem like a party. The soup was delicious, though he wasn't sure how he'd describe what it tasted like if someone asked him, and Aisha served it with generously buttered rye toast and slabs of soft mellow cheese. "This is amazing," was all he could say.

Aisha shrugged off the compliment. "You like everything when it comes to food."

"I guess that's true. What can I say? Food is good." He was about to try to add a specific compliment about this meal being particularly good, however, but Mo jumped into the conversation, apparently approving of where it was going.

"Food *is* good," she confirmed. "Can we have popcorn for dessert?"

"Absolutely."

Aisha was good to her word. After they lingered over their soup—Jase had thirds feeling self-conscious, but Aisha forced him to and wouldn't take no for an answer—and while Mo kept them amused with non-stop chatter about her morning and her plans for rest of the day, Aisha made the largest stainless steel bowl of popcorn Jase had ever seen.

Reluctantly, he said he should probably head out.

"But you can't miss popcorn!" Mo insisted. "Pleeeeeasssse stay. And we're going to listen to Junie B Jones or watch a movie or play a game or maybe all three."

Aisha shook her head, but when she looked at Jase, her eyes were full of laughter. "Yeah, what Mo said. Pleeeeassse."

Jase laughed. "Well, if you're sure I'm not in your way—"

"We're sure!"

Aisha nodded and Jase laughed again. He wanted to say he was flattered, but the words caught in his throat. What he really felt was . . . gratitude and something else he couldn't quite identify, but strangely made him think of the shadow he'd seen flicker in Sam's eyes.

"It is a nice afternoon to curl up with a show, but the TV's in my room. . . . That won't be weird for you, will it?"

"Not at all."

Jase felt that flattered thing again when minutes later Mo insisted on sitting in between him and Aisha on the bed, not just with her mother. "Now you *both* get to sit beside me!"

"Lucky us," Aisha said. "Thank you."

"You're welcome."

"Are you the biggest man you've ever seen?" Mo asked Jase randomly, a second later.

Aisha choked on the mouthful of juice she'd just sipped.

Jase looked at her, then at Mo. "Um, I don't really know? I'm not sure?"

Mo raised her eyebrows and widened her eyes, apparently scandalized by his inability to give a concrete answer about such an important topic. "Well," she said firmly, "you're the biggest man *I* have ever seen. For real."

"Excellent," said Aisha. "I'm glad we got that nailed down."

To Jase's surprise, the movie was on VHS tape. Aisha's TV was tiny and had a built-in VHS player. Jase bet it was older than her and weighed almost as much.

"That's cool," Jase said, indicating their setup.

"Right?" Aisha leaned over the edge of her bed,

pulled open a big drawer hidden by her quilt, and revealed a huge array of Disney movies. "My dad collected old videos for me when I was a kid. Awesome, hey?"

Mo chose "Oliver and Company" and Jase watched it, as enraptured by the storyline as she was—although she was obviously familiar with it because she sang along with every song, word for word.

The popcorn was salty and buttery and delicious, Aisha's bed was a nest of pillows and super soft quilts that looked homemade, and every so often Aisha caught his eye over Mo's head and smiled. After the movie, they played go fish and built domino towers.

It was an achingly perfect afternoon, and Jase knew it was destined to be a memory he pulled out on low days, to remind himself there was good in the world and that he was occasionally lucky enough to be a part of it. It also made him think of Emily, and complicated, confusing grief throbbed through him. He prayed this kind of day, its cozy family togetherness and low-key good fun, was her norm.

"Are you okay?" Aisha asked and he realized he'd accidentally gone quiet.

"Yeah, I'm good. Really good, in fact. Just thinking how nice this is."

Aisha gave him a considering look, then smiled. "It really is, isn't it?" She patted his arm and his heart revved.

All too soon it was dark outside, and Aisha wondered aloud if she should start something for dinner for them.

For them. Jase liked the sound of that so much—but then a stone landed in his gut and squashed the happy feeling. It was dark, that meant it was, what, after six? He'd totally forgotten about Callum.

"I've got to go," he muttered and bolted to his feet.

"It's fine, honestly. It won't be much, but—"

"No." Jase shook his head. "I mean, I'd love to stay but I forgot that Callum wanted to talk to me. He's going to think I blew him off."

"He won't. It'll be fine."

Jase was nowhere near as certain as Aisha was, but that was another of the things he liked about her. She was so optimistic and sure that things mostly worked out. Life hadn't jaded her or made her resigned yet.

"Fine, go—but you have to promise me a rain check on dinner. Pun intended."

Rain check. He wished hard that he'd be able to keep that promise, but his gut warned otherwise. Callum and Jo were happy with what he'd gotten done. Needing to have a private chat could only mean one thing. The inevitable. That his services were no longer needed. That his temporary job was even more temporary than he'd thought.

Aisha's hand on his forearm made him jerk his eyes to her.

"Don't worry," she said softly.

"I'm not—"

She arched a skeptical eyebrow. "Callum's a good guy. Whatever he wants, it's not bad news."

Jase wondered what the heck his face had been saying that he hadn't meant it to. He worried all the way to the office. As much as he was dreading what Callum had to say, he was feeling even worse about breaking the news to Aisha. She really didn't seem to get that he was the kind of person people always considered expendable.

Chapter 11

THE OFFICE WAS DARK AND locked up for the night. Jase tracked Callum down at his house and stuttered an apology for interrupting his evening. Like Aisha predicted, however, Callum wasn't the slightest bit upset that Jase hadn't come to find him the second he was done work.

"It's perfect timing. Jo's out for the night, and I just baked a coffee cake that needs sharing."

Jase chuckled nervously. Would Callum offer him dessert if he was going to can him?

As soon as Jase sat down, Callum put a huge piece of cake in front of him and launched into what he wanted to discuss.

Ed Masterson, one of Jase's references that Callum and Jo hadn't been able to reach (turned out he was snowbirding in Costa Rica) had finally returned Callum's call. He and Callum had gotten to discussing random things, not just Jase's work ethic, which Callum said he'd already proven anyway, but also Jase's construction experience.

"How come you didn't mention it when you applied for the job?" Callum asked.

Jase had just taken a big mouthful of cake. It was delicious, but it felt wrong to eat when he was having an official work talk. He set his fork down. "Um . . . I guess I figured I'd focus on the skills you were specifically in need of."

"Is there anything else you didn't mention that maybe you should have?"

Jase wasn't playing dumb when he shook his head. "I don't think so . . ."

"No mistakes that you wouldn't want to repeat?"

Jase shook his head again—and then it hit him. Shit. "Ed told you about the car incident?"

"Yeah."

Jase was glad he'd stopped eating. His mouth was suddenly so dry there was no way he'd be able to swallow a crumb. "Why? What was the context?"

Callum shrugged. "We kind of hit it off, I guess. Talked about a lot of stuff."

"It was a misunderstanding. No one stole his car. Colton and his daughter dreamed up this . . . road trip, then she changed her mind, but he still wanted to go. I thought Colton had cleared everything with Ed, of course, or I never would've . . . I can't believe he even brought it up. When I agreed to return it, he agreed he wouldn't press charges."

"When you *agreed* to return the car that no one had stolen?"

"No, it wasn't like that. Agreed was the wrong

word. When I *arranged* to return it after I found out he didn't know we had it." Shit, it sounded bad. His only crime had been to listen to one of Colton's crazy schemes and take him at his word that everything was "copacetic," but still.

Jase glanced away, then forced himself to meet Callum's eyes. "It was stupid and sounds terrible, but I give you my word. I'm not a thief. And neither is Colton. He never intended to keep the vehicle. He just . . . doesn't always think things through. And Ed? He said he understood. I worked for him for months after that."

Callum studied Jase for a long time. "I believe you—and Ed gave you a great reference, by the way. He said the car thing was the only hitch in your relationship and that he'd never regretted giving you the benefit of the doubt. I only brought it up because I think it's fair for you to be aware Jo and I know about it."

Jase's face burned and the one bite of cake was like a stone in his gullet. Here it came. How they had to let him go. . . .

"Since we want to offer you a permanent position, we need to know that any similar . . . road trips will never take place."

"What? Pardon?"

Callum looked at him quizzically.

"You're offering me a permanent place . . . here. I'm not fired?"

96

"Most definitely not fired—and really hoping you want the job." Callum laughed. "Sorry, should've led with that, I guess."

Jase could only nod with stunned enthusiasm as Callum outlined what the position entailed, finishing with, "There are a few conditions though."

The first was pretty easy. Callum introduced it by saying that he understood and respected, how, when the job was temporary, Jase wanted to work as much as he could, as many days in a row, to get the job done so he could move on. However, that attitude wouldn't do from here on out. Now that it was a regular job, not a few months of employment, Callum wanted him taking two full days off every seven. Which days he chose were flexible but restraining himself to a forty-hour work week, max, wasn't.

"It's selfishness on my part, man. I don't want to pay overtime, plus I don't want you making me seem lazy by comparison."

Jase nodded seriously and said, "Got it," which earned him a strange look.

The second condition was trickier because it involved Colton.

"If he wants regular hours, we have them for him until fall—as an assistant to you. That said, we need to nail down something more concrete than him only showing up when he feels like it. We need someone dependable, especially since we'll be away off and on."

Jase was torn. He was tempted to answer for Colton, to say he wasn't interested, that Callum and Jo should look for someone else—or that they should save themselves the cost and bother of another employee altogether and let Jase work by himself. He didn't care if he had days off or not, and most work he could do on his own. For the odd time a task absolutely demanded two people, there was Aisha—and no better helper could be asked for.

It had been one thing to recommend Colton when they were both planning to move along in a month or two. It was another to suggest he'd make a good regular employee. And it made Jase extra nervous to have his name and reputation linked to Colton when Callum and Jo were planning to leave him in charge of the grounds when they weren't around.

And yet . . . Colton was his only family. He couldn't just shaft him.

"So will you contact Colton and let me know what he says, or should I call him?" Callum asked.

"I'll do it," Jase promised. "It'll be good too because it will sort of show the chain of command you suggested or whatever."

Chapter 12

THE DOOR TO AISHA'S WORKSHOP flew open and Katelyn bounced in, pink cheeked and rain spattered, carrying a huge plastic tote—equally rain spattered. When her kids flowed in after her, however, she looked positively blow-dried by comparison.

"You came! Hooray!" Aisha exclaimed, leaping away from the bench she was sanding and running to greet them. "I wasn't sure you'd make it, since I left the message so last minute."

Katelyn laughed. "It's never too last minute for a last-minute invite—and it was extra perfect because the kids were less than thrilled by the prospect of a rainy day at home. We happy-danced around the kitchen when I told them you called."

The kids started to race across the room.

"Halt!" Katelyn commanded cheerfully. "Coats off before you take another step—and boots too. We don't want Auntie Aisha's nice dry workspace flooded by the results of your puddle jumping."

"Puddle jumping! That explains it," Aisha said. "I thought you were drowned rats, but really you're just

99

Sawyer and Lacey after puddle jumping."

Sawyer giggled and Lacey shook her head, smiling—but both kids were already looking past her as they hung their wet things by the heater and put their boots on the mat by the door.

"Yep, she's here," Aisha answered their unvoiced question. "Already hard at work. You guys have a ton more wood; I got a bunch of ends from the lumber yard the other day."

"Awesome," Sawyer breathed.

"And Mom gave me more fabric," Lacey said with equal enthusiasm, popping the lid on the tote Katelyn had set down and retrieving a colorful bundle of assorted prints.

"Well, get to it then!"

The kids scooted across the room and through the overlap in the sheets of heavy plastic that separated Aisha's main workspace, where she sanded and painted and made all sorts of exciting messes, from the half of the building where she stored completed projects so they wouldn't get dusty. Mo had her own workshop on that side too, something she'd insisted she needed the past winter, and Aisha had to admit she put it to good use. She had her own workbench, real but child-sized, complete with a vice, a small hammer, nails, and various sanding tools. If she needed anything cut, Aisha did that for her—much to Mo's annoyance, though Aisha held firm that saws were out of the question for a few years. She also had a good assortment of non-toxic paints and glue, stacks of various papers, and felt pens. Her, Sawyer and Lacey's current obsession was doll furniture. Their stoves, made out of blocks of two-by-sixes, then painted red and given ringed elements with black marker, were impressive. Lacey had sold two of them to friends for five dollars each. "A steal!" she'd crowed, making Aisha and Katelyn laugh and wonder if she meant for herself or for her friends, but it didn't matter which.

Katelyn filled the electric kettle at the big utility sink, plugged it in, then dropped three teabags into Aisha's huge pottery teapot. "Getting a bonus shop day is about the only good thing about this weather."

"Exactly!" Aisha agreed. She and Katelyn were the same in that the bulk of their creating happened over the winter months, when they spent a few hours more days than not together in the shop with the kids, working and playing and visiting. Spring, summer and early fall were filled with other chores—work around River's Sigh for Aisha and gardening and preserving for Katelyn. They collected project items and brainstormed new ideas constantly, though.

The kettle whistled and while Katelyn filled the teapot, Aisha unhooked her and Katelyn's favorite mugs from a row of seven hanging in a pretty line above the sink.

"While the tea steeps, let me see how that chair turned out," Katelyn said.

"Right! I forgot you hadn't seen the finished result." Barely able to contain her enthusiasm—and pride—Aisha set the mugs down and zipped over to the storage side. The chair had turned out great. She couldn't wait to show it off.

"Wow," Katelyn said a minute later, squatting to smooth her finger along the gleaming espresso brown claw-foot of the antique chair. "I bet it's every bit as beautiful as when it was new. I can't believe it." She squinted, looking close. "There's not even a hint of those gouges showing."

"Wood filler's miracle stuff, all right."

Katelyn nodded. "And that soft mauve is unbelievable. So gorgeous."

Aisha stroked the crushed velvet seat and laughed. "It is, yes—and yes, it was your idea, so thank you."

"I wasn't tooting my own horn, honest. I forgot I'd suggested it." She patted the chair again, almost like it was a small child she was fond of. "It will be so beautiful in a home library, or in a bedroom—or by a makeup table. I want it for myself!"

They both laughed because it was a common problem: wanting to keep everything one or the other of them made, sewed, or crafted.

Heading back to their tea, Katelyn got sidetracked by a vintage metal-legged foldable card table which Aisha had painted a high gloss black. Its top had been too water damaged to salvage, so she'd re-topped it using MDF and a print of an old Victorian painting of poppies to create the look of a framed "paper top" like many old card tables had. It was visually stunning and incredibly practical, even if Aisha did say so herself.

"Oh! I'm buying this—no, I am!" Katelyn insisted before Aisha could get a word out. Swivelling to take in the crowded shelves and rows of furniture, she shook her head. "When we're here all the time, I kind of get used to it and stop seeing everything, but coming back after being away for a month or two?" She shook her head again. "You have a store here, my friend. A *store*. What are you waiting for?"

It was a good question—maybe even *the* question. Ever since Katelyn stayed at River's Sigh, years back now, seeking emancipation from her psycho ex and trying—and failing—not to fall for Callum's brother Brian, Aisha had talked her ear off about the business she dreamed of opening. And Katelyn, sharing Aisha's love for environmentally friendly fashion and her passion for upcycling in every way, never tired of hearing about it and chimed in with her own ideas too—fitting and exciting because Katelyn was going to be Aisha's first—and most awesome—supplier.

Back then, Aisha would've been certain her shop would be a done deal by now. She was about to say as much, and maybe ask if Katelyn had heard anything about a similar store coming to town, but Katelyn started sharing about a photography project she was working on—staging assorted creations, with the aim of opening an online shop.

"I didn't bring my tablet because I want you to see

the collection as a whole—but soon. Soon!"

Aisha shrieked with excitement, scolded Katelyn for making her wait, then asked all sorts of questions about the process.

They spent the rest of the morning happily chatting, sipping tea and working, Aisha on the piano bench she was sanding then planning to chalk paint and distress (it would make a fabulous end table), and Katelyn seam ripping and salvaging fabric and notions from good quality but unusable clothing. And as ever, when Aisha was in her shop, sanding or painting, gluing or fixing, she just felt *right*. Like no matter how confused or all over the place she was about some things, this she knew: restoring or reinventing things was exactly what she was supposed to be doing, was somehow her being her truest self.

The thought, coupled with Katelyn's brave move forward with her business goals, had Katelyn's question echoing through Aisha. What *was* she waiting for? Nothing she could definitively put a finger on, and maybe never would be able to—and her stalling would soon impede her ability to keep making things. She'd run out of room!

In order to do what she loved and felt compelled to do, she needed to start selling things in a much larger way than occasionally via online marketplaces whenever she thought to post the odd piece. Maybe she should stop worrying about rumors of possible competition and look for a spot to rent, with the goal of a fall opening. Actually, *should* wasn't going to get her anywhere. She *would* do it. It was time. She was ready. A thrill moved through her body and her last bit of doubt melted away. It was a firm decision about a big change. But it was right. She knew it. Finally.

She opened her mouth, about to spill the happy news to Katelyn—then changed her mind. She'd find the location and once it was finalized, she'd invite Katelyn for coffee in town and do a big reveal. She smiled to herself, knowing how much Katelyn would love the surprise and how excited she'd be about what the future held for their designs.

The kids, who'd popped in from time to time for help or to get compliments on what they were working on, finally showed up to say they were hungry.

Aisha was surprised when she glanced at her watch to realize it was twenty to one. "No wonder you guys are starved!"

"We could eat at your place, then work out here for another couple hours," Katelyn suggested. "I don't need to be home until five."

"Yay!" all three kids cheered in unison.

Aisha felt herself blush. "Definitely come for lunch, but um, Mo and I have other plans this afternoon."

"You do? Really?"

"Okay, you don't have to sound so shocked." Aisha laughed. "It's not like I never do anything."

Katelyn's eyebrows lifted. "Well, no . . . but it's

not like you ever usually do anything when you have the opportunity for a full shop day either." She studied Aisha's face. "Wait! Do these 'plans' of yours involve a boy?"

"No, Jase is a man," Mo supplied helpfully.

Oh Mo! Aisha thought and busied herself turning down the heat and clicking off lights.

Katelyn smacked Aisha's butt gently with her umbrella on their way out of the workshop. "I cannot believe you! We spent all morning gabbing and you didn't once think an afternoon with Jase was worth mentioning?"

"He's just catching a ride to town with us. There's nothing to say."

"Oh no, that's so not a thing! You're fessing up all the details—every single one—next time we visit."

Aisha laughed.

Chapter 13

IT WAS STILL POURING AND the trees along the highway blurred like a watercolour painting in the gray "daylight" that felt more like approaching evening, as Aisha zipped along the highway in her little car.

In the back, Mo was singing away to her rag doll, Zimmery—handmade for her by Katelyn and much beloved. It was beyond excellent that she was entertaining herself because in the front, Aisha was finding it difficult enough to focus on her driving with Jase sitting so close, radiating warmth in that oh-so-comforting way of his, and smelling so good.

Aisha fiddled with the stereo and accidentally brushed Jase's thigh. Heat suffused her face. His seat was pushed back as far as it could go, but his knees were still bent awkwardly high and he sat with his head slightly inclined toward the passenger window so he could avoid bumping it against the car's roof. It should've been comical, like he was a clown in one of those mini vehicles, but instead it only made her more aware of his sheer physical presence. Did other people around him notice it as much as she did? Jase filled the whole vehicle, and she was so conscious of him that whether she was physically touching him or not, it felt like she was.

He seemed to feel their proximity too and was (maybe!) as unsettled by it as she was. Or she hoped he was. Or she didn't. Argh, she didn't know! Either way, it had been a pretty quiet drive so far, and she liked that—that he wasn't one of those people who had to constantly talk just to hear the sound of his own voice. He'd commented on how he couldn't get over the beauty of the region—said the mist coming off the river made the place seem mystical—then silently proceeded to take in the passing scenery.

Every so often he drummed his fingers on one of his denim clad thighs, like he was responding to music only he heard. Every time he did, Aisha was drawn to the movement, then had to force her gaze back to the road, away from the view of his legs and the tight fit of his jeans—different ones than his usual work denim. These must be his town jeans, she thought, and it made her smile.

"So what did Callum say?" she asked eventually, truly wanting to know, but also hoping the answer might adequately distract her.

Jase looked over at her. "Did you know?"

It was a strange way to answer the question. "Know what?"

From the back seat, Mo crooned, "Know, know, know whaaat?" to the tune of "Row, row, row your boat," obviously more tuned into the front's occupants than Aisha had originally thought.

Jase rubbed his jaw which had a delicious five o'clock shadow—What is wrong with me, thought Aisha. Focus!

Just as she was starting to worry that maybe Callum and Jo had actually said something negative or terminated his job, he shrugged. "You're looking at River's Sigh B & B's new groundskeeper."

"Like permanently?" Aisha's voice was embarrassingly squeaky.

Jase looked uneasy. "Well, permanent for now anyway. Why? Is that okay?"

"Of course—not that it matters what I think. River's Sigh is their business—but it's all good. We have tons of yard work every season."

"And I guess you guys all vacation in the winter and need a caretaker?"

Aisha nodded. "Yeah, this local guy Jesse used to help us out, but I think he and his wife are going to Hawaii or something this year."

"Nice."

Aisha's eyes were trained on the road, but out of her peripheral, she saw Jase studying her. She shivered a bit and glanced over at him. He immediately looked away and resumed watching the trees zip by—but not before Aisha got a good look at his face. What was he thinking about with such a fathomless expression? It drove her crazy how completely he could mask his thoughts and feelings.

Mo had gone quiet. A peek in the rearview mirror revealed she had nodded off, her little chin bobbing against her chest. The hum of the car's engine and the pooling water on the highway splashing against the undercarriage seemed inordinately loud. They were nearing the four-way intersection that led into Greenridge, and Aisha was about to ask where Jase wanted dropped off, but he spoke first.

"I guess it means we'll be seeing a lot of each other."

Excitement-laced fear rocketed through Aisha. That's exactly what his new position meant. She hadn't known she'd been hoping for that very thing until now, and she was confused by a simultaneous, but conflicting thought: it would be easiest and for the best, by far, if he just . . . moved on.

The stop sign for their lane was suddenly right *there*. Startled, she hit the brakes much harder than necessary. The car slammed to an abrupt stop. Aisha's body lurched against the tight constraints of her shoulder belt and Jase's head thunked against the top of the windshield.

Aisha winced. "Sorry." She checked her rearview mirror again, making sure Mo was okay. She was still asleep, undisturbed by the jostling.

"No worries."

After a logging truck cleared the intersection, Aisha turned right, heading in the direction of the old one lane bridge that would take them into Greenridge on the side of town closest to the library, the first of Aisha's planned stops. "Where should I drop you?"

Jase nodded like her change of subject was a response to his earlier statement, and she guessed it kind of was—but it made her feel like a wimp.

"I want to hit the library and a grocery store. I won't take long either place, but I'm good to sit in a coffee shop until whenever you and Mo are done. Just let me out wherever you want to pick me up. I'll go about my business and make sure I'm back for whatever time you figure you'll be finished."

"I need to go to the library too and I'd also planned to grab groceries. Want to do errands together, or would you prefer to split up?"

"Together sounds good." Was there a hint of suggestion in Jase's voice or was he simply answering her question? Either way, Aisha's stupid stomach leaped again. She glanced back at the still-sleeping Mo.

"To me too," she answered. "But it's complicated."

She was mollified to see Jase's brow crease. Why should she be alone in her confusion?

Aisha jerked her chin toward Mo's car seat. "Can I treat you to coffee and we'll drive around for a bit, so she can sleep a tad longer?"

"Anything you need works for me."

He was so sincere—so *nice*. Dammit! Another point to him!

"Alrighty then."

They got coffee at a drive through, and Aisha gave Jase a guided car tour of downtown Greenridge and what locals called the south side. It took about fifteen minutes, including "doing the bridges."

"There's another residential area on the plateau of that mountain," she said pointing north, "and a couple other pretty well-populated areas on the outskirts of town that have different names, but are really, for all intents and purposes, part of Greenridge."

Jase nodded. "It's huge, super urban."

Aisha laughed. "Okay, okay, no need to be sarcastic."

Mo started to stir.

"Perfect timing."

Like the impromptu lunch and movie/game afternoon the day before, the rest of the day was just . . . lovely. Aisha never felt she and Mo lacked anything being a little family of two, yet she was surprised by how Jase just seemed to fit. He felt like an extension of them, not a guest. Maybe it was because he was so easy going or maybe it was how gentle he was with Mo, not pushy or trying too hard to impress her or ingratiate himself to her—yet shyly pleased whenever she said anything to him or included him. Aisha particularly liked how, when Mo said or did something comical, Jase would meet Aisha's eyes and smile his slow smile, like he was as impressed with Mo as Aisha—and Mo herself—was.

In the library, he was surprisingly quick to return to

the children's section where Aisha was letting Mo choose books, though the reusable book bag he carried was packed full.

Aisha had just told Mo that three times was enough regarding the book they were reading together, but Mo insisted passionately that she needed to hear it again. Her eyes lit up when she saw Jase.

"Will you read this to me, please?" Mo asked. Jase shot Aisha an unsure look.

"You definitely don't have to, but if you wouldn't mind, maybe I could sneak away to pick out some books for myself?"

"Yes, please!" Mo added, like Aisha getting a chance to browse on her own was Mo's top priority.

Jase lowered himself to the floor beside them. Surrounded by child-size furniture that looked exactly like adult furniture but in miniature, he could've been part of a Gulliver's Travels display—though admittedly no version of the story Aisha had ever read suggested Gulliver was so yummily gawk-worthy.

"What?" Jase asked.

Aisha's face flamed and she shook her head. "Nothing." Then she added to Mo, "I won't be long. Be good my little Lilliputian!"

Her comment garnered hilariously similar looks of bafflement from Jase and Mo.

When Aisha returned, after taking slightly longer than she'd planned—she'd gotten pulled into a new series by accident and ended up arranging an interlibrary loan so she could binge read them—it was like neither Jase nor Mo had moved a muscle in her absence. They were both so absorbed in the book on Jase's lap, they didn't notice Aisha approach quietly behind them.

She stared down at their bowed heads, struck by the contrast of Jase's tough-looking shaved scalp, complete with a jagged heart-shaped scar near his crown, something she'd never seen before because he was so much taller than her, and Mo's soft shining curls, which were pulled up into a high, slightly messy bun. The napes of both their necks were visible to her, and they seemed equally tender and vulnerable somehow. The observation made her smile and go slightly misty-eyed. She swallowed hard, then mocked herself. What a weirdo. She must have PMS. It did not go beyond her notice that she used that excuse whenever her emotions got the better of her—and that seemed to be happening a lot lately. But whatever. Getting pregnant as a teenager had made her super conscious of her cycle, whether another baby was a physical impossibility because of no sex life or not.

Jase finally sensed her presence and looked up. For the briefest moment, his eyes gave her the strange impression that he was sad or wistful about something. But then he smiled and his whole countenance transformed. Figuring she was just overthinking as usual, Aisha glanced at the book lying open in his lap. It was the same one she'd read to Mo three times before turning Mo over to Jase.

"Seven," Jase said, like he read her mind.

"And *he* didn't complain once, Mom."

Mo packed up her own books and, staggering under the weight of the bag that she half carried, half dragged, started toward the self-check out machine. Careful not to be overheard by Mo, Aisha whispered, "Suck up."

Jase's face creased with humor. "I can't help it if I'm a competitive repetitive book reader and you're an amateur."

"A *competitive repetitive book reader*, hey?"

"What can I say?" Jase shrugged with mock humility. "Some of us have it, some of us don't."

As Mo "beeped" her own books, something she was obsessed with, Jase said, "You're probably already aware of this, but she knows most of the words in that story. She practically reads it herself."

Aisha smiled. "I think it's more like she has it memorized—and I have no idea how she managed that feat, ha ha—but yeah, she can sight read a few things."

"And she's only four?" Jase shook his head. "Is that . . . usual? Like are most other kids reading by her age too? Or if someone had been closer to seven or eight before they learned, would that be all right?"

It was a weirdly specific question for someone without kids, and Aisha chuckled. "I think as long as you're reading fluently now, you're all good—but yes, Mo is a genius."

Jase didn't laugh at either part of her comment, so Aisha did. "I'm joking—and more than a tad biased."

"You should be. Every kid needs to have a parent in their corner, whether the kid knows they are or not." His tone was so serious that Aisha gave him a double-look, but he'd started pulling out his books to scan and she couldn't see his eyes.

"Well, if that's the most important criterion, I guess I'm nailing parenting."

"I think so." Again, there was no hint of a joke or the suggestion he was even slightly exaggerating.

Grocery shopping with Jase was oddly fun too, although Aisha had to carefully refrain from asking him whether he liked pretty much every item she put in her cart because, of course, he wasn't going to be eating every meal with them.

"Ooolala," she said when she saw him put a Japanese brand of instant noodles in his shopping basket. "So fancy! No generic noodles for you."

His eyes crinkled. "I've seen the food standards at River's Sigh, so I'm upping my game."

Ten grocery carts deep in the checkout line, Jase remembered he wanted ice-cream. Aisha agreed to hold his place, while he and Mo went to find some. A cooking magazine caught Aisha's eye. She was about to pick it up and flip through it, when something two women ahead of her were saying grabbed her attention. Aisha froze and eavesdropped shamelessly, her good mood plummeting. She couldn't even manage to be falsely cheerful when Jase and Mo returned.

"Everything okay?" Jase asked, as they loaded the car with their purchases. "Did something happen?"

"No, yeah—not really." Aisha clicked Mo into her car seat, climbed behind the wheel, and buckled up. Jase followed suit on his side of the car.

"Well, maybe something did. I'm not sure. Are you game for a small detour before we head back to River's Sigh?"

"Absolutely."

And so, her heart beating fast, Aisha drove down main street, then turned onto a small go-nowhere side street, queasy with dread.

She pulled to a stop in front of her destination, and her fears were immediately confirmed. The cutest, most perfect—if rundown and badly in need of re- pairs—heritage house that she'd been coveting for years for her store was already under renovation. And one thing was brand new and already installed: a wrought iron post near the stone walkway with an ornate hanging sign, also ridiculously cute and perfect, announcing The Second Chance Shop. A line below added, Whimsical gifts for the practical heart. And beneath that, hanging as separate entities linked by delicate chains, was a vertical row of creamy placards, forming the following list: New ~ Used ~ Antique ~ Vintage ~ Upcycled ~ Recycled ~ Consignment.

A sturdy but temporary banner hung over the cor- ner of the sign on a diagonal, bragging "Coming Soon" in huge pink script.

It was like the ground split beneath Aisha and threatened to pull her down; she almost cried out. It was one thing to have heard rumors that someone had hijacked her idea, inadvertently or not. It was another thing, entirely, to see it. So perfect. So everything she'd wanted.

"Um, what are we looking at exactly?" Jase asked.

But Aisha . . . couldn't talk.

Mo answered for her in a helpful tone. "That's your store, right, Mom?"

Aisha shook her head and swallowed back what she was sure would be a sob if she let it escape. "No, baby. It's someone else's."

She was aware of Jase's eyes on her as she shoulder-checked and pulled away from her dream, but she couldn't bring herself to say more at the moment. Mo was right. It was Aisha's store, right down to the specifics of what the store was selling. She even loved the tag line "whimsical gifts for the practical heart" and would've used it herself if she'd thought of it. And now . . . what? She had a workshop of . . . absolutely nothing. Someone had beaten her to her dream—and looked like they were going to do a better job than what she'd envisioned.

"Red light," Jase said calmly.

"You're not kidding," she muttered back, then realized what he actually meant. She'd seen the light, was already slowing for it—but understood why he might be worried. She stopped with plenty of time, didn't even have to brake hard, but she appreciated the warning regardless.

"Mama?" Mo asked and Aisha felt transparent and lame. Mo only called her mama if she was sad or sensed Aisha was. "Can I listen to a story?"

"Sure, sweetie. Do you have your headphones?" She glanced in the rearview mirror and saw Mo nod, already wearing her Bluetooth headset.

"It's paired, Mom."

Aisha wiggled her phone out of her back pocket and handed it to Jase. "Would you mind going into the Overdrive app and resuming the Junie B. Jones story? It should be already open. My phone's password is 2-3-2-6."

Jase quietly obliged, and Mo rested back in her seat, looking on the verge of laughter just in anticipation. It made Aisha smile, despite herself. At least one of them was happy at the moment.

As she cut through town toward the highway, the backs of Aisha's eyes burned. Seeing proof that her dream shop was just that, a silly, naïve dream for her, a reality for someone else, on the very same day she'd completely recommitted to going for it was . . . crushing. How had she let herself down so badly? Why had she stockpiled and hoarded and waffled about instead of striking out on her own a year ago? Why, even now, was she almost as preoccupied with Jase sitting beside her as she was with the fact that all her plans had crumbled?

She cleared her throat, coming to a decision. She liked Jase, sure, but there was no safety, no security in that . . . just the opposite, actually. She needed to refocus on her priorities, make concrete decisions about what to do next, and then follow through with actions to bring those decisions, whatever they were, into existence. She had to stop failing herself.

From the backseat, Mo giggled—then giggled again. Aisha and Jase exchanged an amused glance. It was good timing. Mo was definitely distracted and wouldn't overhear, and she and Jase had made eye contact.

"I've been thinking about what you said earlier," she started, shifting her gaze back to the road.

"What was that?"

"That since you're working at River's Sigh permanently, we'll be seeing a lot of each other—and I guess you're right. It does mean that. We will."

"Is that a bad thing?" Jase didn't sound offended, more like he genuinely wanted to know.

One of Aisha's shoulders lifted in a half shrug before she could stop it.

"I'm not very happy with how I've been treating you," she said, darting another quick look his way.

If she'd punched him in the face, Aisha didn't know if he could look more startled.

"How so?"

"I'm normally a very direct person. I try to be super honest, with myself and with others, even if it's uncomfortable."

"Okay . . ."

They were stuck at yet another red light and Aisha spotted a crow just beyond her windshield. Caught in a strong cross-current of wind, it flapped about in an awkward frenzy, then flipped over in the breeze. He struggled to right himself and finally managed to. Instead of flying away, however, he landed in a nearby tree as if attempting anything further was too much at the moment. Aisha so related.

"I like you. I'm attracted to you. I have fun with you. There's something—some draw or whatever—between us. We both feel it, I think."

A half smile creased Jase's face, but was instantly replaced by a pensive, knowing expression. "But?"

Aisha nodded. Just one more thing she liked about him. He wasn't an idiot.

"But when you weren't going to be around long-term, I let myself enjoy the fun of what if, the luxury of flirting, etc." Her grip on the steering wheel tightened. "But now that you're a permanent fixture—and I'm happy you are, sincerely, I am—you need to know that it doesn't matter what fantasies I entertained. I'm building a life for me and Mo. I'm working to be financially independent and to have my own business—which will probably require relocating now." Her voice caught, but she pushed on. "I have no interest in any kind of real romantic relationship, not a serious one, not a casual one, not any kind of one."

"Wow—"

But Aisha wasn't finished. "I just don't have time and I have no desire to make time. Plus . . . " She trailed off, the full truth a hot coal on her tongue. *I'm too scared. I can't risk loving—or losing—another person.* But that was too much to say to someone you weren't even officially dating. "Plus," she repeated, settling for something just as true, but not as nakedly so. "Past experiences haven't convinced me that any benefits of a romantic relationship make the hassle worth it."

Jase blinked and he was quiet for a moment. Then he seemed to come to some inner decision. His eyebrow quirked. "You have fantasies about me?"

Aisha shook her head, but a happy glow of relief flooded her. Oh, good. She'd worried her declaration might cause her to lose him as a friend, but she wouldn't. They were going to be fine. "So not the point, and don't get too excited. I'm strictly PG these days."

Jase turned in his seat—quite the feat for him—and his eyes shone like he was going to make another joke. He opened his mouth, then closed it again.

"Seriously," he finally said, turning away from her again. "I respect what you aim to do. I like working with you though, and I hope things won't be awkward."

"Not at all. And I hope only wanting to be friends

isn't a problem."

"Not at all," he echoed.

"Great." She raised her hand from the wheel to give him a friendly fist-bump. As their eyes and fists connected, an embarrassing spark surged through Aisha. Jase evidently felt it too—quickly, self-consciously, yanking his hand back.

Aisha cranked the radio. The remainder of the drive home was conspicuously loud and eye-contact free.

Chapter 14

JASE SPENT SUNDAY GIVING THE cabin a good cleaning, though it was already tidy, doing laundry, and reading. He was blatantly avoiding the outdoors and any chance of bumping into Aisha. He wanted to show he'd heard her and that he'd respect her boundaries. He also thought it would be good for Callum to see he was honoring the conditions of their agreement.

He tried not to think about his initial reaction to Callum's notice about enforced days off: a body buzzing anticipation at the idea that maybe he and Aisha could go on weekly outings of some kind. With that daydream shot to heck, Jase had no idea what he'd do with time off every week, but he guessed he'd find something.

Sighing, he put his book down. He hadn't been concentrating on the thriller for the last chapter or so, anyway. And he shouldn't delay any longer. It was nearly the end of the weekend. He'd better get busy and text Colton.

He scrounged around for his phone, hoping with all his might that Colton was feeling extra lazy, was all wrapped up in some new distraction in town, or, even better, would announce he was hitting the road with someone else. If he would just decline Callum's offer . . . Please.

Chapter 15

IN THE LIVING ROOM, AISHA pushed back the rich burgundy and gold panel—a gorgeous sari she'd repurposed into a curtain way back when she'd first moved into Minnow cabin—as far as it would go. Then she did the same in the kitchen and dining area. It didn't help. Even with every window as open to the daylight as possible, the living space was gray and shadowy. Thank goodness longer, lighter days were on their way. Seasonal Affective Disorder, a.k.a. SAD, really was a thing.

Though usually a diehard about only using electric lights when necessary, so at *night*, she turned on every lamp in the place. It wasn't good for the human psyche to dwell in darkness. Besides, it made her feel bad for Mo. A bright spark like her shouldn't have to play in the gloom.

As if sensing her mom's affectionate gaze, Mo glanced up from her jungle babies coloring book and beamed approvingly at the closest lamp, which made the table she was working at shine with warmth and the nearby sari-curtain glow. "Cozy!"

It really was. Aisha's heart filled. How had she gotten so lucky? To live in this tiny, beyond-beautiful refuge of natural wood and stone and comfort. And *Mo*. Did every mother feel like this about their child? That just by their existence in the world, yours somehow made sense? As if birthing that little creature was the whole point of *you*, and anything else you might go on to do would always be peripheral to the importance of caring for them? And anyone else you might come to love would always be second to them?

Oh gag, what a sap! But her inner sarcasm couldn't erase the fact that she really, sincerely, did feel that way. And she knew she was fortunate—and that Mo was equally so—because her inner question had been rhetorical. Of course, not all mothers felt that way. Mothers were just people, as varied as they came. And what even constituted "motherhood," let alone being a "good mother" was subjective. Look at Sam. Some people, even Aisha herself at times—all the time?— would say Sam wasn't a mother, or hadn't been one, at least, since she'd given Aisha up for adoption. But didn't that very decision, made with what Aisha truly believed was Sam's genuine desire for the best possible life for her child, show Sam *was* a mother and had always been one, the very best kind of one actually, right from the start?

Aisha didn't feel rejected. She was eternally grateful to have had the parents she did. She just didn't understand the selflessness Sam had shown because in the end *that* was what bothered Aisha about her adoption, now that she had a child herself. She knew how she felt when she was away from Mo. Even when she knew Mo was having the time of her life—and even when she herself was having a good time without Mo—it was like a part of her was missing. No matter how in the moment she was, or how she'd been craving "alone time," if Mo wasn't with her, there was a gnawing awareness of her absence at the edge of Aisha's consciousness. And Aisha saw Sam with Mo, *really saw her*. There was a deep well of love there. The kind of possessive, proud, absolute love you have for . . . your child—or your child's child—and it made Aisha wonder. No matter how cool Sam tried to play it, or how much she insisted she'd done the right thing and had no regrets, a part of her had probably yearned for her daughter . . . and as that daughter? Well, it was a lot of pressure.

Also, if deep down, despite her good life, Aisha really didn't feel the tiniest bit rejected or resentful, why wouldn't she just embrace Sam for her choice and empathize with her? If she truly didn't mind, she would feel compassion for Sam, not just . . . meh. It was a mystery that made her uncomfortable and feel like she didn't know herself very well.

On the heels of that annoying rumination was her unhappiness that she hadn't seen Jase all day—and her unhappiness at being unhappy. He hadn't been in the dining hall for Sunday brunch. Instead, it was crowded with townies (Sam's word for customers who lived locally and came for weekend meals, which Aisha thought was hilarious and adopted immediately). She liked the townies fine. She disliked that she noted and was affected by Jase's absences—disliked it immensely.

"Mom, why aren't black flowers real?"

Mo's question was a welcome distraction from all Aisha's weirdo thoughts, and she joined Mo at the table to discuss it with her and do some coloring herself. Later she and Mo read bedtimes stories, then had a bubble bath, then curled up with a movie in their roomy bed.

As Mo's breathing slowed and she fell into a deep, flush-cheeked sleep, Aisha tried to stave off memories of the last time she and Mo had watched a movie together—and of the lovely, gentle giant who'd filled her bedroom and felt like he'd belonged.

"You can dream," she muttered, finally allowing herself to admit her longing—it was probably normal after all, "but you can't act on it. You and Mo have things to accomplish. Someday there will be room and time for all that with somebody if you still want it."

Although Aisha's whisper had been as quiet as a breath, Mo stirred.

"What, Mama?" she asked drowsily.

"Nothing, sweetheart. Just I love you." Aisha drew her close and Mo snuggled in like a puppy.

All in all, Aisha told herself sternly, except for the

129

blow regarding her shop—something she'd just have to push to the back of her thoughts until a new idea presented itself—it had been a lovely two days off. She was glad she'd been honest with Jase. He'd understood and accepted where she was coming from, which was a relief—so why didn't she feel it boded well for the upcoming work week? Why was she so unsettled? No, scrap that. She knew full well why. She wished Callum and Jo would leave everything be. Why couldn't they just continue to hire the odd workers here or there on a when absolutely necessary basis? Adding another full-time staff member, especially one who lived on the property year-round—even someone as low-key and nice as Jase—would make things different around the place. River's Sigh was supposed to be her steady, safe rock in the ebb and flow of life, and it was perfect the way it was. She didn't want it to be one more thing that was always changing.

Chapter 16

FRAMING THE FIRST OF THREE new woodsheds Callum wanted built was going pretty quickly. A miracle, Jase thought grouchily, considering Colton's mouth worked a lot faster than the rest of him.

Having Colton back working by his side had been fun the first day. He'd made Jase laugh with impersonations of recent people he'd met, reminding him what a good storyteller and observer of human nature he could be. It was almost enough to calm Jase's reservations and give him hope that his brother was going to take the newly re-offered job seriously. He'd even shown up early, with his rucksack of clothing and personal belongings, planning to live on site.

Now, with hardly more than a full shift under their belts and despite their progress, Jase could barely keep from growling whenever he glanced over at Colton, who was measuring two by fours, then cutting them to length according to the list of needed sizes Jase had given him.

The circular saw whined through another piece and the leftover end clattered down. Colton slid his safety goggles up and his hearing protector earmuffs down, so they looped around his neck. "That it?"

"For now. Come give me a hand with this and hold it steady while I anchor it."

Colton walked toward the beam Jase was holding in place, going as slowly as a person could, while still moving forward. Why had he accepted the job if he had no real intention of actually working?

"I'm serious," Colton said, continuing the line of conversation that made Jase want to punch him in the face and was the reason Jase gave him saw duty in the first place—to shut him up. "She's totally into me. That's why she always acts pissed off whenever I'm around. She's trying to cover."

"Or she sees through you and has the good sense to steer clear."

Colton snickered. "No way. You'll see. Fifty bucks says we hook up within the month."

Rage blurred Jase's vision. He took a calming breath and when his head was on straight again, drilled three screws with hard, fast precision. "You can let go now." He finished securing the board while Colton waited for the next spelled out task. "And I'm not betting on whether you can or cannot get a date. It's demeaning to her, and it should be demeaning to you."

"Date? Who said anything about a *date*? I said we'd hook up."

Jase retrieved his level and placed it on the board he'd just fixed in place. He'd already checked before he hammered it in, of course, but he liked to doublecheck. Satisfied everything was square so far, he gave Colton a cool glance. No good ever came of letting Colton see he was getting to you. If Colton decided Jase had a thing for Aisha too, he'd be even more unbearable, wouldn't be able to resist what he'd see as competition.

"I thought you and Becca had something going?" That was a bit of a lie, of course. Jase didn't think it, he knew it—but if that fling had exploded, Colton's free place to crash and endless party invitations had dried up. It would explain not only his interest in Aisha, but also his decision to agree to the more constraining job terms.

Colton shrugged and winked. "Oh, we did. She's a total slut."

Jase didn't bother to hide his disgust. "Nice, real nice."

This was an old battle for them, and Colton didn't bother to pretend he didn't know what offended Jase. "What? She is. So am I. It's called fun, my brother. You should try it sometime."

Jase grunted and delivered one of his old and tired stock lines too. "You and I have very different ideas about fun and about women." And about work. And about life. And about . . . pretty much everything, he added in his head.

Colton laughed. "Well, maybe you have different *ideas* about women than I do—but which one of us actually has any experience with them lately?"

Jase pulled off his leather work gloves and tossed them onto a nearby sawhorse. "I need something to eat."

"You mean we get meal breaks? Lunch at lunch time and everything? How many minutes and seconds do we get, boss man?"

Jase rolled his eyes. "If you didn't want the structured days and schedule, why'd you take the job?"

"I told you. The dough. And the challenge—"

"And I told you, *no*. Leave Aisha the hell alone!" The instant the words exploded from him, Jase recognized his mistake.

Colton's eyes were calculating as he scrutinized Jase and his expression grew merry.

Shit! Maybe by "challenge" Colton hadn't been referring to Aisha at all. Maybe he'd forgotten all about his passing plan to leech onto her—but now Jase had tipped his hand and Colton would be committed to it.

"I just don't want either of us to do anything to jeopardize this gig," he said tiredly, hoping to throw Colton off the scent. "It's solid—good money, nice digs, great food. Let's hunker down for a bit and make bank. When we're flush, if you still hate it, we can head somewhere new."

Or *you* can, he thought. Fingers crossed.

Colton removed his goggles and hearing protection and placed them beside Jase's gloves. For a second, the highest of hopes soared through Jase. Maybe Colton was going to buy in.

"It's a good plan, buddy, but come on, we gotta make it interesting. All work and no play and all that."

One more thing about Colton that irritated Jase: how he twisted the things Mike used to tell them at the group home.

"Let's make it a hundred that sweet little piece will be all over me."

Jase was torn. Should he hunt Callum down right now and tell him he and Colton had to quit, no apologies, no excuses, so Callum wouldn't try to talk him out of it, or should he rush to find Aisha, wherever she was, and warn her off Colton.

Colton brayed like the jackass he was all too often, then let out a low whistle. "Your face! Hoo, boy—you're going to give yourself a heart attack, man. Relax. I'm just kidding."

Jase didn't relax.

"You're getting your panties in a twist over nothing. Aisha's a big girl. She's not going to do anything she doesn't want to do, and I promise I won't misrepresent myself or my intentions."

"That doesn't exactly ease my mind."

Colton grinned. "Cause you're freak, but you're not an idiot."

Against his will, Jase felt a small return smile crack his face. The thing that always made him forgive Colton his shortcomings was how he never tried to pretend he was anything he wasn't—with Jase, anyway. It was his one consistently redeeming quality.

"Okay." Jase took a big breath and expelled it through his nose. "So, for real, how long are you going to work this job seriously?"

"For real," Colton mimicked like they were still eleven, "as long as I can stand it."

Really, if Colton had said anything different, it would've been a lie, intentional or not. "Fair enough. Let's go eat."

"You said that already, *boss*."

Oh yeah, this was working out awesome.

Chapter 17

Aisha came out of the janitor closet, wrestling with the steam cleaner's hose and humming under her breath. There was nothing she liked better than being able to get down to work with no people in the way. The artists' retreat—such a raving success that the group had already booked the same slot for next year—behind them, Aisha planned to take full advantage of the upcoming, slower week. She was going to steam clean each unit's area rugs and furniture— well, not the leather pieces, obviously. She had a great environmentally friendly product for taking care of the leather.

She exited the small hallway into the main body of the dining hall that should've been empty this time of day—and felt the presence of someone before she even registered the motionless shadow.

"Miss me?"

Aisha shrieked and pressed a hand to her chest. "Asshole! You scared the shit out of me!"

"Tsk, tsk, such language from such a pretty mouth."

Colton was leaning against the wall, one leg stretched out, one knee jutting, foot pressed against the wall—as ever, in such a "strike a pose" manner that Aisha was sure he did it for effect. There was nothing casual about Colton's "casual" poses.

"What are you doing here?"

He grinned, straightened up, and took a step toward her. "Waiting for you, of course."

Aisha twitched angrily. "Stop that and tell me why you're really here."

Colton's eyebrow rose and he gave her an intentionally lingering full body glance. "Even the hired help gets a rare break," he said cheekily. "We have labor laws to thank for that—and it's a good thing they exist because your uncle and my bro are two of a kind, unfortunately. They'd work twenty-four hours a day if they could."

Aisha must've looked blank.

"I thought your uncle—or Jase—would've told you."

Aisha dropped the steam cleaner's nozzle, all her plans for a vigorous, productive cleaning day dampened. "Told me what exactly?"

"I accepted."

His words made absolutely nothing clearer. "Accepted *what*?"

"The job, of course. I'll be your five days a week schmuck from here on out."

Aisha narrowed her eyes. Did Colton seriously

think keeping regular hours was something to disdain? What an idiot. It was uncharacteristically poor judgement on Jo and Callum's part, actually. It's not like she'd been keeping an eye on him full-time or anything, but it was transparently clear if you weren't a complete sucker. Colton showed up to work only when *he* wanted to, regardless of what the person paying his wages might need. He put mediocre effort—and that was generous—into whatever he tackled. He had no pride in a job well done.

"I'm not sure what you think that has to do with me. I just work here."

"Right." Colton winked. "Anyway, I wanted to re-assure you. I feel our chemistry too, but it won't affect my work or my . . . reliability."

"Are you high?" The question sounded sarcastic, but she wasn't joking. She didn't know Colton, but she knew his type. It would be just like him to get stoned for work. "Whatever you're feeling, I guarantee it's not mutual. I actually liked it better when you were a deadbeat temp who didn't show up for work—if one can fairly call what you manage to get done in a day *work*."

Colton grinned like she'd complimented him, but then his cocky expression was replaced by something that looked like bashful remorse. He bowed his head and looked up at her from beneath heavy-lidded eyes. "I'm sorry. I know I can come off as sort of a jerk. I don't mean to. It's a bad habit when I'm feeling insecure—and you're so . . . amazing. You can't blame me for feeling out of my league."

Uh huh. Insecure. Right. Aisha didn't buy the line—or his flattery—for a minute. Next thing he'd be telling her that he'd never known anyone like her and she was *so* unique and *so* special and *so* beautiful—and that pretty much from the moment they'd first met, he'd known they were meant to be together, blah, blah, blah, blah, *blah*. Okay, maybe she was getting ahead of herself, not to mention projecting, just a bit, but that minor detail didn't change the facts. Colton was a lot like Evan. She'd noticed it right from day one—and his type would never take her in and use her like a fool again.

"I'm not sure why you're in here talking to me. Jase is in charge. You should be reporting to him."

"You're right. I'll do that." He gave a sharp salute and ambled off. Leaving as—and when—requested was about the only thing Colton could've done that would possibly surprise her, and she had to force herself not to stare after him.

Chapter 18

IT HAD BEEN A LONG time since Jase had seen Aisha angry. In fact, he'd forgotten all about her bad temper days. But when she showed up where he was clearing a blockage that was damming the creek and flooding lower parts of the property, it was obvious her furious side was alive and well. She closed the distance between them like she was on fire, her hands clenched in fists, flaming color raging in her cheeks. Her eyes practically sparked when they landed on him.

Jase put down his saw and climbed the bank. "What's up?"

"Did. You. Know?"

"Know what?"

"When you told me you were staying on permanently, did you know they were offering Colton a full-time job too?"

Somewhere deep inside, an observation registered with Jase. By referring to Jo and Callum as "they" instead of by their names, Aisha linked herself with him, as separate, as *other*, from "them." Obviously, it was done unconsciously, but even so, something inside him leapt at the significance. Then shrank in shame, all too aware of how undeserving he was of being linked to her in any way.

"Uh, yeah." He winced. "I actually arranged it for Callum."

Aisha made a derisive half sniff, half snort sound. "Why?"

Jase wasn't as confused by the question as he wished he was. He already knew she was sharp as a blade. She'd seen him and Colton working together, and Colton wasn't careful around Aisha like he was around Callum. Of course, she knew Colton was . . . a questionable choice.

When he didn't immediately answer, she repeated herself and elaborated. "Why would you do that? What were you thinking?"

Jase studied her agitated face, struggling for the right words. He'd assumed her outrage was because she intuited how Colton was. But something in the flush of her skin, which had spread from her cheeks, down her throat, all the way to the hint of cleavage at the soft curve of her shirt's neckline, made him pause. Maybe it was something else about Colton becoming a permanent fixture, something non-work-related, that had her unsettled.

Aisha looked around, and her frown deepened. Jase wanted to take her face in his hands and smooth away the stress lines furrowing her brow.

"Why are you staring at me?" she snapped. "And

where is he, anyway? Already on a break?"

"Nine thirty would be early for a break, even for us slackers."

"For *you* slackers, hey?"

"We spent the last two days organizing and using up the lumber Jo and Callum had on hand—I don't know if you knew, but we're building new wood-sheds?"

Aisha nodded.

"Anyway, I sent him with a list to the hardware store. He took Jo's pickup—Jo knows, don't worry—but he'll only pack back the smaller stuff. They'll deliver the lumber."

Aisha nodded again and plunked herself down on one of the freshly cut stumps, looking deflated and glum, but no longer angry. Jase loved how she wore every emotion so vividly—much like her clothes, actually. He didn't necessarily know what triggered each mood or what reaction to always expect from her, but he didn't have any trouble picking out what she was feeling. Her face was . . . captivating. Yeah, that was the word, all right, even if it was kind of old-fashioned.

"You're still doing it," Aisha said, her voice soft now.

"Doing what?"

She nudged at a splintered branch with her snub-toed boot. "*Staring*."

He sat down beside her. "Sorry."

"It's all right." She turned a little, so that her body faced him, then gave his upper arm a friendly, feather-light punch. "I'm sorry I bit your head off yet again. I don't mean to be such a snarky cow."

"You're the furthest thing from a cow."

"Oh, but I *am* snarky?"

Jase responded to her teasing tone with an equally teasing exaggerated shrug. When he spoke though, he was serious. "What is it about me and Colton that pisses you off so much?"

A fresh wave of deep pink suffused Aisha's face. "I don't know," she mumbled, for once seeming as tongue-tied as he always felt. "Colton puts me on edge or something. That's the only way I can really explain it. I know he's your foster brother or whatever, and I get that you're tight, but I don't like him—or trust him."

At this proximity, Aisha's eyes were even more amazing, and today she'd enhanced them further, adding a dusting of fine gold sparkles to the sweeping black arc of pencil that created the cat's eye look she favored. It was so pretty he couldn't tear his gaze away. No wonder she called him out for staring at her! He always *was*. With that, he consciously forced himself to glance away and focus on something else for a minute—though it didn't work that well. Sure, his eyes weren't on her for the moment, but she was still all he could see.

"You probably think I'm awful and judgemental."

Jase shrugged, torn between wanting to defend Colton and wanting to tell Aisha to listen to her gut.

"He's just so cocky—so positive everyone wants him. He reminds me of my ex. Mo's dad."

Jase's shadow-self, a perpetually awkward, shy kid that he could never outgrow, braced and waited for the blow. In his experience, baby daddies got a bad rap, but then again, Aisha never talked about Mo's dad. Her lack of griping was more telling than if she complained about him all the time. It made him think Mo's dad might really be a bad guy. There were enough of them around, for sure. Even with his dark suspicions, however, what she went on to say still managed to catch him by surprise.

"I hated the kind of person I became when we were together—or maybe already was, just that he brought out in me." Aisha squinted into the distance, clearly looking back at something that made her uncomfortable. "He was charming and flippant, never took no for an answer, and could always figure out exactly what to say to keep me buying his line—or, at least, doubting my own opinions. He thought he could take anything he wanted, *get* anything he wanted—and eventually it led to sex I didn't really want to have."

Jase nodded. His heart hammered, relating too much and wishing for her sake it wasn't something they had in common. He wanted to tell her about Bonnie and how she'd been with him—but he was a guy. No one ever thought the guy didn't want it. Even all the way back then, his friends thought he had it made. That he was *the man*.

Aisha went on to explain how Evan tried to talk and cajole her into having sex, then badgered her, then, finally, forced himself on her one heated night.

Afterward he'd acted like it was a big step forward in their relationship, said most girls had doubts at first, that it was normal. It hadn't felt normal. It had felt like rape—but she hadn't broken up with him. She kept going out with him. She kept making out with him. And then she'd ended up pregnant. And not only that, she discovered another girl in her school was pregnant with his kid too, though she ended up losing the baby.

Aisha braced her elbows on her knees and pressed her face into her hands, and Jase worried she was crying and wanted to comfort her but didn't know how. After a moment or two, she regained her composure and lifted her face—which was notably free of tears.

"It was so . . . humiliating. Like some Jerry Springer freak show." Her voice was flat in a way he'd never heard it before. She stood up from the stump abruptly and paced the wood chip strewn ground. When a twig snagged her pantleg, she picked it up and fiddled with it. "But it was also good because it finally allowed me to see through the mind games he played, to know the things my gut whispered were true. He was just manipulating me, using me. I don't know what I was thinking. That's honestly what bothers me most. That I wasn't true to myself or to my values when I was with him. Instead I was this person I didn't recognize. This stupid, vapid, weak . . ." Her voice trailed off, and her piercing gaze shot up Jase's.

"You can't tell anyone!"

"I won't. I *wouldn't*."

Aisha snapped the twig she'd been holding. "My Dad and Sam know. Evan came weaseling around when Mo was small, pretending he wanted custody. I explained to Sam and my Dad so they'd understand why I was so adamantly against having him around us."

The twig, in many pieces now, dropped back to the earth. "I never talk about this—have never told anyone else besides them the details before. Sam was helpful, actually. Said it didn't *feel* like rape. It was rape. Said it wouldn't have mattered if we'd had a happy consensual sex life and then he'd forced me sometime. That would be rape too. Sex you don't want, that you say no to, is rape."

A new twig, a larger one, found its way to Aisha's hand. Her voice was raw and her sigh sounded like it hurt her. "And I agree . . . but what do you say about something like that when you keep going along with it, when it becomes voluntary? What does it say about the kind of person I am?"

Jase felt like he was caught up in that old "Killing Me Softly" song. It was exactly like Aisha was telling his whole life with her words. For a long time, he'd lived every day with the shame of being coerced into something he didn't want to do but did anyway—and then kept doing.

Years later, he'd realized it was wrong . . . that he'd been a kid and a pretty innocent one, sexually anyway. He'd been taken advantage of, but it was like Aisha's rhetorical question.

"Sex . . ." Jase cleared his throat. "I don't know. When you're a kid, or young, I mean . . . it's complicated."

"And it's not now?"

Jase blinked. "Well, that's good."

"No . . . it was a question. You don't find it complicated now?"

"Um, I don't know." He shook his head, then shrugged. "I don't have sex these days."

Aisha looked surprised. Then her mood changed abruptly, and she laughed. "Me neither! I might as well be a nun."

"Well, not having it does get to be a habit."

"Was that a pun?"

He nodded sheepishly. He wasn't trying to make light of things . . . not at all. Just, well, sometimes you had to make light of the pain you carried or it would sink you.

"A *habit*." Aisha echoed, then rolled her eyes and groaned. He smiled in relief. She obviously appreciated the lame joke.

A beat later, she prodded, "So?

"So?"

"Do you think I'm a bad person for judging Colton based on how he reminds me of someone else?"

"Not at all. But you should know, Colton's not some terrible guy. He's not like . . . your ex—" Jase broke off with a shrug. "I mean he's a bit of a player, but he's not a rapist. He'd never do something a woman didn't want him to—and he's trustworthy around kids, not a pervert or anything, and he won't steal from you guys."

"Wow, so he's not a pedo or a thief? What a rave character reference."

Jase ducked his head, feeling stupid. He did think those attributes were noteworthy and spoke about a person's character, but he guessed Aisha's insinuation that they were the bare minimum was one more sign of how different the worlds they'd inhabited as kids must've been, despite any similarities in their past relationships—and, really, in all practical ways, how different the worlds they inhabited now as adults still were.

He couldn't think of how to word his thoughts about all that, however, so he changed tracks entirely. "Okay, so Colton reminds you of your ex. That explains your reaction to him, I guess."

"My *over*reaction, you mean."

Jase shrugged. "If you say so—but what about me? Just guilt by association or what?"

The pink in Aisha's cheeks had faded, but now it

glowed again. Jase sat up a little straighter. What was this now?

"You already know," she grumbled.

"I really don't."

"Yeah, right."

He widened his eyes and held his hands up.

"I already told you in the car on the way back from town the other day."

"Told me what?"

She apparently thought he was teasing her or something because she exploded cheerfully. "Don't rub it in! So I was attracted to you or whatever when I first saw you and it made me a bit mental. It's not a big deal."

"Oh, sorry, right. Uh—"

"You sound confused."

"Um . . . I just, I mean, well, obviously I remember our conversation in the car and stuff. I just didn't know you were . . . attracted to me so early on."

Aisha shook her head. "You really have *no* idea, do you?"

"Um, no, I really don't," he said again, but chanced a grin. "About what? You're going to have to be more specific."

"Not on your life."

"Okay . . . but going forward can I safely assume, in general, that my *general* existence no longer makes you furious, only Colton's does?"

Aisha burst into warm, happy laughter, and she

was suddenly her usual cheery, undaunted self. For a shining moment, everything was right in Jase's world. "Yes, rest easy, Jase. Your *general* existence *in general* does not make me angry anymore. The opposite actually."

Make that two shining moments, Jase thought.

Chapter 19

NOW THAT COLTON WAS SHOWING up and pulling his weight, Jase didn't need Aisha's help as much. A good thing, she kept telling herself. She was more than busy enough—so busy, in fact, that the question about what to do regarding her shop-fail was easy to ignore. That said, another idea—one that first flashed when she'd told Jo she wanted to live at River's Sigh forever but not be a squatter—was more difficult to quiet. Initially she'd thought it was nonsense. Buying shares in River's Sigh? It was too big a dream. But the possibility kept popping back into her head with increasing frequency, and it made so much sense, felt so right. Aside from Jo and Callum, who cared more about the place—or worked harder to help it flourish—than her? But it would mean choosing to not be fully self-sufficient or self-reliant. She'd never be the boss, never be in charge, and her and Mo's security would always depend on other people. It went against everything she'd previously thought she should work toward. What was best though? Her old way of thinking or this new, slowly emerging one? Argh! This was why it was good she had enough on her plate to keep her out of her head most of the time. Thinking drove her crazy!

Busy or not, however, she couldn't deny that she liked working with Jase. Liked it a lot—and she'd given up trying to pretend it was just the change of scenery involved with doing a different kind of work or the novelty of hanging out with someone her own age that she appreciated. Jase was the draw, and she knew it. Every chance she got to be an extra pair of hands for him, she was happy to oblige. And that's how she found herself outside this glorious afternoon, under a pristine blue sky and brilliant sun, revelling in warm air that smelled deliciously of quickening sap and tender new growth, and that carried the promise of coming summer.

Jase, however, appeared to view summer's approach as more of a threat than a promise, and he'd stewed about it to her and Colton in the dining hall that morning. He wanted the third woodshed up and roofed, and as much of the mountain of firewood split and put away as possible before peak season hit.

"Jo and Callum aren't going to hold it against you if there's still some wood to do when there are guests around. They know how much we need now that we're so busy and so many of the cabins have wood heat. Besides, customers find it charming."

"I'll hold it against myself. This place is gorgeous and all that wood lying around is a mess. I told Callum I could build a shed from top to bottom in two days."

Aisha rolled her eyes. "And I heard him tell you not to kill yourself to do it—and it's not like you're sitting around idle when you're not working on the sheds."

"Yeah, but there's no lack of things requiring attention. I've tagged trees that need falling on the west side of the property, you know, by that outdoor stage thing?"

Aisha nodded.

"But I haven't tackled them yet, and then the whole area will need clearing and cleaned up, but if we can fill those sheds, that'll see the cabins through this year, at least. The rest of the wood I do will be next season's. Jo also wants me to put in a big vegetable garden. After that—"

Aisha listened to the rest of his list, which could easily take them into the next century the way he kept adding to it. How Jase not only thought about work for the day, but always had an eye for tasks that needed done in the future reminded Aisha of Jo. The observation made her smile and quickly interrupt him, before he buried her in the details of every single other possible job he, Jo and Callum had discussed. "I don't have any real construction experience, but I can take orders and swing a hammer—plus, you already know I heft wood like a champ."

"More like a champ and a half."

Aisha grinned. "I'll come find you when I'm done cleaning cabins. It should go pretty quick. A lot of guests have No Service Needed signs on their doors. Then I'm all yours for whatever you want."

Hearing the possible, though completely unintentional, double entendre in her words made Aisha's breath catch with embarrassment, but her discomfort was instantly replaced with a happy flattered feeling as Jase's eyes lit up.

"Really? You don't mind? You have time?"

His eagerness was as transparent as hers—and so cute that Aisha giggled, feeling a lot like a thirteen-year-old with a crush. Then, to her huge mortification, Jo chuckled from somewhere behind her too. Dammit! She hadn't noticed Jo come in and would've greatly preferred not to be caught making a flirty ass of herself. Yes, Jo was her aunt and they were close, but she was also her employer. Meh! It was super awkward how tightly knit all aspects of her life and relationships were. She didn't want to dim the light in Jase's expression though, so she tamped down the snarky comment that would've been her usual default when caught feeling obvious feelings and answered Jase with equal enthusiasm, knowing she was grinning like a mad person and not even minding that much. "Yep, nope, and yep!"

The office phone rang and Jo went to answer it, just as Jase replied, "Great!" His gaze held so much warmth that heat tingled through Aisha—heat that chilled when Colton looked up from his oatmeal. He was so not a morning person. Aisha could count on one hand how many words she heard out of him before noon on any given day—a welcome respite from his norm, truth be told—and she was surprised when he intruded on their conversation now.

"You guys realize you'll be screwing down tin and banging nails, right, not each other?"

Jase glowered, but Aisha was getting used to Colton and merely crossed her eyes at him. When he laughed, she further startled herself by chuckling along with him.

Anyway, that had been the morning. Now, with lunch done, she was practically jogging alongside Jase to keep pace with him. She was a brisk walker, but good grief, his legs were at least a foot longer than hers, maybe more. Colton caught up with them too, and as they strode toward the worksite together, Aisha found herself comparing and contrasting the two guys and herself, yet again.

As laughing with him earlier that morning instead of wanting to slap his smirking face showed, she was getting along better with Colton now. And she was (mostly) immune to his crazy good looks. The more time they spent together, or near each other, at any rate, the more he seemed to shrug off his you-know-you-want-me shtick and act like a normal person. Still, it was pretty clear that he was merely working for the paycheck. But maybe she was too critical. That would describe most people, and why shouldn't it? That's why you took a job, after all, for money. It was an extra bonus if you could combine supporting yourself with work you were passionate about, but there was honor in every type of honest employment.

Aisha shook her head at herself. She really was a dork. But it was true. She wasn't lying or exaggerating to Jase whenever she went on about this kind of stuff. She had no financial stake in River's Sigh—or not yet, a tiny part of her mind prodded—but she was definitely invested in the labor she did here. It was fine that Colton wasn't like her, obviously. It even made sense that he wasn't—but it did make the similarities between her and Jase all the more noticeable.

As she exited Woodshed One to fetch another armload, she admired Jase's broad back and realized he must have stopped shaving his head. Normally he wore a bandana while he worked, but he'd taken it off. No one would call his hair long by any stretch, but it was almost ready to need a comb. It looked soft and touchable—but then again, she'd wanted to rub her hands over his tough-looking bald head too.

He was bent over a sawhorse table, meticulously double-checking the plans he'd designed for the third woodshed that was going in by the barbecue pits, closer to the big group cabins Callum and Jo were planning for some time in the future. It was more complex than the first two sheds and would include an insulated room at the back for gas and saw storage.

As if feeling her eyes on him, he glanced up and smiled. She gave a small wave, acknowledging their wordless exchange, and his smile deepened before he returned his attention to the diagrams.

Jase was motivated by . . . what? The need to take care of himself and keep a roof over his head, sure—but he was a traveller. And young. It wasn't like his cost of living could be that high.

"True confessions time, Jase," Aisha teased. "Do you have any deep dark secrets or bad expensive habits?"

Colton, who was filling his arms with logs on her left, guffawed. "Our boy Jase? Not a chance. He's too boring."

Jase grinned. "What Colton said—unless tattoos and books count. Why?"

Why, indeed?

"Just curious," she muttered, turning away quickly to load her arms with the biggest pieces of wood she could find. Tattoos and books did cost money, but in and of themselves weren't enough to explain his work ethic.

Maybe there was something specific, a big-ticket item, he was saving up for? Yeah, that was probably it. Maybe he wanted to travel around Asia or go back-packing in Europe. Or maybe he wanted to buy a house and settle down somewhere? Not bloody likely, but she couldn't help entertaining a smidge of hopeful delu-sion. And it wasn't her fault. Her dad was a romance writer! That kind of wishful thinking, believing happily-ever-after was a thing, rubbed off on a person—but she would go to her grave before admitting it!

She and Colton were making good progress in Woodshed One. It was half full already. She started a new row, making sure the pieces were butted up tight against the ones behind them, then snuck another look at Jase as she emerged from the shed again. Over by his sawhorse work table, he had straightened up and was staring out into nothing, like he was envisioning the structure he was about to build, seeing it take form in front of him.

While she'd been inside stacking, he'd stripped off his nylon shell and fleece. He was wearing nothing but a soft looking, faded waffle knit shirt, so worn the cuffs were ragged.

"Running hot today," he said, misinterpreting her gawking. (Thank God!)

Aisha wanted to lick her lips and say something semi-lewd to be funny, but she resisted. Considering she'd been the one who laid down the law about not getting involved, being super flirty or overtly hitting on him would be pretty ignorant.

But he looked so totally huggable and—

He clasped the back of his neck with one of his large hands, distractedly kneading the thick muscles at the top of his spinal column. With how hard he worked pretty much every hour of the day, Aisha could only imagine how tight and sore he must be sometimes, though she had never heard him complain. She had a delicious massage oil that Callum's sister-in-law Noelle had sent her, infused with rosemary, calendula, and eucalyptus that she'd grown herself, specifically for easing muscle aches and pains. For a second, she envisioned straddling a shirtless Jase as he lay on his stomach while she rubbed his back.

She practically had to bite her tongue to keep herself from groaning. Yikes, girl! Rein yourself in, will you? She'd definitely check her calendar when she got back to her cabin. She must be close to ovulating because her hormones were out of control.

Jase turned toward her suddenly, inclining his head in a silent question.

"We're making good progress!" she said brightly—as if that's what he'd been wondering about when he'd felt her eyes on him again. Aisha forced herself back to mulling over his . . . work ethic.

No matter what he might or might not want to spend his money on, she couldn't help but feel it was more than money he worked for. Couldn't escape the notion he was trying to prove himself somehow, show his worth or something. She shook her head. She was probably projecting again. Either way, she decided to give her full energy to the work at hand and stop thinking.

The hours passed pleasurably. With Colton there all afternoon, it was a louder, chattier work session than usual, but Aisha couldn't help but feel, despite all the chatter, that a lot less had actually been said—at least by her or Jase. That was all right though. Colton was actually pretty funny and even if he hadn't been, seeing the obvious satisfaction in Jase's expression as he surveyed their day's work would've made putting up with Colton worth it. And the odd time Jase met her eye and smiled like he was reading her mind? Well, that was just icing on the cake.

The last of the light was leaving the sky and the air was cooling fast, when they finally called it a day and started trekking back toward the dining hall. They'd made good progress. Woodshed One was full to bursting, and Jase had done all the measuring and pre-cutting he needed to do. He was ready to pour a cement slab in the morning and once it had cured, building would begin.

As they trotted along at a much more leisurely rate than earlier in the day, Jase put his layers back on and even zipped up his shell.

Aisha grinned. "Oh, so you're a mere mortal after all and feel temperatures like the rest of us, hey?"

"Oh, I'm better than mere," he assured her. Then winked.

She laughed out loud, then wondered why when Jase was cocky she found it cute and when Colton was, it grated on her last nerve. No doubt because when Jase mouthed off, he was joking or was actually confident about something real, whereas Colton thought he was all that and a bag of chips in pretty much every aspect of life.

The sky was a pretty periwinkle blue dotted with a sprinkling of first stars, and the air smelled of wood smoke and roasting meat. Aisha sighed at the beauty—and her stomach rumbled at the aroma. She wished she'd accepted Jo's dinner invitation, but then again, she hadn't seen much of Mo today at all and couldn't wait to have some down time just with her.

Walking the wide gravel trail without talking, the cheerful glow from various cabins' windows lighting their way, Aisha thought the two guys were enjoying the quiet companionship the way she was. But then Colton let out a whooshing exhale.

"This place! It's like falling back in time a hundred years." His tone made it clear the words were anything but a compliment.

Jase's response, almost like he hadn't heard the scathing criticism in Colton's voice, was an absolute contrast. He sounded reverent as he breathed, "Totally."

Colton bounced on his heels and turned to walk backwards, facing Aisha, as if looking for a co-conspirator. "What do you say we escape back to the twenty first century for a bit? Go to town and unwind, maybe go to the show, or have some drinks? Jase will DD—and don't use work as an excuse. I already know you have tomorrow off, and this morning Callum checked in to 'make sure' Jase and I were taking the weekend off too."

"That's true." Jase's voice was so glum that Aisha

would've laughed if she wasn't preoccupied with how to respond to Colton. It was pretty presumptuous of him to assign Jase the job of "designated driver" and to assume she was a drinker like he apparently was, but she didn't bother to say either thing aloud. Since she had less than zero interest in "unwinding" with Colton, Jase's willingness or unwillingness to drive for them was irrelevant.

In the spirit of maintaining a positive work environment, however, she tried to sound gracious, or, at least, not openly dismissive. "Thanks, but I already have plans. I'm hanging out with Mo tonight."

"Oh, come on, girl." Colton dragged out "girl" in a way that he no doubt intended to sound flirtatious, but that made Aisha grit her teeth. "It'll be fun. And you've earned it. Just because you're a working mom doesn't mean you have to be stuck at home with your kid every night."

"I don't *have* to be anything. I *want* to and I *get* to. I'm lucky."

Colton grunted and, continuing to walk backward, directed his attention to Jase's casually loping form.

"Nope," Jase said before Colton could get a word out. "Don't look at me. I've got a date."

"With what? A book?"

Jase made a finger gun and pretended to shoot Colton. "Got it in one—and people think you're just a pretty face."

"And there you have it. Nights *in* for the win!" Aisha laughed and held up her hand for a high five—which Jase was quick to give.

"Lame." Colton pivoted to face forward once more. "You guys suck. Seriously, Jase, it's like you've moved us into some senior living complex or something. It's so boring my ball sack's literally starting to sag."

Aisha wouldn't have given a rip if Colton had called her boring, but she was defensive of River's Sigh. Even the tiniest negative comment about this beloved place stung and was just . . . wrong. (And what boredom "literally" did to his scrotum was beyond weird. What did his testicles have to do with boredom? No, forget it. She didn't want to know. Also, she really hated it when people misused the word literally.)

She paused at the fork in the trail that would take her to Minnow cabin, where—she checked her watch—Sam was probably already waiting with Mo.

Although Jase and Colton would be continuing straight toward the dining hall, they followed her lead and stopped too.

"Okay, so here's the thing. I'm happy to hang around here 24/7, and I *never* run out of things that interest me, but I get that maybe going out and doing something on your day off would be appealing."

Colton perked up immediately, but Aisha kept her eyes on Jase's face, watching for his reaction. "I'm busy tomorrow, but I was—I am—planning a day trip on Sunday—out to these amazing natural hot springs.

You can come with me if you want."

"Are bathing suits optional?" Colton asked.

Aisha rolled her eyes. "Do what you gotta do."

"I'm in."

Aisha looked at Jase again, willing him to read her mind like he occasionally seemed to. She didn't want to go with Colton by himself. Shit!

"Jase?" she prodded.

He shifted from one foot to the other, then finally mumbled, "I won't be a third wheel?"

Colton started to say something that sounded suspiciously like, "Yeah, you will," and Aisha practically yelled over him. "Not at all. Definitely, the more the merrier. Definitely." Then, before they could say anything else, she added—also at a hearty volume—"I'll meet you at your cabin at ten. See you Sunday!"

She was down the trail, Minnow cabin within her sight, the guys out of it, before they could say good night.

Chapter 20

JASE AWOKE TO THE EARTHY aroma of fresh coffee and sat up, smiling broadly. Not wanting to waste a moment of leisure, he'd set the coffee maker's timer before he went to bed and it felt super luxurious.

He crept down the ladder from the loft, so as not to disturb Colton who was asleep in the living room, fixed a big mug, and ascended the ladder again. Settling into his library room—that's right, he'd claimed it as his—he spent some time jotting observations. Then he read for a couple of hours, during which he refreshed his coffee three times and made himself a big bowl of cereal and a peanut butter and banana sandwich for breakfast, all without so much as a hair stirring on Colton's head.

After filling his gut with food and his mind with thought-provoking images and ideas, he headed outside to stretch his legs and roam the property just for the fun of it, promising himself he'd turn off the part of his brain that looked for work that needed doing and assigned said tasks to his constantly evolving internal to-do list.

Now that he was used to having them, Jase enjoyed days off immensely. Maybe it was because he'd been commanded to take the break by Callum, so even he couldn't find a reason to feel guilty or worry he was shirking some unspoken responsibility. Or maybe it was because he was totally stoked about spending a whole day with Aisha tomorrow. He was trying, he really was, to put it out of his mind and not dwell on it—but he was utterly failing. Even the fact that Colton would be there, hitting on her like crazy, didn't dim his anticipation. And the hot springs sounded like just what the doctor ordered. His neck and back would love it. Then again, maybe it was purely the day and the place that was making him happy. How could a person be anything but happy at River's Sigh?

He found himself at the creek almost without thinking about it, but that wasn't a surprise. Something about the rush of water burbling over the flat rocks sounded like the hushed chat and laughter of old friends.

Sitting down on a massive fallen tree that ran parallel to the creek, he took several deep breaths. With each inhale, he filled his lungs until they almost hurt, then held the air for as long as he could, like a kid dunking in a swimming pool, trying to best his friend's record. When he couldn't last another second, he exhaled noisily.

The air was so clean he could practically feel it detoxifying him. He couldn't get over the idea that someone could own a place like this, could make it their home—this perfect mixture of cozy domestic bliss and rugged untouched nature. It was tangible proof that if you were willing to put in the time and effort, you could build something amazing—a real home.

Jase always thought it was pre-existing family circumstances, so *luck*, that led to this kind of a life, this kind of community, but the other day, Callum had told him about River's Sigh's humble beginnings. How creating something like this had been Jo's dream for a long time, how she'd started out all alone—with, from the sounds of it, a background not any easier than Jase's—with nothing to put into it except elbow grease and determination. And now, over time, she and Callum had built . . . this.

The sense of tentative possibility the story sparked deep within Jase was painful. It was one thing to hope in secret. It was another thing to know someone who had done what you hardly dared admit to yourself you wanted to do.

In the end, it was too much to dwell on for long, so he pushed the thoughts down again. Callum and Jo called their job offer "permanent," but Jase had lived long enough, seen enough, been through enough, to know that "permanent" got messed up all the time— often due to random happenings, not anyone's "fault." The only thing you could truly count on was that you couldn't truly count on anything. But until the day he got the boot for whatever reason? Well, he was going to treasure this place and its people like they were his own.

After a while Jase left his log and decided to explore further along the creek, hoping to find a spot Jo mentioned once. She had asked him if he liked fishing and when he said he didn't really know because he'd only gone once as a kid, she'd said he was welcome to borrow a rod anytime he wanted and described the trail that led to the river.

The shade was much deeper here than in other parts of the property, and the deciduous trees arching above his head had buds, but very little green. It was still pretty, just in a quiet, laden with potential way, not a showy, overt one. Except for the soft tread of his boots and the occasional bird call or swish of an evergreen bough as he pushed past, it was silent—a deep, ancient silence like nothing he'd ever experienced. It was surreal to think that some of the trees surrounding him had been there, doing their thing, for hundreds of years, and would continue on for centuries beyond him. He'd never really thought about the permanence of plant life before. So hah! Some things *were* permanent. It was on the tail of that thought that he heard it—a keening whimper.

Keeping still, he listened for a beat or two. Just as he decided the tiny sound was his imagination or the wind and was about to resume walking, it came again. Jase looked around, scanning the mossy crooks and crannies formed by tree roots and large rocks for movement. Nothing. Thinking the noise had come from his left, he veered from the vague trail and pushed through a jungle of broadleaf plants that looked like something out of a comic book, standing as tall as he did and flaunting huge, hairy, evil-looking thorns.

Every so often the whimper sounded again. He thought it might be getting louder, but it was difficult to tell. He still wasn't entirely sure it wasn't just the breeze, blowing through something or against something in an odd way.

He eased through a copse of closely growing jack pines. Their trunks were so skinny that if standing alone, the slightest breeze would probably bring them down. Together, however, they stood a chance, each breaking the strength of the wind, shielding their brothers. And suddenly Jase was on a narrow pothole-riddled road—gravelled at one time, now mostly just dirt. He turned in a circle but saw no movement. And the sound seemed to have disappeared. Where was he anyway?

Jo's conversation about her fishing spot came back to him. She'd mentioned there was boat access to the river close by too. Maybe this was the road to the makeshift boat launch?

A whimper again. Unmistakable this time. And definitely louder. Jase stooped and studied a tangle of wild berry bushes and greenery. Still saw nothing out of the ordinary—well, except for a black garbage bag of trash a few feet away that some loser had tossed here instead of disposing of properly.

Jase looked at the bag and his frown deepened. With an intensifying sense of foreboding, he moved to retrieve it. At the very least, he'd get rid of it properly, not leave it littering up the place. At the worst—no, he didn't want to think it.

But there was the whimper again. And now that he was watching for it, the bag twitched. He dropped to his knees and fumbled with the bag's knotted neck—then realized the side was torn.

Jase stretched the ripped plastic, creating a large opening. For a long moment, he could only gape, almost unable to comprehend what he was seeing.

He'd only been a little kid when he learned that crying got you worse than nothing, just showed you were vulnerable and made you a target, so he was surprised by the burn of saline at the back of his eyes and the painful lump that formed in his throat. The rage, however? It was a familiar companion and scorched through him. He didn't try to tamp it down, like he normally would.

Jase let out a seething string of the foulest expletives he knew—but did so in a low, crooning whisper, not wanting to cause more fear. It didn't matter what a person thought of animals. How could anyone do something like this?

Three listless puppies lay in a foul-smelling mess of urine and watery feces. Jase leaned back on his haunches and covered his mouth, swallowing back nausea. He couldn't leave the dogs here, but—

He bent over them again, resolve pushing away his squeamishness. He had less than no idea how to tell how old they were, but they didn't seem super young—their eyes were open, or at least two of the pups' eyes were anyway—and their breed was unclear too. Before reaching to pick one up, he removed his sweatshirt, turned it inside out so the softest, fuzziest part would be against their skin, then lay it on the ground.

With a hot, queasy rush of grief, Jase realized one of the puppies looked wrong—because he was *wrong*. He had a broken leg, at the very least, and he wasn't moving at all.

Jase looked closer, then briefly closed his eyes. The small dog was definitely dead. It made him feel like something broke inside him. How were the other two even still alive? He had no clue, but alive they were. He scooped them out of the mess, one at a time, and put them onto his sweatshirt.

Immediately, it became clear who the little fighter was, whose piercing whimper had caught Jase's attention and saved her and her brother. She had a little white and gray face—so gray it almost looked blue—and she was making noise again and nuzzling at his hand like she knew he could be a potential source of food. Her surviving sibling was so scrawny he remind- ed Jase of a thin cat—though now that he was really studying him, his frame was too large. The puppy made a mewling shape with his mouth, but no sound came out. Jase winced at the sight of his gummy, infected looking eyes.

"Hang on, guys. You're safe now. You're safe." The tiny creatures seemed soothed by his voice, so he continued whispering. "Where there's breath, there's hope." He didn't remember where he'd heard the saying, just knew how much it had always resonated with him. "Where there's breath, there's hope, guys. Keep breathing, okay? Keep breathing."

He gently folded his sweatshirt so that it covered all but the snubs of their little noses, then got to his feet and carefully scooped up the bundle. Holding it softly but securely against his chest, Jase retraced his trail back to River's Sigh, moving as quickly as he could while trying to avoid jouncing and jarring his terrifyingly-still parcel.

Jase broke free of the tree line surrounding Sockeye cabin, the most secluded of River's Sigh's already-very-private cabins, and breathed a bit easier. If he kept this pace, he'd be at the office in another ten minutes max. Jo would definitely lend him her truck. Definitely.

He didn't get as far as the office before being stopped. Aisha appeared on the trail, Mo skipping along beside her. For the first time since he'd met Aisha, instead of a rush of joy at seeing her, he wanted to run in the opposite direction. He didn't want her—or little Mo—to be subjected to this disturbing sight. The dogs might not make it. He might be too late. It was too sad.

Aisha saw him and broke into a grin, then did a visible double-take, dropped the book bag she was carrying, and broke into a run.

"Mom—mommy! Wait for me," Mo wailed and started to sprint, trying futilely to catch up.

"Jase! What's wrong? Are you hurt?"

"No," he managed to grunt. "Not me." He turned slightly, sheltering her from the dogs.

She immediately slowed and approached cautiously, then as if feeling Mo's presence as the little girl neared, she held out a hand to her side, reaching for her daughter. "Slow down, sweetie, and be careful. Jase has a—" She looked closer and a pained, pinched sound of surprise escaped her.

"Is that a puppy! Can I see?"

Aisha's hand shot out and caught Mo's wrist before she could rush past her and crowd Jase. "Oh no," Aisha breathed to Jase. "It's more than one. Two? Are there two?"

Jase nodded.

Aisha crouched down to look Mo in the eye. "The puppies Jase has are sick, munchkin. We have to get them to a vet—a doctor for dogs—before you can look at them or touch them, okay?"

"I need to borrow a vehicle—or can you drive us?"

"Yes." Aisha was already in motion again, gently

tugging Mo along with her. "But Jo and Callum aren't here, and my car's getting new brakes. The mechanic is a friend and he's going to drop it off later, but I have no idea when."

Jase sighed in frustration.

"It's okay. I have a spare booster seat in case Mo's ever being babysat by someone who doesn't have one, and I know where Jo stashes her spare keys. She won't mind us borrowing the truck."

Half an hour later they were at the four-way stop leading into town. Ten minutes after that, they were hustling into the vet's office—with only minutes to spare before it was due to close.

Mo had gotten a bigger glimpse of the puppies once they were inside and talking to the vet's assistant. Her eyes got very large and very shiny, and the tip of her nose and ears went red, but she didn't cry or make a sound—and for some reason that made Jase need to swallow another lump in his own throat.

Aisha was calm and thorough, asking all the questions Jase wanted answered but hadn't thought to ask, and giving as much information as she could in return—which wasn't much because all she had to go with were the paltry details Jase had provided during the drive.

"We'll report it to the police," the assistant said, then added, "and we'll post on our social media pages and ask for anyone who might have information about the puppies—" she checked her notes—"left near the boat launch by River's Sigh B & B to contact us privately."

"I'll pay," Jase said, but fury and sadness made his words sound aggressive, almost threatening.

Both Aisha and the vet assistant looked momentarily alarmed, and Jase considered what he must look like, all tatted up and angry-eyed, wearing nothing but a sweaty tank top and dirty jeans. He shrank into himself and shuffled from foot to foot, then looked to Aisha, feeling desperate. "I mean, I have money. Don't put them down. If there's even the smallest possibility they'll make it, give them that chance. I can leave my credit card, or pay a deposit, or . . . whatever."

The vet tech smiled sadly. "They look like they're in rough shape—not necessarily too young to be without their mother but dehydrated for sure."

"Please."

"Dr. Aman will check them over, and I'll get back to you. Do you have a limit?"

Jase shot Aisha a glance, knowing he should understand what the tech was asking.

"I think she means a cap," Aisha explained gently. "Like what is the maximum you're willing or able to pay before you'll choose to have them put down instead."

Jase supposed he should feel lucky he and Colton hadn't been dogs. Who would've paid? He closed his eyes for a moment, numbers flashing in his mind like the red and blue lights of squad cars he got all too used to having show up at his house. He saw his bank account balance and how much he'd made working at River's Sigh B & B so far. He saw how much he wanted, needed, to amass this quarter—but it didn't matter. He'd figure something out.

"Can we, I mean, I . . . Can I play it by ear, like have the vet see them, let me know how much he thinks it will cost, then I'll decide?"

"Absolutely. So how about I take them into the back now? I'll be in touch with you Monday and let you know if they survived the next twenty-four hours and what Dr. Aman thinks."

Jase nodded numbly and gave his cell number, then added too much information, that it was text only, that he didn't get good reception where he lived, but that he'd check it regularly and call as soon as her text came.

On the way out of the vet's office, Aisha took his hand and looped her fingers through his. The simple touch made him nauseous with gratitude and longing. He couldn't bear it. As quickly and gently as he could, he disentangled himself from her and went around to the passenger side of the vehicle, feeling more alone than ever.

He paced outside the pickup, while Aisha strapped Mo into her booster seat. It was a tight squeeze with the three of them in the cab, and much easier to fasten the seatbelt without his big carcass in the way. When Mo was securely buckled in, Aisha came around the passenger side just as he was opening the door to climb in.

"Are you all right?" she asked but kept a physical distance this time—and like a moron, Jase wished she'd take his hand again.

"No—yeah, I don't know." He shook his head. "People just really suck sometimes, you know?"

"Yep." Aisha nodded, her shoulders and upper body swaying lightly in agreement.

"Think they'll make it?"

Aisha glanced at the vet clinic like she expected to see the puppies through the glass door.

"I don't know," she said slowly. "Stranger things have happened. I think there's a chance."

"Really?"

Aisha smiled and nodded again. "Really."

Jase wondered if she was merely being kind, trying to shelter him the way he'd wanted to shelter her and Mo from even seeing the dogs.

It was a quiet drive home. Intuiting he didn't want to talk, or possibly wanting time with her own thoughts herself, Aisha turned the stereo on and set the music to a volume that was comfortable enough to listen to, but that made conversing impractical. As they zipped along in the lengthening shadows, the trees an increasingly dark blur along the highway, Jase comforted himself with the idea that the Aisha and Colton outing tomorrow would be a good distraction—and for tonight, he'd keep his mind off the pitiful dogs by retreating into a book.

When they arrived home, every window in Jo and Callum's house, the dining hall, and the office blazed with light, and there was a small army milling around the circular parking area.

Aisha rolled to a stop beside her car, which had been returned, and Jo sprinted over.

When Aisha swung the truck's door open, revealing herself as the driver, Jo did a double take. "Oh, it's you. *You* had the truck!"

"Yeah . . ." Aisha said, sounding confused. "I texted you that I did. Didn't you get it?"

Jo's gaze flicked toward Jase, but she wouldn't quite meet his eye—and in that instant Jase saw what she'd thought. He felt sick. Callum's assurances that they believed Jase's version of the story about the mix up with Ed's car had merely been politeness, not real trust. Jo, at least, believed he was capable of stealing her truck, or worse maybe.

Attention fully back on Aisha now, Jo shook her head. "I didn't get your message. I don't know why."

"Oh, man. I'm sorry. I hope you weren't worried." Aisha was slower on the uptake than Jase, or perhaps it was just that she could afford to be a bit oblivious because she was part of the place and belonged in a way he could never hope to. Either way, it was only now that she noticed that the glob of people—Sam, Jo, Callum, Callum's brother Brian, whom Jase had only met in passing, and a tall unfamiliar man standing close to Sam—were all wearing identical stressed expressions.

"What's going on? Did something happen? Is something wrong?"

Jo shook her head. "No, a few wires got crossed, that's all."

Before Aisha could reply, the stranger approached. It was obvious Aisha hadn't noticed him until now because her face lit up when she saw him, and she jumped from the vehicle. "Dad! When did you get back?"

The man opened his arms and Aisha walked into them and gave him a big hug. Jase climbed out of the passenger side and was about to help Mo out of her booster seat, when he noticed that the man—Aisha's father, apparently, so the "Charlie" he'd heard so much about—was glaring in his direction over Aisha's head.

Jase glanced over his shoulder, trying to glimpse the offensive person who was earning such overt suspicion and disdain. Then Aisha's dad spoke again, yanking Jase's focus back to him.

"Is this the guy who took off with your truck, Jo?"

Something rock-like thudded in Jase's gut, and his limbs grew heavy. *He* was Aisha's dad's target—and now that he was noticing, he thought he recognized similar, if not quite as intense, expressions on everyone else's faces. He wanted to respond, even opened his mouth to do so, but the familiar sensation of marbles on his tongue instead of words made him mute.

Aisha pulled free from the hug. "What? Of course not—and what a rude, aggressive thing to say, especially since it was clearly *me* driving." She pivoted to Jo, her face lined with such incredulous disbelief that it was almost a parody. Jase would've laughed if he didn't feel so humiliated and ashamed. "Jase has been working here for months. You should know he wouldn't steal your old beater."

Jo held up a conciliatory hand. "Hold on, Aisha. Let's not blow everything out of proportion. I was wondering where my truck was, but no, of course, I didn't think Jase—or anyone—had stolen it." Her tone grew more earnest and she fixed a concerned gaze pointedly on Jase. "Honestly, I didn't."

"It's all right. The truck was gone. I was gone . . . I get it," Jase mumbled uncomfortably. "I really don't steal things though. I promise."

Aisha was still pink in the face. "Okay, so we're all good and everything's crystal clear now? Great. I'm going to get Mo to bed. I'm really sorry about the misunderstanding and that my text didn't go through. If you are mad though or have any concerns, it's me you have an issue with. It was my idea to take the truck."

She outlined what Jase had found and why they'd needed to rush to town. Immediately the group's body language changed. They finally seemed to fully believe that Jase hadn't jacked the truck or gone out joyriding or run off with Aisha and Mo against their will or something. He tried not to take it personally, but it was pretty difficult.

Aisha turned to her dad. "Do you want to come for story time with Mo and catch up a little?"

Charlie put his arm around Sam and smiled down at her, then looked back at his daughter. "Maybe tomorrow instead? I've been away from Sam for too long as it is."

"Sure. Anytime's good." Aisha buried herself in the truck cab, releasing Mo from her constraints and grabbing her bag. Jase knew Aisha missed the look Sam shot at Charlie and couldn't tell if she heard Sam's whisper or not.

"Are you certain, hon? I don't mind if you want to have a little visit before we head home."

Aisha popped out of the cab a second later, her big bag slung over her shoulder, and an obviously sleepy Mo propped on her hip—which explained why the little girl hadn't been fussing to get let out of the truck earlier.

"Night all," Aisha said, addressing the group as a whole. "It's been weird."

Jo chuckled. "Well, that's not completely unheard of for us, is it?"

Jase hesitated. He wanted to walk Aisha to her cabin, but she hadn't invited him—and he couldn't help but feel doing so would only intensify Aisha's father's negative view of him. It was blatantly clear that Charlie was not a Jase fan, though what Jase could've possibly done to earn the guy's ire was beyond him. Fine, Charlie thought he'd borrowed the truck without asking—but that had been cleared up immediately and he was still giving Jase dirty looks.

Yet again, Aisha saved him from having to speak for himself. "Coming?" she asked. "I'm starving and bet you are too."

"I could eat."

Mo perked up. "You can *always* eat."

"True words, little mama."

Mo giggled hysterically. "I'm not a mama!"

With Mo twined around her like a small monkey, Aisha started across the parking lot, and Jase followed.

As they neared the mouth of the trail that opened up from the parking lot, Aisha muttered, "Shoot, the hot springs. I almost forgot." She turned back to the group, most of whom were chatting, though Jase noticed that Sam and Charlie seemed to be staring after him, Aisha, and Mo.

Aisha seemed to think so too—and to also find it strange. Her brow furrowed. "Uh, sorry, Dad," she called. "I just remembered. Tomorrow's no good. I'll be out all day, but how about you, or you and Sam, come for dinner on Monday or Tuesday?"

Charlie and Sam looked at each other and Aisha held up a hand. "You don't need to decide right now. Talk it over and let me know."

Without waiting for a reply, Aisha resumed walking, but her demeanour had changed, and she was preoccupied. As they neared Minnow, she turned to Jase. "Would you mind terribly if I rescind the dinner offer? Mo's wiped. I'm wiped—"

"Yeah, no problem," Jase said quickly, meaning it, even though he was awash with disappointment.

"You'll be okay? Not too sad or worried about the puppies?"

Jase cringed inwardly. She must think he was such a weak dope. "Yeah, I'll be fine. They just really got to me."

"I get it. Totally." Aisha nodded. "Are you up for tomorrow still?"

Jase nodded. "Absolutely. I'm looking forward to it." He started to retreat, then stopped. "Aisha?"

She paused on the porch and looked at him over Mo's head. "Yeah?"

He scuffed the dirt with his boot. "Thank you for today—for driving and everything, so I could keep holding them. Having you with me at the vet . . . it really helped."

"I'm glad," she said, voice soft. "But I wish we'd spent the day together under happier circumstances."

"We will."

"Well, yeah, like *tomorrow*." They both laughed a little and Mo's head lifted from Aisha's shoulder. "Are we home yet?"

"We are, baby." Aisha pressed a kiss to Mo's crown. "We'll go inside in just a sec."

"Okay, well, I guess I'll see you tomorrow."

"I'll come by your place to pick you and Colton up as soon as Mo and I are awake and ready," Aisha promised.

Colton. Right. But even thinking of him and where on earth he might be didn't faze Jase at the moment.

"Sounds good."

He was almost at the fork in the trail, when Aisha's voice, bright and light, came to him once more. "I really am going to have you for dinner sometime."

"Sure she is! Likely story."

Her laughter tinkled in the night air, and the heaviness that had dogged him since finding the puppies finally lightened a bit. Aisha had meant it when she said she wanted to be friends with him. He could tell by how she treated him. They really were *friends*—and it had been years, since high school even, that he could honestly say that of anybody other than Colton. The realization softened the sadness of the day and eased the embarrassed, angry shame of the rest of River's Sigh obviously assuming the worst about him. As he strode down the trail toward the comfortable bed and book that awaited him, the clouds above parted and he was stopped in his tracks. Hundreds of stars winked and blinked overhead, shining so brightly the whole night glowed.

Chapter 21

AISHA JOGGED THE TRAIL TO Jase's cabin, Mo sprinting alongside in her slightly clumsy, uncoordinated kid way. *Jase's cabin, hey?* The thought hit her. Technically, it was Jase and Colton's, but she never thought of it that way. Everything about Colton suggested he was only here temporarily, no matter what he said— and half the time, even when he was with them, he wasn't really *with them.* Jase, on the other hand? He seemed as integral to River's Sigh as the creek or the cabins. No, scratch that. Colton was the creek, always on the move. Jase was more like one of the beautiful ancient trees or one of the huge boulders by the river. It boggled her mind to think that in the beginning she'd resented his presence, saw him as an intrusion. . . .

Heat rose through her that had nothing to do with her pace. The expressions on everybody's faces, even Jo's, when they'd rattled into the parking lot together last night filled her brain. It was insane—especially considering it had been Jo and Callum's idea to offer him a permanent job. Why would they do that if they didn't trust him?

"We're getting ice cream at the little store, right, Mom?"

Aisha snapped back to the glorious present, smiling down at her daughter. "Yep, we sure are."

Mo's uncanny memory never failed to surprise and amuse her. She'd only taken Mo to the hot springs once, but the little general store on the remote, sparsely populated stretch of road to the Nisga'a territories was firmly planted in her brain as one of her favorite places. Aisha couldn't blame her. The hard ice cream really was crazy good—and the size of the cones made her eyes widen with delight just like Mo's.

They were at the door to Jase's cabin now and Aisha looked around before knocking, realizing with a start that it was missing something. No cute little cedar sign identified the place. It hadn't been named. That was an oversight she, Jo and Callum needed to remedy.

Mo shrieked with delight. "I never saw this before!" She lifted the ornate bee-shaped brass knocker and let it drop. The metal sound was somehow musical. She lifted it again, and before the knocker stopped reverberating, the door opened and a shirtless Colton, obviously fresh from the shower, greeted them with a grin. Aisha's stomach fluttered despite herself.

"Come in, come in. Lurch is busy in the can, but I'd be very happy to entertain you." He winked.

Mo scooted under Colton's outstretched arm, not needing to be invited twice. "Where's Jase?" she asked, Colton's "Lurch" reference way over her head.

"You showered *before* going to the hot springs to swim?" Aisha's tone clearly added, are you a moron? to the end of her statement, but she didn't feel bad about it. Colton deserved it. She didn't like how he always subtly—or not so subtly—slammed Jase. As ever, Colton was immune to her disdain.

His eyes glinted. "There's nothing wrong with being clean before you get wet and dirty."

Aisha rolled her eyes and pushed past him into the cabin, wishing she was seeing Jase's space for the first time without Colton's presence making everything all greasy.

Mo spotted the area rug in the living room and ran over to it, exclaiming over the brightly coloured fish that decorated the hand-tufted navy rug. If someone had described the carpet to her, Aisha might have felt it was too cabin-kitschy or something, but it was perfect in this space with the bright pine walls and the amazing background of green visible through every expansive window.

Knowing the fun design would keep Mo hooked for a while, Aisha let herself study Jase's habitat to her heart's content. The detail that stood out to her the most pleased her immensely. The cabin was immaculately clean, not a dish left out, the windows bright and streak free, the hardwood floor shining. Even the tea towel hanging on the oven door was crisply folded.

She moved deeper into the open concept cabin, still looking for traces of Jase, and stroked one hand over the shale-covered breakfast bar. It was the only design element she hadn't been crazy about when Jo shared the plan. Shale was porous and hard to keep clean, but Aisha had to admit the rough black stone was gorgeous, adding drama and depth to all the light wood surrounding it. As she stepped around the counter, she caught sight of the only thing in the whole space that was remotely out of order. The couch in the living room was pulled out from the wall, and the cot from upstairs was tucked behind it. A couple of crumpled pillows lay atop its bunched up quilt, showing it was being used as a makeshift sleeping area, which was odd, considering the loft had two bedrooms. She should know. She'd made them up for the guys' first night at River's Sigh.

Colton caught her staring at the sloppy bed and winked, jerking his thumb toward the closed bathroom door. "His majesty, the King of Delusion, likes to fantasize he owns the place, so being the easygoing prince that I am, I crash here and let him have the upper level. We share the rest because he can't figure out a way to lock me out of the bathroom or exile me from the kitchen."

Colton stayed down here, while Jase had the two rooms to himself? That was a bit weird—and yet, if Colton was right about the reason why, it was kind of sweet in a sad way. Owning your own place, especially a small cabin like this one, lovely as it was, shouldn't seem like the impossibly far-fetched dream Colton made it sound like it was. She was instantly rankled again on Jase's behalf.

Suddenly she spotted something that took her mind off of how irritating Colton was. A library book titled *The Practice of Poetry*, plus a tablet with a black Moleskine folio case and a digital pencil rested on the arm of the big recliner, which had been moved from its original position. When Sam and Jo first staged the cabin, they'd placed the huge comfy chair so it looked into the room to facilitate conversation. Now it faced toward the breathtaking floor-to-ceiling corner window that Aisha still coveted, perfectly positioned to capture the view of the creek shimmering through the trees.

If the book wasn't enough to give it away, Aisha's dad was a total weirdo when it came to writing accoutrements. She recognized the trappings of another writer immediately. She glanced at Colton quizzically.

He held up his hands like she was about to throw something distasteful at him.

"Don't look at me. That's all our boy Jase too. Do I look like someone who'd waste my time writing anything, let alone poetry?" He said *poetry* like the word carried a bad smell.

"Nope," Aisha agreed. "You really don't seem like someone with anything remotely near to an interior life."

Colton grinned, not slighted in the least. "Touché."

But Aisha's thoughts were all on Jase. A poet? It was a surprise because, come on, poets weren't exactly a modern phenomenon . . . and yet, at the same time, it made sense. Fit with what she was learning about who Jase was perfectly.

She had to put her hands behind her back and link her fingers together to keep herself from sneaking a peek. At that moment, as if sensing his sacrosanct work might be at risk, the bathroom door opened and Jase appeared, fully clothed but obviously freshly showered. Aisha shook her head.

"Jase!" Mo exclaimed. "You have fish on your carpet."

"I know. Cool, hey?"

Mo bounced up and down. "Yeah! *So* cool."

Aisha felt as transparently giddy as Mo.

"I love your cabin," Mo added. "It's almost as nice as ours."

Jase's slow smile appeared. "I love my cabin too."

Was it Aisha's imagination or did he put a soft inflection on the word *my*? Or was that just wishful thinking on her part? In the beginning she hadn't wanted him or Colton around, period. Then she was excited about the prolonged stay. Now she was afraid that she was starting to see Jase as a permanent fixture in her life in a way that he didn't—and why would he? He was here now, supposedly permanently, but how long would that *really* be? He was a traveling poet. A drifter. He'd return to his wandering ways when the novelty of staying put wore off. And it's not like she'd given him any encouragement to see her as anything other than a friend—the exact opposite, in fact—so why did the possibility that he might not stay bother her so much? Dammit, the stupid internal rhetorical question made her furious with herself. She knew exactly why. It didn't matter how much she didn't want a relationship right now, or maybe ever. Her stupid heart was in a relationship. With Jase. Even if he didn't know it. And it was going to hurt her. She had to do something to break her connection with him.

She wished she hadn't had the genius idea of them visiting one of the most romantic places on earth, but it was too late to cancel now. She clapped her hands, like she'd been waiting impatiently, although nothing could be further from the truth. She would've loved more time to poke around the place Jase lived.

"Daylight's burning. Let's move."

Chapter 22

THE DRIVE TO THE HOT springs took almost two hours and included a stop around the halfway mark at the little general store, perched by its lonesome on the side of the road in an area that made River's Sigh look like the heart of city life.

The shop's quaint storefront and rustic post and beam covered porch made Jase feel like he'd fallen back in time or accidentally ended up in some sepia-toned photo. Inside, however, its wares were surprisingly eclectic and upscale, with a special predilection for things that appealed to that most modern of personalities: the foodie. Authentic dim sum and Chinese dumplings imported from Vancouver filled a massive freezer at the back, and the packed shelves carried spices and sauces for any taste, no matter how diverse.

Aisha, Mo and Colton had ice-cream. Jase had elk pepperoni, seaweed snacks, and a big bag of salt and vinegar kettle chips. Then he shared Aisha's ice-cream when she insisted. She'd chosen "Old-fashioned Apple Crumble" and as Jase sampled it, he imagined the warmth of her mouth, suddenly ice-cream cold and tasting of vanilla and cinnamon. It made him embarrassed, but was also . . . well, kind of delicious to think about.

Mo was already asking if they could stop at the store again on the return trip as they piled back into Aisha's car.

Jase didn't often feel small—or not size-wise at least—but this place dwarfed him. The dense forest and unending spread of trees on one side of the roadway, the vast fields of nothing but lava rock as far as the eye could see stretching out in the other direction. . . .

But overwhelming all of it was Aisha. Aisha. *Aisha*. Before hitting the road, he'd worried that his preoccupation with how the puppies were faring would ruin the outing, but he should've known better. In Aisha's company, his darkest thoughts lightened, and his keenest worries lost their edge. Plus, Mo's sweet silliness and exuberance made it impossible not to see that even though painful things existed, pure good did too. He even appreciated Colton's attempts to be funny because of how he triggered Aisha's laughter. If he could just listen to her laugh all day, every day, he really wouldn't need a lot more out of life. The realization filled him with such a warm glow that he could almost ignore the wistfulness that followed on its heels. Aisha had—and was—everything he wanted for himself. But he understood why she didn't want them to be anything more than friends. He came from nothing and had nothing to offer her. But still, it was hard not to wish . . .

Aisha pulled to the side of the road and killed the engine, cutting off Bob Marley's crooning voice. "We're here!"

Jase and Colton looked out the window at the exact same time, then both shot Aisha identical questioning looks.

Mo answered for her. "It's that trail!"

Jase craned his neck in the direction Mo pointed and saw a shadow that might indicate a break in the foliage. That was a trail?

"Are you kidding me?" Colton harrumphed as he undid his seatbelt. "I thought we were getting a break from extreme nature."

"Why would we want a break from nature?" Mo was genuinely confused.

Aisha laughed. "Exactly." She slid out of the car and fetched their backpacks from the trunk.

It wasn't a long walk in, maybe fifteen minutes or so, and very easy as the hidden path turned out to be a series of well-built, sturdily connected boardwalks. The beauty surrounding him almost bowled Jase over. It was surreal, with ferns almost as tall as he was and cedar trees so massive that three men his size could link hands and still not be able to reach all the way around them.

Colton interrupted his reverie with a grouchy, "Gross, what stinks?"

He wasn't entirely out to lunch. Jase had become aware of an unpleasant scent, metallic and eggy, growing steadily stronger the further they walked.

Mo giggled. "Uncle Brian says the water smells like egg farts."

"Mo," Aisha said reprovingly. "It's just sulfur. Lots of minerals have odd odors when heated."

Mo shrugged agreeably. "I know. And the minerals make the water so healthy. They detoxi-fly you."

"Detoxi*fy*—that's right."

Colton made an exaggerated gagging sound. "I think Uncle Brian was more on point."

Mo tsked, then added, "That's rude," like she wasn't the one who brought up Brian in the first place.

Jase paused and stretched his arms above his head. They weren't even in the water yet, but he felt so good. It was like in some weird way the four of them fit together, were almost a family or something, like the way Aisha was with Jo and Sam, silly and bantering and often chatting about trivial things—but genuinely close.

"Look, there's a lizard!" It was Colton again, but he'd dropped his carefully honed nonchalance and sounded thrilled.

"It's a salamander, actually. Salamanders are amphibians. Lizards are reptiles," Mo corrected. "Lots of people make that mistake though. Aren't they the cutest?"

"Totally." Colton laughed with delight, and he and

Mo took off ahead, apparently on an amphibian hunt.

Jase snuck a look at Aisha who was gazing after them. Unaware of his eyes on her, her features were unguarded. The soft-eyed affection and warmth in her expression made him suck in a breath.

After a moment, she turned to him. "So you're a poet and I didn't know it, hey?"

Shit. Double shit. *Colton.*

Her eyes sparkled with light and mirth. If he wasn't so preoccupied with how cute she was, he'd be totally humiliated.

She stopped walking and leaned back against the railing of the boardwalk, almost provocatively. But then again, he found every movement she made provocative. "Will you write a poem for me?"

"You're assuming I haven't already."

She inhaled sharply, like his quick—for once—response had stroked something in her. Shyness compelled him to look away, but he forced himself to hold her gaze. Damn—it was as powerful as sex almost. She visibly swallowed, and he knew she felt it too.

Like it was mutually discussed, they commenced walking again, matching each other's rhythm and striding hip to thigh—him so much taller than her, yet somehow a perfect match, regardless—close and in sync.

And then they arrived. Three pools lay before them. Two of them were like Japanese-styled soaker tubs, gorgeous deep bowls with cedar plank sides. The third was more natural, what some might call rough—just a large wood-framed rectangle with a silty gravel bottom.

Colton and Mo had already stripped down to the bathing suits they had on under their clothing and were wading into the more rustic pool.

Aisha peeled off her vintage Billy Idol sweatshirt and lace-trimmed leopard print jeans. And there she stood in all her glory.

It was a strange, archaic way to think of her, but he couldn't help it. "Glory" fit perfectly. Not that she was naked. In fact, her bathing suit was conservative by modern standards, but it didn't matter. Her candy apple red boy shorts and halter top threw him into thirteen-year-old-male high alert. Did she know how gorgeous she was? If, yes—that was super hot. If not—dang, that was super hot, too. Either way, he was doomed.

He averted his eyes because it was the only decent and responsible thing to do—but, damn it, he noticed Colton noticing her too. Jase stripped down to his shorts in a confusing state of mingled possessiveness and arousal, which, oh-gawwwd, he hoped wasn't showing through his shorts—which were loose and came to his knees, thank you very much.

He crossed the slightly slippery deck, surveyed the greyish water, and gingerly climbed in, unsure what to expect—and was immediately seduced. The temperature was . . . amazing. Settling on his butt, he stretched out until nothing but his head was above the water and let out an involuntary groan of pleasure. Aisha plopped down beside him and laughed. "I know, right? It's crazy heaven."

It was. It really was. Until it wasn't.

Chapter 23

AISHA DIDN'T KNOW WHY SHE did it—no, that was a lie. She knew exactly why. She'd felt so close to Jase all day, like she, him, and Mo were a family or something, out on an adventure—complete with Colton, the annoying in-law, ha ha.

She watched Jase's endless patience with Mo as he listened to her non-stop questions and answered them thoughtfully, unreservedly admitting when he didn't know something—like when she asked him how long it took toads to have babies and if they mated and then laid fertilized eggs, or if they were like fish and the daddy fish came along *after* the mom fish laid the eggs. His and Aisha's eyes had met on that one, and his eyebrows had popped up comically.

"I have no idea, but it's definitely information you can find if you ask your Mom for help."

Mo sighed contentedly and moved on to something else. She liked concrete answers of any kind, be it specific information or a clearly stated, "I don't know." Wishy-washy I thinks, maybes, or pretending you knew something when you didn't irritated her. It was a quality Aisha really liked about her daughter.

Colton was good with Mo too, actually, but Aisha couldn't shake the feeling that it was with an eye to her for approval. Where Jase seemed to genuinely appreciate interacting with Mo for Mo's sake—and only involved Aisha when they exchanged unspoken isn't-she-the-greatest looks—Colton glanced at Aisha first, like he was checking she was watching as he made Mo laugh or helped her in some way.

And then in the largest hot spring pool, after they'd lounged and lazed about for a long time, and every one of Aisha's knotted muscles was soft and delicious feeling, Mo hopped out and ran to her backpack to grab a ball. The pack had a tricky zipper though and often caught the lining, making opening it—or closing it again to free the fabric—difficult. Aisha climbed out, conscious of both guys' eyes on her and knowing her butt was on full view—but whatever. She looked good. They didn't have the corner on hotness or anything. The thought made her giggle, and Mo shot her a look, looking so much like Sam—and like she was reading her thoughts—that Aisha instantly stopped.

After fighting with the zipper for a good minute, the ball was finally freed. Mo threw it to Colton, then flitted back to the water's edge and hopped in. Eyes on her daughter, Aisha didn't notice the spot she was planning to re-enter was two steps down, not one. Instead of stepping onto the pool's gravel floor, her foot hit slippery wood—and she was off-balanced. She felt herself go down. Shit, this was going to hurt—

She never hit the edge. Instead, iron arms reached out and caught her. Jase had seen what she had not and lunged—very successfully—to save her from a fall. But maybe she had ended up in worse danger. She tried but failed to hold back a surprised gasp. Her embarrassingly audible inhalation of breath wasn't triggered by the notion of falling, but rather by the sensation of where she'd landed and what it did to her insides.

Despite the fact they were both in their bathing suits, with the amount of their flesh that touched, they might as well have been naked. The satin-sleek hardness of Jase's oh-so-warm wet skin as Aisha slid against him made her feel drunk. Every ounce of her being wanted to twist in his arms and wrap her legs around his torso and—

Their eyes met, and the mutual molten desire in his, like he was reading her mind and about to put her wishes into action, sent heat rioting through her, along with a need so strong that her lower parts literally ached with it. The pure animal urge, the biological drive of it, was absolutely exquisite in every way—and utterly terrifying.

It felt as if time stopped and the moment was unending, but in reality it couldn't have been more than a few seconds. Mo—bless her jealous, innocent heart!—tugged on Jase's arm possessively. "It's my turn! I want to be picked up and thrown."

The reciprocal wanting in Jase's face morphed into confusion as he glanced down at the hyper child dangling off his arm, then back to Aisha, whom he still held. Lord have mercy, if she didn't feel like a scantily clad Scarlett O'Hara cradled in his arms that way, securely held against his chest.

Aisha forced a light laugh and explained what Mo was talking about, understanding immediately how her daughter had misconstrued Jase's embrace.

"The last time we were here, her Uncle Brian kept lifting everybody up and tossing them in." As she spoke, the huskiness in her voice—and what caused it—made her blush.

Thankfully, Mo was oblivious, though the same couldn't be said for Colton. As Mo continued to bounce and splash and tug Jase's arm, Colton sidled over to Aisha and held out his arms, mimicking Jase's posture. "What about me? I want some of that too."

Mo began to chant, "Dunk me, dunk me!" Laughing and ignoring Colton, Jase plunked Aisha down and obligingly scooped Mo up.

As Aisha watched her shrieking, giggling child relish every second of being doted on, she was hit with profound longing for such a dizzying array of complex things that it almost triggered tears. And that was what precipitated her stupid move: overwhelming terror about the bond she'd formed with Jase despite her best intentions and her remembered plan to kibosh whatever was between them.

The steamy water was no match for the heat still coursing through her and with something like despair, she turned to Colton, half-joking, half-challenging. "Well?"

"Well what?"

"I thought you said you wanted a turn?"

One of Colton's eyebrows shot up and Aisha had to admit, with his damp hair hanging over one eye and his mouth curved in a rascally grin, he was cute—but he left her cold inside. It was too late, though. He lifted her up and simultaneously pushed toward her, so that she was seated on the wide wooden ledge surrounding the pool, and he was straddled by her legs.

She sensed, rather than saw, Jase freeze. She couldn't look at him. Colton's hands ran up the sides of her outer legs from knees to thigh and rested on her bikini clad hips. Then, before she even realized what was happening, what she'd triggered, he leaned down and pressed his mouth to hers. Stunned, a second elapsed before she pushed on his chest and broke the kiss. Colton looked down at her with a flirty smile and hungry eyes. Shit, shit, shit! She did look at Jase now, but his freezing had apparently worn off. He had turned slightly, so she couldn't see his face.

"Ready, set," he called.

"Go!" Mo yelled and careened up into the air, then down into the warm depths with a big splash.

She surfaced almost instantly. "Again, again!"

And Jase obliged again—and then again and again

and again, seeming to find the game as entertaining as Mo did—but there were no shared looks or smiles directed at Aisha, whose heart hurt way out of proportion to what had just happened. What had she done? What was she playing at? What kind of a terrible person was she?

On the trip back to the car, an exhausted Mo riding on Jase's shoulder, Colton brushed his hand against Aisha's like he was trying to link fingers.

She jerked away almost violently. Instead of looking hurt or confused by her vehement rejection, he studied her face without a hint of flirtation in his expression. Then he nodded slowly and resumed moving along the boardwalk.

His unspoken whatever-it-was baffled Aisha, but she didn't focus on it for long. She was too busy beating herself up and watching Jase's departing form as he steadily increased his distance from her, stride after stride.

If anything the "moment" with Colton had been a fraction of the length of her "moment" with Jase, but it didn't take a genius to know which one carried more weight and would send out bigger ripples.

Chapter 24

JASE PACED THE STRETCH OF driveway where he always had good reception as the vet tech talked, then thanked her and ended the call with shaky hands. His heart was thudding so hard, it felt like it was pounding out of his chest. He glanced at the time on his phone. Would Callum and Jo mind if he took a couple hours off now instead of on the coming weekend? Would Jo let him borrow her truck? After the greeting party on Saturday he felt even more uncomfortable asking than he would normally. He wanted to see if Aisha was free to come with him—yearned to do so. Craved it. Which, of course, was exactly why he shouldn't. What part of her telling him she didn't want him that way was he not getting? Did she have to sleep with Colton for it to sink in? God, he hoped not. Just their kiss, no, even before that, just Colton's hands on her, filled him with . . . the desire to jump on the next bus out of town.

He forced the image of Aisha in Colton's grip out of his mind and returned to his cabin and the breakfast the vet's office had interrupted. While few things affected his appetite, the news had. It seemed too good to be true, and his stomach was too jumpy to finish. He took his bowl of now soggy cereal to the toilet and flushed it, then returned to the kitchen, filled the sink, and washed his bowl, utensils and orange juice glass— then did up Colton's toast plate and peanut butter smeared knife, which lay where he'd left them at whatever time he'd vacated the cabin. Jase didn't want to think about what might've motivated Colton to get moving before he absolutely had to.

He pulled on his fleece-lined jean jacket, then checked his phone once more on the way out of the cabin. He had time to track Jo down and ask to borrow the truck and see if he could swap hours from his weekend. If she wasn't receptive, maybe he could zip in on his lunch break. It wouldn't be ideal, but it would be enough time if he booted it.

He was nearing the dining hall when Aisha popped out from behind a stand of cedars, like she'd been purposely lying in wait for him. He grimaced at the notion. In his dreams, maybe. But it turned out, that was exactly what she'd been doing.

"You're here," she said. "Great! I was hoping I wasn't too late to catch you before you started your day."

He could only nod to her enthusiastic greeting, his senses warring between misery and elation. Seeing her made his day—and it shouldn't.

She sensed his discomfort. "Look, Jase, I want to clear the air about . . . yesterday."

He resumed walking. "You don't have to explain anything to me." He hoped she could tell he meant it because he really did. He cleared his throat. "You were perfectly clear about wanting to be friends, and I appreciated your frankness. I'm sorry you could tell I was . . . disappointed about you and Colton having a thing. I value your friendship—and my place here. I won't jeopardize either of them."

She made a sound he couldn't interpret, and he cut a look at her. She was staring straight at him, though her forward march hadn't wavered.

"What?"

She shook her head. "I'm not interested in Colton, not the way you think. Not in any way. I'm just a jerk."

Something deep inside Jase went still and waited. Sharp-edged hope prodded him. He didn't want to hope.

She looked away, then brought her eyes to his again. "I . . . used him—and I feel terrible about it. I was, *I am*, scared. I meant what I said about not wanting the complications of a relationship, except, then, whenever I'm with you, dammit, my resolve is weak."

The tiniest of smiles tugged Jase's mouth. One thing about Aisha: she may be confusing, might run hot or cold, but no one could say she didn't at least try to keep you in the loop.

"I don't know." She exhaled gustily. "We were having such an amazing day, like we always do—like we just fit each other, you know?"

"Yeah, totally."

The dining hall loomed beyond a wall of cedar hedging. Without so much as a glance to cue each other, they both stopped walking.

Aisha turned toward him and looked self-conscious. As ever, the rare time she appeared anything but unflappably confident, it struck Jase as incongruous—but maybe it really wasn't. Maybe deep down, on some level, everyone was insecure about, if not most things, some things, at least.

"And then you Superman in to save my clumsy Lois Lane ass. . . ." Her tone was casual, her jokey wording an obvious attempt to downplay the surprising heat of that moment, but the bloom of roses across her cheeks told him she was revisiting it the same way he was. Their eyes locked.

"And, well, you know what happened," she croaked—and it was a good thing she spoke because he sure wasn't able to.

"Anyway, I feel bad. Bad because I know it hurt you because despite how kind you are to say that I 'told you clearly' we're just friends, I know I've been sending mixed messages—and also because it was a shitty thing to do to Colton."

"It's okay. Colton deserves it." He grinned to show he was mostly joking.

She laughed. "Not nice!" Her expression sobered again. "I've already apologized to him too. He was . . .

really gracious about it. Didn't give me a hard time even jokingly."

A second later, she asked, "Are we good?"

Jase nodded. "Always." Then, as if it was the most natural thing in the world, like it was a reflex or something, he reached out and lightly touched Aisha's rosy cheek, such a marvel of heat and softness. She didn't seem to mind—the opposite, in fact. She held his gaze, smiling. "Do me a favor though?" he added.

"Ugh," she said, twinkling up at him. "I guess I kind of have to, considering."

"I'm serious."

She nodded, biting her lip.

"Don't play me, okay? I really like you. As a friend, or . . . more if you ever want it. And seriously, if you decide you're ready for a relationship and want to go for it, and it's not with me, I'll be good with that too. I get being confused and going back and forth. Just be honest. Don't make me have to guess what we are or make me feel I have a chance if I don't." He sighed heavily, feeling winded. Talking about this kind of stuff was exhausting. He'd much rather split wood for twelve hours.

She nodded again. Then quirked an eyebrow and purred, "If I promise to let you know when it's serious, can I flirt with you outrageously?"

Something warm and happy bounced inside Jase. She made him feel like a kid—and he didn't know if he'd *ever* felt like a kid before, or not in that innocent, optimistic way people meant when they said such things, even when he was one. "I'd be disappointed if you didn't."

They'd resumed moving forward again, and Aisha had her hand on the door to the dining hall, when she turned to him. "What are we here for anyway?"

"The pups!" Shoot. He couldn't believe they'd slipped his mind. "They're going to be fine! They were dehydrated, plus need antibiotics, and are a little malnourished and underweight, but nothing dire. They couldn't have been there too long." He explained in a rush the rest of what the vet tech had said.

"What are we standing around for?" Aisha bounded down the stairs they'd just climbed. "We'll take my car. Let's motor!"

"But—"

Aisha flapped a dismissive hand, still in motion. "Jo, of all people, will understand the urgency. I'll text her on the way—or you can since I'm driving. Just make sure she actually responds so we can avoid another inquisition and near burning at the stake."

Their eyes met and Jase loved that they could laugh together without making the slightest noise at all.

Chapter 25

MO SNUGGLED INTO THE "MARSHMALLOW fluffy"—her words, not Aisha's—bed in Jo's guest bedroom, and her eyes closed the instant her head hit the pillow. Aisha was sure she'd be asleep in seconds if she wasn't already. Still, she hovered for a moment, watching Mo's breaths slow and lengthen, taking in the occasional flutter of her long lashes. She pressed one more kiss to her forehead.

When she finally made her way to Jo's living room, boisterous laughter told her the informal meeting to discuss Caren's upcoming art show was already in full swing.

There was a large space beside Sam open on the couch. Aisha pretended not to see it and hoped Sam was focussed enough on her discussion with Caren and Audrey, the Art Gallery director, that she'd be oblivious and not feel snubbed. She plunked down on the floor beside Katelyn—and noticed Katelyn had her tablet with her. It could only mean one thing.

"They're done? You're ready?"

"They are—and yep, ready as I'll ever be." She

darted a shy glance at Caren, who was laughing and saying she'd suggested to Jo that they skip offering food altogether and just go heavy on the wine and spirits. "After all, it might make people more receptive to my show."

"I don't think Caren will mind if I steal a few minutes to update you."

"She totally won't." Aisha laughed. "I doubt she'll even notice, so let me see already! I've been stalking your Instagram, but you never share enough."

Katelyn unlocked her screen and obediently handed over her tablet. As Aisha started to scroll, Katelyn leaned in close too, peering at the rolling images as if they were totally new to her, not like she was their creator.

"Awesome," Aisha breathed. And they were. Each one of Katelyn's beautifully displayed designs was more gorgeous or more intricate or just . . . *more* . . . than the one before.

Aisha stopped swiping. "Oh, wow. Just . . . *wow*. Mark this one sold!"

Katelyn's bell-like laugh tinkled. "I knew you'd like that one."

"*Like* doesn't even begin to describe it!" It was a mermaid cut formal gown with a court train, constructed from pieces of worn-soft denim in various shades of blue so faded the dress almost appeared silver in some of the photos. It was absolutely stunning—yet managed to be romantic and bad ass at the same time. One of Aisha's favorite combos.

"Have you had a marriage proposal I don't know about?"

Aisha scoffed. "Come on! You know me better than that. Like I need a wedding to wear a wedding gown?"

She studied the dress for another minute, then moved to a series of 70s inspired flared jeans of various widths from a gentle sweep, barely more than boot cut, to a crazy wide "elephant bell" as Katelyn referred to them.

"It's hard to believe my Etsy shop is a go. It's really happening."

"Yeah, it's cray." Aisha had meant to say crazy, but a lump suddenly formed in her throat, bungling her speech. She swallowed hard. "I'm so happy for you. It's wonderful." Both statements were completely true. As was the next one. "But I'm so sorry."

"Sorry? Why sorry?"

Aisha shrugged. "That, you know, I never got any of my big plans off the ground. That I'm not your vendor. That I wasted your time."

"No way. Don't you dare feel bad. We were both constantly brainstorming and daydreaming. I always knew that, and when you do have your store—because it will happen—I'll just have one more place to carry my goods."

"You bet," Aisha agreed, but if anything, her impatience with herself was only intensified, not softened, by Katelyn's assurances.

"In a lot of ways, this is best for me right now anyway. I can update my shop as I have new things ready, but without the pressure of worrying I'm letting you down stock-wise if I'm working slower—and I'll do a pop-up shop whenever I have a surplus. Plus, flexibility really suits an exciting little change in my household."

Katelyn's hands, which had been flapping animatedly as she discussed her launch plans, rested on her deceptively flat stomach.

It took Aisha a good second to figure out what her friend was saying—and then she shrieked. "What? Really?"

Katelyn nodded, her cheeks pink with pleasure at Aisha's obvious delight. "She—or he—might be a Halloween baby."

Aisha wrapped her arms around Katelyn's small frame and hugged hard.

Katelyn laughed. "I take it you're happy for us?"

Aisha could only nod, and then Jo appeared beside them, a bottle of shiraz and a newly filled glass of wine in hand. She handed the glass to Aisha—who only then registered that Katelyn was drinking a murky green smoothie, not wine. But then again, Katelyn was much more of a health nut than the rest of them, so Aisha wasn't necessarily clueless for not making the connection earlier.

"Hi, you!" Jo exclaimed. "I'm glad you could

make it."

Aisha quirked an eyebrow. "Of course, I made it. Why wouldn't I?"

"Sam thought we might lose out to the lure of cute boys—and cuter puppies."

Aisha shook her head and Katelyn teased, "Oooo, she's not saying anything! That means she did consider standing us up."

Aisha was fuddled for a moment. And embarrassed. She actually *had* considered blowing off tonight in favor of hanging with Jase and the dogs—but she'd decided she needed this more. Obviously, she'd made the wrong choice!

"If you had ditched us, who could blame you? Those little fur balls! I was tempted to myself." Jo's merriment fell away. "I don't know . . . Maybe it's time to get another dog. I was so sad after saying goodbye to Hoover, I was positive I didn't want another one. Now I'm not so sure."

"Only you would be tempted by the dogs, not the men," Sam called from across the room.

Aisha pantomimed gagging and Katelyn giggled.

Jo went around the room with another bottle of wine and a platter of Bruschetta. "I thought it would be fun to enjoy a test run of some of the tidbits we'll be serving on Caren's big night."

Aisha lifted her glass for a refill, surprised at how fast the first glass went down, and helped herself to three of the crispy toasted delights. "Mmmm," she said through her first crunchy bite. "Delicious."

Jo smiled. "We have Caprese salad inspired skewers too. I'll bring them out shortly."

Caren stood up and raised her glass. "Before anyone gets too deep in their cups, I want to thank you, Jo—so much—for all the ways you support me. Not everyone would get behind their wacky mother-in-law's pet projects the way you do, and I want you to know how deeply appreciative I am to have you in my life."

"Hear, hear," Aisha cheered in agreement, while Jo, in typical Jo fashion, tried to insist she didn't do anything at all. Finally, she gave in. "Thank *you*, Caren. It's my pleasure to help—and if you ever feel the need to gift someone a painting, you know how much I love your work."

They all laughed and toasted Jo, then Caren lifted her glass again and made a sweeping gesture with her free hand to encompass the whole group. "And the rest of you, so busy, I know, yet still so generous and kind . . ." Caren's eyes shone with a light mist of sentiment. "Thank you all in advance for helping out at the opening. Jo insisted none of you minded, that it wasn't a big deal, but to me, it's huge, so thank you."

"Like Jo said, you're very welcome—any time," Katelyn said, then added, "Do we get a sneak preview since we're helping out?"

Caren laughed like Katelyn was hilarious.

"I think we can take that as a big fat no," Jo said

and the whole group giggled again, all well aware of Caren's almost strange secrecy about her painting. "But I have to say, I'm super curious about your new work. Callum says you've outgrown your studio and spread into your garage—and that it looks more like an electrician's shop than an artist's workspace."

"How intriguing!" Caren's delight seemed genuine but detached, like the observation was made about some other artist not her. It was abundantly clear she wasn't going to take the bait and give any clues about what they could expect to view.

With the full bulk of the catering, including the menu creation, in Jo and Callum's capable hands, the remaining details surrounding the gallery show were quick to sort.

Aisha would not only run the bar, she'd help with serving and cleanup. Katelyn was acting as art handler and assisting with staging and lighting. Jo made a crack about whether they'd be blindfolded while they worked in order to prevent them from seeing the paintings ahead of time.

"I've actually considered it," Caren deadpanned.

The night was not exactly *young*, as the ravished platters of appetizers and empty wine bottles clearly revealed, but was by no means old, when Jo suggested they play a game. Aisha cheered. Her parents hadn't been into board games, and she'd only learned upon coming to live at River's Sigh how much she enjoyed them. Caren and Audrey departed, and within a short time, the other guests—friends of Jo's and Sam's from town—begged off because of early morning starts.

With only the four of them left, Aisha, Jo, Sam, and Katelyn, Scrabble was quickly decided on, despite a small groan from Sam. They all knew she enjoyed word games at least as much, if not more, than they did.

Jo poured three round-bellied glasses of port, Aisha squealed with glee—and everyone laughed at her enthusiasm. But seriously, what went better with Scrabble than an old man's drink like port? It was too bad cigars were so gross. A glass of port, a cigar and Scrabble would be amazing. Aisha wasn't much of a drinker usually, but she did enjoy the chummy excesses of girls' night. Katelyn had—of all things!—a mug of Ovaltine.

Aisha giggled uncontrollably. "You make port seem like the drink of youngsters!"

"*Youngsters*? Who says *youngsters* nowadays?"

Now Sam and Jo giggled too. It was very possible that all of them, except Katelyn, of course, were a little hammered.

They each picked a tile to see who'd go first—Sam with the letter B.

There was a silent minute or two as they each scrutinized their tiles, then Sam deliberated out loud. "Hmmm, what to start us out with, what, what, what? Maybe cat or hat . . . or maybe I'll go all out with cats, plural."

Jo groaned. "Please tell us you have something longer than four letters."

Sam assumed a Southern drawl. "Well, since I do live to please y'all, maybe I'll lay down this itty-bitty baby. Toenail. And in a sentence: Toenail. Jo is as funny as an ingrown toenail—something she could prevent if she'd ever get a pedicure."

Sam set her tiles down with quick clicks, counting aloud as she did, one, two, three—all the way to seven—then sat back. It took a micro-second for what had happened to sink in, then Aisha, Jo, and Katelyn simultaneously exploded.

"No! Are you kidding me?"

"Rigged. Totally rigged."

"That's it, I quit!" The last comment was Aisha, but she was totally joking. Sam getting an extra fifty points right at the start for a seven-letter word would just make the game that much more interesting.

"Don't hate me because I'm beautiful—and brilliant."

"We don't," Jo muttered, her eyes twinkling with an old joke that, she'd once explained to Aisha, dated back to a makeup commercial from their teen years. "We hate you because you're a bitch."

"Yep," Sam said with great satisfaction, "A bitch who is going to kick your butts."

The game progressed—digressed?—from there, and it was a blast, except for one thing. Scrabble leant itself well to gabbing.

"Come on," Jo cajoled at one point. "Seriously, Aish. Tell us what's going on with Jase. You're with him all day, every day—and on your days off."

"Nothing," she insisted and tried to figure out what to play. Suddenly she plunked down four tiles. Pals. It was a super lame word, but it made her grin. "Like the word says. We're just friends."

All three of her friends-slash-family smiled at her in an infuriatingly knowing manner.

"Just give me my points and stop thinking what you're thinking!"

"And just what is it that you think we're thinking?" Katelyn queried, adding Aisha's dismal score.

"That that's what each of you guys said once upon a time. Jo was 'just friends' with Callum. You were 'just friends' with Brian. Sam and my dad are probably still 'just friends' if you listen to him."

Sam laughed. "Now I need to ask him what he *does* say."

"My point is that some people can say they're only friends and actually mean it."

"That is a true fact," Jo agreed in a maddeningly cheerful way, "but for the sake of inquiring minds and all that . . . if one of them did happen to be more than a friend, who'd be the lucky guy? We can't decide. Jase or Colton?"

Ah, crap. They really weren't going to let this drop? She wished she'd had less wine. She didn't want to talk about this. She really didn't. But she also did—

and that was definitely down to the shiraz. Or maybe the port.

"I don't know. Ever since Evan . . ."

Dammit! Both Sam and Jo went absolutely silent and still, listening intently. It was her own fault they were making such a big deal about this. Never talking about the creep made him seem like a bigger deal than he was in her past.

She shrugged almost angrily. "You know what? Never mind. I didn't come out of her uterus"—she jerked her chin towards Sam—"for nothing. I refuse to answer based on the fact that anything I say will be used as fuel for more of these kinds of annoying conversations." She took a large swallow of wine. "But that said? Colton? Come on. Give me some credit. I have better sense than to fall for a man-whore." Or she did now, anyway.

Katelyn, who still referred to some types of conversation and words as "rough talk," looked uncomfortable, but Sam nodded approvingly. "That's my girl."

Normally that kind of comment from Sam would make Aisha want to pull her hair out, but tonight, strangely, she found it comforting or affirming or something. And before she could censor herself, the following question popped out of her mouth. She couldn't help it. She really wanted to know.

"So you don't like Colton, but you do like Jase?"

Sam looked startled but rallied quickly. "I have

nothing against Colton, per se—but I think your take seems accurate. He appears to . . . appreciate . . . any and every female. He's also way too aware of how pretty he is. Jase, on the other hand . . . definitely more interesting. Still waters and all that. At first I thought he was all brawn and no brains, but I've overheard him talking to Colton—they're both different, looser or more at ease or something, when no one else is around."

Or when just I'm around, Aisha thought with a smidgeon of pride. Then she wanted to smack herself. She was the girl who fit in with the cute boys. Goodie! What was she, twelve?

"And Callum likes him, says he's intelligent—not a compliment he hands out often."

"What about my dad? Does he like Jase all right?"

Sam's animated face lost all expression. "Why wouldn't he? They've hardly met."

Hardly met. That was true because Charlie was always conveniently busy whenever Aisha invited him for coffee when Jase would be around—but it also totally sidestepped the question. Aisha wasn't fooled, and she hadn't been kidding when she said she hadn't come out of Sam's uterus for nothing. They, whether Aisha liked it or not, have similarities she couldn't deny. One was bluntness. By assuming a poker face before answering, then skirting the direct question when she did respond, Sam had tipped her hand: Aisha's dad didn't like Jase. But why not?

Sam was saying something else now. "But in the end, it doesn't matter what other people think of him, not me, not your dad. What do you think of him?"

She was saved from having to answer because Katelyn grabbed her arm and used her to help hoist herself to her feet like she weighed four hundred pounds or something—which was hilarious because Katelyn was tiny as anything and the bean she was carrying wasn't even showing yet.

"Sorry," she panted. "Pathetic, I know, but I've hit the wall. I'm asleep on my feet. I can't wait till my second trimester. If this little one's anything like my others, it'll be easier times then." She grinned a little. "Unless the conversation is going to turn to sexy talk. Then I could probably get a second wind."

"Eeeek," Aisha said. "Keep your sexy talk for Brian. He'll appreciate it more."

Sam and Jo laughed.

"Oh yes, get me home to Brian. Good idea."

"Let me guess? First trimester makes you extra horny too?"

"No," Katelyn said seriously. "I'm always 'extra horny' as you so delicately put it—but it is extra fun when you don't have to worry about getting knocked up—again." She winked.

Aisha grinned, happiness welling through her. It was so great to see Katelyn so free. Free to be silly, free to joke about anything, free to just be herself. She knew firsthand that Katelyn hadn't always, even remotely, had the freedom to talk off the top of her head, without analyzing everything she said, carefully trying to avoid setting off her ex.

Aisha gathered the empty container that had held Katelyn's crazy delicious black bean brownies. "I'll walk you out."

Chapter 26

At Katelyn's car, Aisha gave her another hug and told her again how happy she was for her on both fronts, her upcycled clothing launch and the wonderful news that she was expecting.

Katelyn returned her hug but lingered by her driver side door in no apparent hurry to leave. "There's something I wanted to ask you."

"Oh yeah?"

Katelyn nodded. "I would've brought it up inside, but I know you're reticent to talk about some kinds of things in front of Sam."

Aisha lifted an eyebrow. "Okay?"

"What's the hold up, the real one?"

"What do you mean?"

"Aisha," Katelyn's tone was gentle but firm—and Aisha recognized it at once. Katelyn was using her "Mom voice." Before she could tease her about it, however, Katelyn cut to the chase—and to Aisha's core. "You have the start-up money, you have a solid business plan, and you have more than enough stock—so why haven't you moved on anything?"

Aisha stared up at the sky. It was a deep, velvety blue, like her favorite pair of pre-washed dark denim jeans—almost eleven p.m. and not completely dark yet. The moon wasn't full, and it wasn't a Christmas card worthy crescent either. It was a sort of lumpy three-quarters or something—not its best look. And the indecisive clouds scudding across it didn't help. The nerve of her thoughts made Aisha smirk. Critiquing the esthetics of the moon's phases? She really did have Sam's blood.

Katelyn, as if sensing Aisha was thinking, not stalling, waited like she had all the time in the world.

If the moon, if nature, couldn't make a decision, couldn't be fully one thing or another for any length of time, how could Aisha blame herself for not being able to either? She was in a lumpy, scudding, indecisive phase too—and pretending otherwise hadn't helped her one bit.

"Have you ever really wanted something, and worked hard and long for it, only to wonder, when it's close to attainable, if it's really what you wanted at all?"

"Are you saying you don't want your shop now?"

Aisha shrugged. "I thought I did, and recently I totally recommitted to the idea, vowed to stop letting my nerves rule me, and made a firm plan to rent a space—and the exact same day I did all that, I discovered the rumor isn't a rumor at all. Someone else *is* opening my store and with a perfect name to boot. The Second

Chance Shop."

Katelyn made a sympathetic sound and Aisha shot her a wry look. "Don't feel too badly for me. It was a terrible blow—at first. But then, I don't know . . . It was so easy, almost a relief, to put it out of my mind. And that's made me face something I think I've known for a while but resisted. My dreams have changed."

"That's huge . . . to what?"

Aisha shrugged. "That's the million-dollar question, all right."

Katelyn laughed. "You really have no idea what you want instead?"

"That's just it . . . nothing. I want nothing instead. I love my life and the home I've built here with Mo—and everyone else. Is that totally lame?"

"Not at all." Katelyn's smile was so sincere and sweet that tears of relief filled Aisha's sinuses. She should've known Katelyn wouldn't judge her. She was the most accepting person ever.

"I've been giving it a lot of thought. What I really want is to buy into River's Sigh B & B. To have a personal stake in it. Please don't mention that to anyone though, not even Brian, because I haven't broached the subject with Jo and Callum yet."

"I won't . . . but wow."

Aisha nodded. "I think I've wanted it for a long time but was afraid to admit it because it's a lot to take on—financially, but also emotionally. It makes me *never* in charge, always dependant on other people for my and Mo's security, at least partially."

"But we're all dependant in some way on someone or something else."

"I know. I just like to fool myself that I have more control than I actually do."

"You and me both." Katelyn patted Aisha's arm sympathetically. "But what about all your amazing creations?"

"No change there. I'll definitely keep making things and upcycling like a maniac."

"Phew, I'm relieved to hear it! Your becoming an official part of River's Sigh totally makes sense, though. I can't believe we didn't brainstorm that idea before."

Aisha smiled. "Right? Anyway, I'll still need to figure out something selling-wise, if only to have room to salvage more, but I'll find a way."

The night air was cool, but Aisha was warm all the way through with how good it felt to finally admit what she really wanted, to stop hiding from it. Since she was on a roll, she might as well go for broke. "And I want to stop being such a coward in my personal life too, but I'm afraid—afraid to change things up, afraid not to. What if I go for something and it totally wrecks what I have? Or what if I chicken out and regret it my whole life?"

"This 'something' you speak of is Jase?"

"Yeah."

"I get it. I really do. It was like that when I was trying to get my courage up to leave Steve. I felt paralyzed because as badly as Steve treated me and as increasingly scared as I was, I was also financially secure with him, and my kids, at the very least, had a solid roof over their heads, more than enough clothes, and excellent food. I worried that if I couldn't be sure I could provide all that, maybe I should stay put. Your dilemma and mine aren't remotely the same, of course." Katelyn laughed self-consciously. "My only point is that all change is hard. Is terrifying. Even when it's potentially super positive—or maybe especially then because it feels like there's so much riding on it."

It felt like they were going to keep talking for a while, so Aisha opened Jo's tailgate and boosted herself up to sit on it. Katelyn joined her, settling close.

"I just want to hold on to what I have, you know? Keep Mo and everything and everyone I love as they are: safe."

Katelyn's voice was as soft as the gray clouds rolling across the night sky. "*Safe.*" The word was a blessing from her mouth. "Who doesn't want that? The only problem is that there is no such thing. We can't predict the future, and ninety-nine percent of what we worry about doesn't ever come to pass, just drives us crazy in the present and ruins everyday special moments. And inevitably the thing that really kicks us in the teeth, the thing with the potential to ruin or destroy or maim us for life, comes totally out of the blue."

"Wow, that's amazing," Aisha said. "You should put it on a T-shirt."

Katelyn giggled. "Too wordy. Maybe on a maxi dress?" Her voice grew shy. "Sorry, that was kind of a lecture."

"Don't be sorry. I loved it—and I needed to hear it. Rant on, sister."

"Don't go for 'safe,' Aish," Katelyn said. "And don't do anything from a place of fear. Do what your heart really desires. Go in that direction. It's scary to listen to, but it will never steer you wrong."

"Okay, in real life, *that's* the T-shirt—but man, I hope you're right." It was all Aisha could find to say in her jumble of thoughts and emotions. She looked up at the sky just as a massive cloud shifted again, revealing a swath of black velvet decorated with three Disney-worthy stars that twinkled down on her.

Katelyn seemed about to say something else, but a whimpering-keening sound interrupted her.

She and Aisha made the connection at the same time. "Puppies!" they squealed and hopped off the tailgate.

The cute snuffling noises and squeaky yips got louder as they headed to the trail that led to the cabins. Then, about fifteen feet in, bingo! Two tumbling balls of legs and tails frolicked clumsily under the light cast by one of the cabins—followed by a laughing Jase.

"Oh, hi!" he said when he saw them. "I hope we're not being too loud."

"Not at all," Aisha said. "We were leaving Jo's when we heard the cuteness overload."

Jase grinned and crouched to scoop up the female puppy, his big hand cradling her round, hairless belly. "Cuteness overload about sums it up, all right."

"Hi, you beautiful guy!" Katelyn rubbed the little male's flapping ears, and he collapsed in joy. "What are they anyway? They're a lot bigger than I imagined them when Aisha first told me their story. I pictured tiny pups, but these look like they'll be massive."

Jase laughed. "They're tiny to me, but you're right. The vet figures they're Mastiff-Shepherd crosses."

Mastiff. That explained the female's fuzzy brindle and the little fella's fawn coat. The breed was so perfect for Jase—gentle and giant—that Aisha shook her head. "I can't believe how far they've come in such a short time."

"I know. It's awesome, hey?"

Katelyn looked up from the dog belly she was scratching. Glancing first at Aisha, then at Jase, she straightened and stretched. "And that's a day for this old pregnant lady, I think."

"I'll walk you to your car," Aisha said quickly.

"No, no. It's just right there. You stay. Play with the pups."

But Jase had already put the puppy he was holding down again. "We'll all go."

"It's not necessary," Katelyn protested.

"It's good for them," Jase said. "I'm hoping to tire them out, so they'll sleep through the night."

Katelyn groaned. "Don't remind me of cute things that don't sleep through!"

The puppies ambled after them with great energy all the way to Katelyn's car. Just before Katelyn climbed into the driver's seat, she pulled Aisha into a goodbye hug—and whispered in her ear, "Remember our T-shirt."

"What?"

"Don't go for *safe*."

It was all she needed to say.

"I'll see," Aisha promised. "Thanks."

The puppies were much less enthusiastic about the trek back to Jase's cabin, but with much coaxing, laughter, and praise—and frequent pauses for piddles—they made it.

Jase's cabin's porch light glowed a friendly welcome.

"Where's Mo tonight?" Jase asked, but his eyes held a deeper question.

"A sleepover at Jo's. We had a meeting with Callum's mom, Caren, about her upcoming art show, and it was easier to tuck her in there—and then Jo and Mo decided she should stay the whole night, so they could have a pancake feast in the morning."

"Fun."

Aisha nodded, but her breath hitched. Had she arranged for Jo to keep Mo, knowing—or hoping, at least—that this moment, time alone with Jase, might happen?

"Do you . . . want to come in?"

Chapter 27

AISHA PICKED UP THE BOY pup when he struggled to climb the stairs and snuggled him under her chin. Jase held the other pup in a similar position. The dog *was* tiny against his big chest, and Jase looked as happy as a little kid.

Did she want to go in? Oh yes, but—

Don't play me, okay? Jase's long ago simple, but serious request played back in her head. If she went into his cabin, it would be saying something. They both knew it. Her stomach flipped. She thought about Katelyn's advice—and how, before driving away, Katelyn made it clear it wasn't just about some business or career thing. It was about how to live: how Aisha should approach *life*.

Jase grinned his slow grin. "We'd have the place to ourselves. Colton is off being Colton—don't think I'll see him until Monday."

Aisha looked into his warm eyes and what she saw there made her tingle all over and feel happy and sure. She mentally added a line to her and Katelyn's epic T-shirt: Don't do anything from a place of fear—and don't *not* do something you need to because of fear.

Returning Jase's smile, Aisha opened the door wide.

Inside the house, Jase quickly tucked the dogs into the kennel he'd borrowed from Jo and stashed in the bathroom, then he turned out their light, shut the door and returned to the kitchen. Aisha thought the speed with which he settled the dogs into bed was strange, until he turned to her and said, "Don't get me wrong. I love the puppies—but this, *you*, here . . . It's too rare a treat to squander."

Something in Aisha's stomach flipped. "So, um, what do you want to do? Watch a movie or something?"

Jase reached out and caught her hand. "Or something," he said, placing her palm on his chest, just below his sternum. She could feel his heart beating and it was as if her own blood's rhythm changed to match his.

His eyes locked on hers, asking permission. When her chin lifted in reply, he bent and dropped his mouth to hers. All her tension left her in a huge shuddering sigh—and then she kissed him back.

They stood like that for a long while, kissing, exploring lightly—mouths only, bodies close but not quite touching.

Yet even this barely-skimming-the-surface level of physical contact plunged Aisha in way over her head. She could hardly breathe for wanting him. Her senses bobbed and swam with awareness of his proximity. So close, so damn, teasingly, torturously close. His scent. The homemade soap she stocked each River's Sigh cabin with—new for this season, cedar and spice, mmm!—but also just *him* . . . and maybe a tinge of puppy. How the hell was that hot? But somehow it was, it really, really was.

She was drowning in the desire to grab him and pull him toward her and force him to stop kissing her with such restraint. For a heady second, she wondered if his hands-off approach was way sexier than if he'd grabbed her straight off. This was not like kissing the few other boys she had in her life. That was fruit punch compared to wine: sweet and sugary versus a mind altering, sway-inducing, full-body rush of heat and blood. And it wasn't remotely like being with Evan. That relationship, she knew now, with the worst of its horror and shame softened by a few years of growing, was always more of a curiosity thing, a desire to escape the void she felt after her mom died, a desperate attempt to feel *anything* except sad (and, wow, had that backfired!). It had never involved true, real wanting. It had never kindled a connection she could feel even when they were apart. Not like this.

No, she thought suddenly. No more thinking about any of that. Only of Jase. Better yet, no more thinking, period. Only feeling.

Like Jase read her mind, he took her by the hips and sashayed her backwards.

Aisha tried to see over her shoulder. "Where are—"

"Shhh." He put a gentle hand to her face, redirecting her gaze to his once more, then silenced her with his lips, continuing to walk her backwards. When the ladder to the loft bumped lightly against the back of her calves, Jase lifted her like she was a feather and deposited her on the second rung. Instinctually, she placed her hands on his shoulder for balance. Her breasts were inches from his chest, her pelvic bowl much more in line with his—

"Better access." He grinned, eyes gleaming with humor—and unmistakeable heat. "Plus, it wouldn't do to get a crick in my neck just when it's getting good."

"No, no, wouldn't do at all," Aisha said breathlessly. His big hands still framed her hips, and his thumbs moved in soft circles over her hipbones, while his firm fingers kneaded the V at the base of her spine and massaged the top of her buttocks. She sighed in pleasure and felt him smile against her mouth.

He pulled away long enough to whisper, "Like that?"

"It's . . .okay." But she knew the raggedness of her voice gave her away. *Like* didn't begin to describe the sensations rolling through her.

He gently nudged her legs apart with his knee and slid his leg further until she was basically riding him. The pressure of his thigh against her humming parts was . . . excruciatingly pleasurable. He was still kneading her ass and as his tongue explored and prodded her mouth, it all felt so good she just couldn't contain herself—

A tiny moan escaped her, and he untangled his limbs from hers and stepped back. Her whole body objected.

"Get naked," he said, but it wasn't his usual sweet, tentative tone. It was commanding, authoritative. Sexy as hell.

She balked—but only because she knew she should. Or felt she should. Or . . . damn. She didn't know.

His voice softened but was no less sure. "We won't do anything—I won't do anything—you don't want to."

Keeping her eyes locked to his, Aisha complied. She put her hand on his chest and pushed, so he stepped back some more, then she hopped off the ladder.

She shrugged one shoulder out of her boat necked top, then the other—then slowly, very slowly pulled it up over her head and let it fall to the floor. She waited a moment before easing off one platform wedge—and then the other. His eyes darted up to meet hers, then locked on her fly, which made her smile. She slowly undid the button, then released the little side hook and dragged the zipper down. Finally, still taking her time, she shimmied out of her 50s style capris.

She smiled at the heat in Jase's eyes as she stood there in her panties and bralette. Thanks to Katelyn's ongoing passion for creating retro "undergarments," she had a plethora of cute scanty things and she was so pleased to be wearing them.

"You are . . . so beautiful." Jase's whisper was reverent, and he ran a finger down her cheek, across her clavicle and back, then down to the hollow between her breasts and up again.

She inhaled sharply, her eyes closing.

And then he was smoothing his hands over the curve of her shoulders and down her arms. The sensation of Jase's strong, slightly calloused hands against her skin was delicious and she shivered while her insides melted.

"I knew your body would match your heart."

"That sounds like something only a poet would say," she whispered back.

They laughed together and somehow that was so hot too.

"Your turn, buddy."

Jase didn't need to be told twice. He yanked his sweatshirt and tank top off as one and tossed them aside, then dropped his jeans and stepped out of them, balancing on one foot then the other to pull off his socks. While Aisha had enjoyed watching him respond to her unhurried clothing removal and thought him doing a slow reveal sometime in the near future was a marvellous idea, there was something flattering in his impatience to be free of his clothes.

He stood before her in nothing but tight-fitted boxer briefs that hugged every ridge and bulge from hip to mid-thigh. Oh my. Apparently, he enjoyed seeing her reaction to his near-naked state too. That rare flash of cocky confidence glinted in his eyes and in the quirk of his smile.

He scooped her into his arms and carried her up the ladder to his room. She hated—and adored—how his sheer physical prowess made her zing. "You Tarzan, I Jane!"

He grunted good-sportedly.

And then they were upstairs, on his bed—on bedding that Aisha no longer had the privilege of cleaning every day, but that was pristine all the same—and then they were both very, very quiet.

Despite her excitement, Aisha was sure that at some point, something Jase did would be an awful trigger—but nothing could be further from it. Every way he touched her, only made her strain against him harder, only made her want him to touch her more . . . And every way she stroked him, explored him, only made her feel . . . like she was actually a woman, in control, with power over her pleasure and his.

And in the end, it was Jase, not her, that pulled back and paused the endless caresses and intensifying longing, sounding breathless. "We . . . should stop for now."

He pulled her hard against him though, and she growled into his neck with frustration. "I know you're right, but—"

"We have time, little mama."

"Dude, *no*," Aisha exclaimed and to her relief, a surge of mirth cooled her ardor just a tad. "I've been meaning to tell you since the first time you said it. The little mama thing—so terrible. Not sexy. Not sexy, *at all*."

Jase chuckled, low and deep. Pressed against him, Aisha felt the rumble of it go through her whole body—setting all her parts a jangle and aflame once more. Dang it, okay . . . Maybe everything he did was sexy to her.

Jase laughed again, like he was reading her embar-rassing thoughts—and then, giving her a lip-bitingly-scrumptious view his glutes, he headed down the ladder and retrieved her clothes.

Chapter 28

THE EARLY MORNING SUNLIGHT WAS already warm and wherever it settled and rested, filtering down through the trees, the grass glowed electric. Jase looked around, the feeling of awe he was growing so familiar with, welling up in him. Like they sensed and shared his sentiments, the puppies bumbled about in clumsy, ecstatic leaps, tripping over their own paws and each other in joy.

With more than an hour to spare before he needed to start work, Jase sat down cross-legged to watch their antics—and, too late, realized the lawn was damp with dew. Oh well, a soggy butt was a small price to pay.

"Oh! They are more perfect every day!" The breathless exclamation came from behind him and expressed Jase's own feelings. He turned his head, and saw Mo bounding toward him with the same energy and loose-jointed lack of coordination as the pups, her slightly lopsided pigtails bouncing. She flopped down beside Jase in the grass, and the puppies, as delighted with her as she was by them, frolicked over and proceeded to climb on her lap, frantically licking her face and arms. Mo squealed with glee—and Jase wanted to do the same when Aisha came into view from behind a tree.

"Hey," he said.

Aisha's eyes crinkled and she plunked down beside him. Close. His heart leapt. "Hey yourself."

"Mooooom," Mo crooned dramatically. "They're sooo cute. I could die."

Aisha laughed. "I don't think anyone's died from cuteness, Mo-bean."

"Good thing," Jase agreed, "or with you guys and these two mutts around, I'd be a goner."

Aisha groaned but her face was all smiles.

The male pup got carried away with the excitement of fresh air and so much affection and nipped at the dangling sleeve of Mo's dress. "Oh, bad plan, Mo. Don't let them bite, even just playing. It's not good training. They'll be big dogs."

"Right," Mo agreed immediately. "No biting, Cutie," she said in a firm no-nonsense tone. The dog backed away, probably more out of coincidence then comprehension, then plunked to his belly, definitely more out of gawky awkwardness than submissiveness—but Mo knew to reward the desired behavior. 'Cutie' did a full-body wiggle of pride and ecstasy when she rubbed his head and affirmed, "Good dog! Smart dog!"

"So can we?" Mo asked a second later.

Jase had obviously missed something. "Can we

what?"

"Name this one Cutie?"

We. Mo's casual inclusion was like cocoa on a cold day—and when he locked gazes with Aisha, her expression was a warm blanket with a book on the couch to go with that cocoa. His breath caught as Aisha gave a small, almost apologetic nod. "Mo likes you okay, but when she found out you're keeping the puppies? Let's just say you might be stuck with us."

'Cutie' had started roughhousing again, making Mo giggle and Aisha smile.

"I could live with that."

"Being stuck with us or sticking that poor dog with a horrible name like Cutie?"

"Mom!" Mo protested. "Cutie is *not* a horrible name. It suits him!"

Jase laughed. "Well, they do need names all right. I can't keep calling each of them 'dog' forever. I'm not Sam."

Then, looking between Aisha and Mo and the somersaulting dogs, Jase realized something he wasn't sure he'd ever fully put together before. The elusive home he'd been searching and saving for his whole life . . . He'd been mistaken. He'd thought it was something he needed to buy or build, a specific place or structure. It wasn't. It was people. Two people, it turned out. These two people. Although the very thought of it, that it was even a possibility, took his breath away.

Mo hopped to her feet and the pups tumbled after

her as she called to them. He put his arm around Aisha for a second and squeezed—then whispered, "Is it okay to touch you in front of her?"

Aisha's smile was brighter than the sun and was the real force that made River's Sigh B & B glow for him. She stretched her face toward him and lightly brushed his lips with hers. "Yes," she whispered, then settled back on the ground, her leg and hip nestled against his.

The happiness that buzzed through him was muted slightly by another realization. If they were really going to be close, if she was his home, there couldn't be any closed doors or hidden spaces from each other. And that meant, as hard as it would be, as much as it shamed him, he needed to tell her . . . everything. And he would soon. The very next time they were alone, in fact.

"Cutieeeeee," Mo trilled, trying to call the dog who'd become distracted by a clump of dandelions. "Cutieeeee!" The pup looked up suddenly and took a step toward Mo. "Good boy, Cutie! Good boy!" The dog liked the sound of that and took another three steps, his ears bouncing enthusiastically. "Cuuutie!" He took one more step.

"I guess 'Cutie' it is," Jase said.

Mo cheered. Aisha groaned. Jase laughed.

Chapter 29

AISHA WAS RUNNING ERRANDS, THEN planned to meet Katelyn and Caren at the Art Gallery—and she felt like she was walking on air as she trotted around town. Every once in a while, grinning like a fool, she actually looked down to see if her feet were still on the ground. She was heady with the sight and scent of the huge banks of fuchsia roses that the Greenridge Beautification society had planted along most of the downtown sidewalks. She was heady with . . . life.

The only thing that would've made the day better was if Jase had been free to accompany her—and maybe they could've gone out for lunch. She always thought it was so romantic when she saw couples out for lunch—more so than dinner, maybe because a dinner date was so obvious, but sneaking away for lunch was somehow . . . mysterious and sexy?

Couples. Out for lunch. Out for whatever. Couples! Is that what she and Jase were? Yes, maybe not in so many words, but obviously, *yes*. She checked her ballet flats. Yup, still on the pavement. A woman, seeing her laugh, gave her a tentative smile—and a wide berth.

First off, to make sure she didn't forget, she stopped by a liquor store and the craft store to grab a few things Jo had requested for a last-minute surprise birthday party she'd decided to throw for Callum. "He insisted I not go to any fuss, but I don't want him to be lost in the shuffle of his mom's show. I like celebrating him, you know?" she'd said as she handed Aisha the list, and Aisha smiled. It was clear as day to anyone that knew them that Jo and Callum both still celebrated that they'd ended up together. Their relationship was something to aspire to.

Next, Aisha went to the bank, returned library books, got new ones, then browsed two of the secondhand stores, resulting in a bag of T-shirts that she had big plans for. Returning to her car to stash her loot, she checked the time on her phone. Wow, she'd really overestimated how long her errands would take. She had more than an hour before she needed to be at the art gallery.

Hoping it wouldn't wreck her lovely mood but unable to resist the temptation, Aisha decided to check out her house—er, *the* house. The Second Chance Shop. She still hated that she loved the name. And she hated how—even while knowing it was for the best because she had other plans—it still stung a bit that someone else owned her shop.

She breathed in sharply when she pulled up in front of it and parked. The renos were done, and it was so dang cute. She got out of her car and mounted the steps. It looked ready to go, like it should be open—but the door was locked up fast. She pressed her face to the window on the door, then moved to the big front window that ran the length of the old-fashioned porch, then jumped the railing and stood on a cherry red bench to peer in a quirky bay window that jutted out the side of the building. Nothing but shadows no matter where she peeked. Darn. But then again, maybe it was for the best. What would she have done or said if the shop owner was there? *Hey, just to let you know . . . you stole my idea!*

"Can I help you?" A low female voice came from behind her, sounding slightly amused, sardonic even—but without any overt hostility or wariness.

Aisha was so startled she almost fell off the bench. Aiming for a calm she didn't feel and a composure she hoped wouldn't be noticeably fake—after all, it was totally normal, everyday stuff to pull a peeping Tom on a locked store, right?—she pivoted on her red perch and looked down.

The woman, shorter and softer-looking than her resonant voice suggested, returned Aisha's gaze, one eyebrow raised. She wore a faded silk-screened T-shirt that said "Shazam!" in a red, blue and yellow starburst, vintage comic book style, with faded jeans and old Converse All-stars. Great, just great. Not only had the woman stolen her store, she had an envy-evoking fashion sense too. Well, in Aisha's opinion anyway. Sam, no doubt, would have a hernia about a "grown woman wearing skateboard shoes."

The woman wiped her forehead with her forearm and Aisha noticed for the first time how pink and rosy her face was, like she was glowing from the inside out, or sweating heavily—but it wasn't hot out. Very mild, actually.

"I'm not casing the joint. I promise."

The woman laughed. "Honestly, at this stage in the game, I'd be relieved if you were. Come in the night, take everything, and burn the place down. I'll get the insurance money and split."

This woman was opening *her* store and not even grateful for it? Aisha's expression must've shown her resentment and disapproval because the woman laughed again.

"Relax. I'm totally—mostly—joking."

The twinkle in her eye was irresistible and Aisha found herself smiling against her will. She hopped down from the bench and stuck out her hand. "Aisha."

The woman shook firmly. "Nice to meet you, Aisha. I'm Madeline—and if not planning a minor heist, what are you doing?"

Ah, what the heck, thought Aisha. She might as well come clean. At worst, Madeline would think she was pathetic. At best . . . well, maybe she'd be encouraged and feel better about the work load she'd signed up for, because she'd beaten someone to the punch.

Aisha spilled her guts about her thwarted plans and confessed the confusing mixture of jealousy and relief that had tortured her since learning The Second Chance shop was opening in the very building she'd wanted for her own similar store. As she talked, Madeline's expression grew increasingly incredulous, like she couldn't believe what she was hearing—a response Aisha found beyond irritating.

"*What*?" she finally asked, interrupting herself mid-description of her packed-to-the-rafters workshop.

Madeline's eyes widened. "I'm sorry, what do you mean *what*?"

"You look like you don't believe a word I'm saying."

"I don't. It's crazy."

"*What*?!"

Madeline didn't answer with words, or at least not right away. Instead she gestured at Aisha's outfit. "Yours?"

Aisha looked down the length of her body, then smiled. She'd forgotten what she was wearing: wide-legged overalls, created from three different pairs of jeans, that featured ornate, mismatched antique buttons. An ivory lace inset—material taken from an old 70s wedding dress—ran up the front of one leg from the ankle all the way to the top of the bib, giving a whimsical feel to an item of clothing that otherwise could've looked quite utilitarian. A tassel-fringed kimono in a black, pink and cream cabbage rose print, and soft ballet flats completed her ensemble. She was especially proud of the kimono. No one, except possibly Katelyn who had taught her the trick of using old bed linens and curtains for sewing projects—so much fabric and such good quality, so cheap!—would ever have guessed the romantic garment had originally been a pair of sheer drapes.

"Yes," Aisha said proudly. "The overalls and this kimono are both my own designs."

"I noticed your outfit right away, even when your back was turned to me. Both pieces are gorgeous. Just gorgeous. Is your other stuff, the items you've been stockpiling to sell, as good?"

It wasn't the time for false modesty. "Better. As much as I love clothes and have fun creating the odd thing here or there, my friend Katelyn is the real genius when it comes to wearable art. I'm more into practical household items. I do super interesting things with old furniture."

"Like what?"

Aisha whipped out her phone. "It's easier if I show you some examples."

Madeline scrolled through photo after photo with a growing expression of awe. Not one for poker playing, our Madeline, Aisha thought—betting her own growing feeling of excitement was just as transparent. She got compliments on her creations all the time, but something about Madeline's interest felt . . . bigger.

Madeline's gaze shot up from the phone and pinned Aisha. "These are all of yours, things you made or fixed or upcycled?"

"No."

Disappointment flicked across Madeline's face. "I don't understand then—"

"I mean yes. Those are all mine. It's just not nearly *all* of them. I wasn't kidding when I told you I have a workshop, more like a warehouse, full. I spend winters pretty much doing nothing but making stuff."

Madeline grabbed Aisha by the arm and yanked her toward the store's front door. "Come with me."

Excitement warred with trepidation. Aisha couldn't wait to see inside The Second Chance shop, but she hoped she wouldn't be hit by a sudden attack of new regret or envy. She already liked Madeline and wanted to wish her well without any nagging bitterness or sour grapes. After all, it wasn't Madeline's fault she'd copied Aisha's plan. She hadn't even known that Aisha or her dream existed.

There was a ton of merchandise out on the floor already, including a whole wall of all-natural soaps and beauty products, shelves of eye-grabbing miscellany, and artfully arranged knickknacks and home décor items. Aisha wanted to stop and take everything in, but Madeline was on a mission, pulling Aisha deeper into the house.

As they went, Aisha realized Madeline had kept the original rooms and was using them as themes for organizing and displaying stock. A glimpse of the kitchen showed a crazy wealth of cooking and food related goods. The dining room had to-die-for tables and assorted chairs, some in groups of four to six but some utterly unique and without partners. She wanted to look at the dishes. She loved old dishes! But still Madeline pulled her onward.

She stopped when they reached an arched doorway. Then she waved a hand as if to say, "Here it is," like it was something she and Aisha had already discussed.

Aisha peered into a large, empty, white-washed room. Huge old-fashioned multi-paned windows along the far wall revealed a massive rose bush, heavy with the pink blooms she'd been so enamored with earlier in the day.

It was a gorgeous space, absolutely, but felt anti-climactic after all the treasures Aisha had wanted to paw through. She didn't understand why, with all the work Madeline had done so far, this was what she was eager to show off.

"What were you going to name it?" Madeline asked.

"Pardon?"

"Your store. If you opened it, what were you going to call it?"

Aisha cleared her throat. Since she'd pretty much decided, or had it decided for her, that she wasn't opening her own place, she hadn't even told Katelyn her latest name idea, the one she'd immediately known was *it*.

"Reclaimed," she said.

Madeline stared and Aisha felt compelled to explain. She waved her hand in a slightly defensive gesture, as if to ward off criticism, and jerked her chin almost curtly. "It's sort of symbolic. I feel really strongly about reducing the amount of materials that go into our landfills by reusing and repurposing materials that have already been manufactured—and showing people that pre-loved stuff can be as useful—and as beautiful and fun to shop for—as new, so the name is literal, like I mean I'm reclaiming junk or 'garbage' and giving it a new life. But it's also a weird metaphor for something I'm trying to work through." Aisha couldn't believe she was about to tell Madeline, a total stranger, something she hadn't even been able to express to the people closest to her yet. But maybe the fact that she and Madeline didn't have a relationship was exactly why she felt she could. There was no pressure, no judgement, no need to worry that something she said would be taken too seriously or not seriously enough, that it would unintentionally wound—or give false hope. She could just say it, test it, out loud.

"I was adopted at birth, and my parents—the ones who adopted me—were awesome. It really was, corny as it sounds, like we were meant to be a family. Like I was born for them, and they had been created to be my parents." Aisha darted a glance at Madeline to see if she was coming off as a total flake, but Madeline seemed rapt.

"Then, when I was thirteen my mom died. My dad handled it the best he could, but it was a really shitty few years for both of us. And then I got pregnant at seventeen."

Madeline blinked.

"Yes, I have a four-year-old," Aisha confirmed, hoping it would stave off the "you look too young to have a child" comment she often got. "Anyway, for the first time in my life, other than the odd moment of curiosity, I really wanted to find my birth mom. I needed to figure out what to do and I thought hearing her take on giving me up would help me. And it did, except that in the process, she and my dad met and," Aisha's face heated because she still found the whole thing embarrassing, "they fell for each other and got . . . *married*."

Madeline smiled but looked sympathetic. She reminded Aisha a little of Jo in some ways, if Jo was older, and it gave her what she needed to finish her rant. "Anyway, long story short—oops, too late!"

Madeline smiled again.

"I have this huge extended family that I love very much and am so grateful for—and my dad is doing great. I pretty much never worry about him anymore. I kept my daughter and I can't believe I ever wondered if I should."

Just shut up, Aisha willed herself—but Madeline still seemed genuinely interested.

"And I have Sam, my birth mom, who, I have to

admit because I try really hard to be honest about all things in my life, is great. It's like I, personally, have been reclaimed, retro-fitted into this new family, and while I appreciate it, value it, feel super lucky because I honestly do know I'm a bit of a spoiled brat and I have so much . . . I also feel guilty. I just really want my mom, my real mom, and I know it's ridiculous, but I sort of feel like accepting Sam, fully letting her in or whatever, is like . . . a betrayal." There she'd said it. Stupid as it was. "So yeah," she finished lamely. "*Reclaimed*. I already know the value of reshaping and remodelling pre-existing entities, and I'm deeply hoping I can appreciate the new version of my family."

"It sounds like you already do," Madeline said thoughtfully. "The process of making something over *is* a process, sometimes a tedious one. Plus, even when something's 'done,' it never really is. Every item can be adapted again and again. Relationships are similar. They're never static. They change and grow—for better or worse—just like us."

"Yeah," Aisha said, surprised by how thoroughly Madeline seemed to get what she was trying to say.

Madeline crossed the airy room's beaten up hard-wood floor—beautiful because of its damage and the wear and tear it had seen over its many years, not in spite of it. Flattening her hands on the wide window-sill, she stared out. "Reclaimed," she whispered. "It's perfect, unbelievably perfect."

Aisha had started to follow Madeline toward the

window, but now she stalled halfway across the floor, suddenly uncomfortable. They didn't know each other at all, and their conversation had been strangely intimate. Maybe the woman was a total nutter—absolutely brilliant business idea aside.

Madeline turned back to Aisha, her eyes still far away. Then she straightened up, shrugging her shoulders and shaking her head as if to free herself of a weight Aisha couldn't see.

"So . . ." Madeline clapped her hands once. "This might sound crazy, but I think you're my hold up. I was supposed to have . . . a partner in this scheme, but . . . things changed." She gave a wry smile. "I've been postponing my opening, talking to different vendors . . . but I have a lot of new merchandise and like my sign says, I, like you, am committed to offering secondhand or upcycled items. This room is entirely Reclaimed, if you want it—as hands off or hands on as you want."

Aisha could hardly breathe. What was happening?

"You can be in charge of displaying your work, or I'll do it . . . I would prefer to sell your stuff on commission, but if you'd rather set up a monthly lease agreement, I'm fine with that."

Madeline misinterpreted Aisha's inability to respond and pushed on, sounding apologetic. "I can't, at this stage anyway, afford to buy all your stock outright and just sell it myself, but if that's what you'd prefer, I could start with a few of your bigger ticket items and incorporate them throughout the store. . . . "

"I . . . I . . ." Aisha was rarely speechless, so having a riot of thoughts coursing through her and no ability to formulate them into words was frustrating. She shook her head. "I didn't come here to try and weasel my way into your store." What? *That's* what she came up with in response to the most amazing offer, ever? What was wrong with her?

"I know that . . . but sometimes things work out in ways we couldn't possibly foresee—or so I hope." Aisha caught a hint of sadness in Madeline's eyes, though her voice was cheerful.

"What I meant to say is I'm crazy excited and I accept! I'll fill this room and have it look just as lovely and interesting as the rest of your store—and commission would be fantastic. Does 60/40 work for you? Like 60 for me, 40 for you, I mean?"

"Absolutely!"

"And, it's not a deal breaker or anything, not by a long shot, but if the designer friend I told you about, Katelyn, wants to be included, can I display and sell her pieces alongside mine?"

"Absolutely," Madeline said again. "It's your space, you figure out what you want in it—so long, of course, as she's willing to accept the same terms you and I set up."

At a loss for how to fully express how thrilled she was, Aisha stuck out her hand. "I am so, so glad we met."

Madeline's exuberance matched hers as she pumped Aisha's hand enthusiastically. "Ditto!"

"We should probably go over some concrete details a little more specifically," Aisha added—then remembered concrete details she was supposed to be working out with Caren and Katelyn. She glanced down at her phone which she still clutched in her left hand. "Rats!"

Madeline looked understandably confused.

"I'm really sorry. I have another engagement. When I stopped by to spy, I had no idea I was going to be offered the best opportunity I could ever imagine."

Madeline bowed her head modestly and grinned. "And to think I was mildly depressed earlier, feeling the shop was lacking . . . and then here you are, the very thing I knew I needed but couldn't find on my own."

Aisha glanced at her phone again, hating that she did so, but Madeline understood. "We could talk all day, but you need to go. Give me your cell number. I'll text you, so you can add me and have my contact info."

All Aisha wanted to do was stay and hammer out the details, but it wouldn't be fair to Caren, so she thanked Madeline again, rattled off her number and headed out.

By the time Aisha arrived at the art gallery, her phone had already pinged with a message from Madeline.

"Please don't get cold feet! Come by with your

wares anytime next week! Bring Katelyn too, if you want."

Aisha sent back a string of excited emoticons—then, hearing Sam's voice in her head about the difficulties young people and women faced in business, wished she'd could yank her reply back, but settled for sending a calmer, more restrained and professional follow up text that thanked Madeline for the opportunity, suggested she draft a consignment contract, and told her she'd see her Monday.

Madeline sent back a thumbs up, clapping hands, a party popper, two champagne glasses and a cry-laughing cat face.

Aisha's insides squeezed with barely suppressed laughter and a feeling of joy that she'd later sum up to Katelyn as "Squeeeee!"

As she ran up the stairs that led to the gallery's massive glass doors, she checked her feet again. Still firmly hitting the ground with each step. It was impossible to believe.

Chapter 30

Q.T.—Jase's way of honoring Mo's dog name wish in a way that wouldn't make him cringe every time he made a vet appointment—and Cedar were snuggled in their kennel, happily exhausted from a long play session. But even knowing they'd sleep the whole time he was away, Jase was having second thoughts about going out. He wished he could bring them with him. They'd give him something to focus on if he was feeling out of place, and they'd be such an easy, effortless topic of conversation if he couldn't think of anything to say. He should've at least asked Jo. She was so soft-hearted about animals—and about most things, actually—she probably would've said yes, but it was that very fact, that she'd likely oblige him even if she wasn't a hundred percent on board, that kept him from making the request. Bringing two rambunctious, not-completely-house-broken puppies to a surprise family birthday party? He may not, as Colton constantly jibed, get out enough, but even he knew it wasn't the best plan.

He checked himself in the bathroom mirror, one

more time. The shirt he'd bought in town after Jo invited him, a navy button-down in a soft faded fabric that kept it from seeming too weirdly fancy, looked all right—he thought—with the gray Dockers cargo shorts he'd also purchased. He'd noticed Callum and Brian wearing similar, so figured he'd fit in.

As nervous as he was, he was excited too. He'd eaten in the dining hall countless times, and there wouldn't be anyone at the family party that he hadn't met, at least in passing, before—but this felt different. Monumental somehow. To be included at a meal in Jo and Callum's house, without any other employees or B & B guests around made him feel hopeful, like maybe because Aisha accepted him, wanted him, her amazing family might expand to include him too.

On his way out the cabin door, he grabbed the bouquet of ferns and wildflowers he'd picked for Jo—assured by Aisha that Jo would appreciate blooms he'd picked himself as much as any purchased floral arrangement—and scooped up the bag containing the present he'd gotten for Callum: a collection of three different spice rubs, made from locally grown, dried and blended herbs. He knew how much Callum loved anything cooking and food related, so hopefully the gift would be received okay.

Aisha's sunny smile flashed in his mind and the words she'd spoken to calm his nerves replayed in his head. "It's not a big deal, I promise. You're my . . . Well, we're together, so you belong. Period."

He'd smiled back, like, hey, she was right, what could he say? But really, he'd wanted to correct her. Her casual "we're together" and "you belong"? Both were big deals to him. The biggest. And he would do his best to be interesting, to be polite, to make her proud of him.

Still, remembering the twinkle in her eye made him feel calmer and filled him with anticipation that outweighed his anxiety. No matter what happened, it would be a great night because she would be there.

As he strode to the door, Colton lifted from the couch and stretched like a cat. "You're finally ready, Cinderella?"

Ah, Colton. The gift that kept giving. But even the fact that Jo had invited Colton too—and that Colton, for once, didn't have plans off-site the minute the workday was done and had accepted the invitation— didn't dim Jase's enthusiasm.

He shut the cabin door firmly and managed, barely, to walk to Jo and Callum's, not run.

Chapter 31

AISHA STOPPED JUST BEFORE THE cedar archway that beckoned visitors into Jo and Callum's welcoming living room. Her dad and Sam were already there and clearly audible—but equally clearly trying not to be. If they'd been talking in their regular voices, Aisha would've barged in like normal, alerting them to her presence before she heard anything. Their hushed tones, however, put her on alert before she was even completely aware of it. She hesitated, not wanting to interrupt them if they were having a highly personal conversation.

And it turned out they were. About her.

"I don't like it." Charlie's voice was quiet and intense, and Aisha was about to automatically sympathize with his side, whatever it was—but then he added, "He follows her around like a lost puppy—no, like some big stupid overgrown galoot of a mutt. If he was a kid like her, it'd be one thing, maybe, but he's not. No home. No history. No prospects that he'll share. He won't even look me in the face when I talk to him."

It was totally obvious who Charlie was talking about—and totally unfair and *uncalled for.* Fury roared through Aisha, and she went completely rigid, fists clenching in indignation and outrage on Jase's behalf.

"He's shifty," Charlie added.

"He's *shy*," Sam contradicted. "And while I understand how you might feel differently, it's not really up to you, like it or not."

"I'm not going to stand by while some user tries to ingratiate himself into her life."

"Honey, come on," Sam soothed. "I know you're protective, but this is too much. He seems sweet and kind, and no one can argue that he's a hard worker. You're being too harsh—and hey, for me to think someone's being too harsh is really something. You should listen to me."

But Charlie wasn't done, and he wasn't able to maintain his lowered voice anymore either, apparently. His next words were a scathing explosion. "He's a loser. He has nothing to offer her and Mo. Nothing!"

A sharp inhalation sounded behind Aisha, the kind you make when you slip with a knife and sink the blade deep into your tender flesh. Even before the pain registers, you know the damage is done. She instantly knew, sickness roiling through her, who it was. Tears burned in her sinuses as she turned.

Jase—yes, looking big and puppy-like, but in a good, sweet, lovely way—stood behind her, head lowered, looking sucker punched.

EV BISHOP

What the hell was wrong with her dad? Why was he being such an asshole? It wasn't normal for him.

"Jase." She was barely able to squeeze more words out when she saw the hurt in his eyes. "He didn't mean it."

"Yeah, he did."

"Okay, maybe—but he doesn't know what he's talking about. He doesn't even know you."

Jase shrugged. "He's right though, isn't he? All those things he said . . . he's right."

"He is not right! You're—"

But all the nice, reassuring things—the *true* things—she was going to say got cut off. Charlie and Sam heard her and had the nerve to show their faces through the doorway. Jase broke eye contact with Aisha the moment they appeared.

"I'm, uh, not in the mood for a party," he whispered. "Got some work I should do." He thrust the bouquet and present he was gripping at her. "Tell Jo and Callum I'm sorry, please. I'll see you later."

"Jase—"

But he was silently gone, down the hall and out the door into the night, moving like his nature—soft, gentle, sure-footed.

Aisha turned on her father, her heart a raging storm that she could hear in her ears and feel thumping in her temples.

"Unbelievable," she seethed, each syllable like a separate word. "Just . . . unbelievable."

She pivoted, about to launch after Jase—but then Colton, who had been in Jase's shadow, and whom Aisha thought had left with Jase, shot past Aisha and halted inches away from Charlie.

Colton's face was full of violence, his low growl more ominous than if he'd shouted. "You shouldn't talk shit when you don't know shit, old man."

Charlie blanched.

"Colton, I know how it sounded, but take a breath, please. Let us explain," Sam started—then stepped back when Colton's venom-filled gaze swung to her.

"Jase is a good guy. The *best guy.* Your daughter, or any guy's daughter, would be lucky to have him. You don't like that he's quiet and keeps to himself? That he works with his hands and his back instead of with a douchie computer in some douchie office? You think *you're* better than him?" Colton snorted and for a second Aisha worried he might spit in her father's face to emphasize his point. "He's too polite to say what you need to hear, and he cares too much what you think because he cares about your precious princess here."

Colton glanced at Aisha briefly, then punched Charlie with his hard-eyed glare again and laughed without humour. "Thankfully, I have no similar hang ups, so you know what, big guy? *Fuck you.* Jase is ten times the person you are. No—twenty times."

Aisha was shamefully surprised by Colton's fervor. She'd thought he was a party guy, plain and simple, out for himself and whatever was easiest and most fun in the moment, the type to slink off at the first sign of conflict or uncomfortable emotion.

Regardless, one thing was clear to her now that hadn't been before. It went both ways. She thought it was just good-hearted Jase watching out for Colton, but the relationship was obviously reciprocal. *He's my brother,* Jase had once said, like it explained everything.

"Now hold on a minute," Charlie said, his hands raised in a conciliatory gesture. "I didn't mean any offence."

"Yeah, sure. You had no idea what you were saying. English is your second language, right? What you *mean* is that you didn't intend to get overheard—but hear me. You call Jase a loser and act like he's some shiftless drifter without a pot to piss in. The opposite is true. He's been saving for a place of his own since we were like, fifteen. And every penny he earns outside his savings and the little bit he lives on goes to his daughter. I never knew any grown ass men who took care of their responsibilities the way Jase does."

Charlie stepped back and his whole body sagged. "I . . . I don't know what to say. I'm sorry."

Colton was saying something else, something like how he wasn't the one Charlie should be apologizing to, but Aisha couldn't hear clearly over the clanging words repeating and repeating and repeating in her brain. "Jase has a daughter?"

"What?" Colton's head jerked like she'd slapped him. "You didn't—oh, shit. Shit! I thought . . . I thought you knew. You guys are so close and—*shit.*"

Aisha held up a hand to stave off Colton's verbal diarrhea. "No worries. I would've assumed the same thing." Actually, screw "would have." She *had* assumed the same thing. That she knew Jase. Sure, he didn't find talking about some stuff easy, but he'd told her about his childhood, about his mom, about the long list of foster families. It was another thing she would've put money on, actually: that he'd shared his past as honestly and openly with her as she had with him because he cared for her.

She barely noticed Colton leave. She was too preoccupied with a flood of humiliating memories and could barely refrain from shuddering with mortification. She'd been so stupidly transparent with him—and he hadn't even bothered to mention he had a kid? There could only be one reason why he hadn't.

She'd been so utterly sure he was nothing like Evan. That he was, as Colton described him, a good guy. The *best* guy. Wholly, unconditionally, decent and trustworthy. But the reality? The truth? She'd been duped by a skilled liar and manipulator again.

Jo was suddenly in the archway to the living room, a huge cake in her hands. Her gaze darted between speechless-for-once Sam, pale-faced Charlie, and irate Aisha. She shook her head once, as if deciding she didn't have time for whatever she'd missed. "Quick, guys! The car's pulled up. Everybody else is already hiding. Come get ready to yell surprise."

Yell surprise. Well, that had already happened. Torn, Aisha looked in the direction that Jase and Colton had defected. She desperately wanted to do the same—in the opposite direction. But she didn't want to let Jo down either.

Heavy hearted and dreading the whole festive "fun" evening, Aisha let her aunt herd her into the living room.

Chapter 32

CUDDLING THE PUPPIES ON HIS lap, deriving some comfort from their snores and the feeling of their now-chubby bodies pressed up against his, Jase watched for Aisha from his deck into the wee hours of the night. She didn't show up, and he wasn't so dense that he didn't know what that meant. She'd either taken an alternate route home that didn't run past his cabin, or she and Mo had stayed over at Jo's. The latter seemed unlikely, as Mo occasionally had an Auntie Jo sleepover, but Aisha never did. Either way, he had no doubt that she was avoiding him.

Having no clue how to even begin to fix things between them made his body feel like one giant muscle cramp. Still, despite every desire to go find her and try to explain, he resisted, wanting to respect her space. She knew where he was, and she was the furthest thing from shy. If she wanted to see his face, she'd show up. If not . . . well, he wouldn't insert himself where he wasn't wanted.

Around three a.m. he dragged himself inside, settled the dogs in their kennel, and went to bed. But sleep wouldn't come, and he lay staring into the darkness. He wished Colton hadn't taken off. Lord knows, he wasn't angry with him—and he was ashamed that Colton had worried he would be when he barreled back to the cabin to tell Jase he'd "let the cat out of the bag."

Of course, Colton assumed Aisha knew about his past. What kind of idiot, even remotely serious about a girl, wouldn't tell them something as big as the fact that he was a father? Even if he was the most piss poor one in the world.

He'd told Colton that, of course—reassured him that he wasn't mad at all—but Colton had still taken off, with all his stuff.

"I'm done here, and you should be too. I'll hitch into Greenridge and crash with Becks for a bit. Text me by Tuesday. Let's go somewhere bigger. This place sucks."

Jase couldn't even reply, let alone start to make new travel plans. Sadness hammered his brain. He'd wrecked everything. Everything.

One question and one question alone banged through his skull as sleep finally dragged him into oblivion: how long would he have to wait to find out how badly his cowardice had messed everything up?

As it turned out . . . not long. Not long at all. Aisha was on his porch, arms crossed, her body tense as a fist, when he bolted out of the cabin door at the crack of dawn, desperate to get to work.

"You know it's not you *having a kid* I have a problem with, right?" she said, skipping all preliminary greetings. As ever, he was awed by her. She was such a take the bull by the horns kind of person. He was more like, sense conflict? Run! It was actually a feat that he was still here for her to yell at, a miracle he hadn't already hit the road with Colton.

"I—I know. I'm sorry."

She gave a terse shake of her head. Even her hair, straightened for the previous night's party and now pulled back in the tightest ponytail he'd ever seen, was severe. "Not good enough. Not good enough by half."

What could he begin to say in his defence? She was right.

"You're a liar."

"I didn't lie. I just didn't tell you everything." *Yet*, he wanted to add. *Yet*. But he didn't get the chance.

"Not telling someone vital facts is like lying."

"I—"

"No, *I*," she interrupted. "*I* thought we were *friends*. I told you stuff I haven't told anyone. I shared things that were so," she swallowed hard and her voice dropped, "so effing humiliating."

Worse than everything this fallout was going to cost him, was what it had cost her. He hated that he had hurt her, had made her feel betrayed.

"And to know it was so obviously one-sided." She shook her head again, speaking softer yet, like she was baffled. "I just don't . . . for what? So you could get in

273

my pants? Then why didn't you already?" Her voice sharpened again. "God knows, you had your chance."

Jase felt gutted. He hated the resignation in her eyes, as if that's all she could expect from a guy.

Did he want her that way? Hell, yeah—but it was the smallest part of what he wanted from her, what he craved from her.

He finally managed, "Haven't you ever been ashamed? Had anything happen that hurts so much you can hardly bear to think about it, let alone talk about it? I wasn't lying . . . I just . . . don't go there."

The minute the words were out, he wanted to cut off his tongue. The raw pain in her face; it was like he'd hit her.

Of course, she'd been ashamed. Of course, she'd hurt. But she'd chosen to share her pain with him, while he . . . he'd lied by not saying anything back to her.

Aisha's already pale face blanched even paler. Then she laughed a hard, bitter little laugh. "Of course, you don't 'go there,' Jase. You don't go anywhere emotional, do you? And I'm a fool for thinking any-thing different."

If only she knew. If only—but she didn't give him a chance to try to fix things or, more likely, to botch things further. She turned on her heel, took the stairs two at a time, and strode away.

"Do—do you want me to leave?" he called.

She paused and the hard edges of her seemed to

slump, but she didn't turn back. "If you remember, I never wanted you here in the first place."

"That's not exactly an answer." Yet it was, clearly. Still, he had to try. Before she resumed her steadfast march, he managed to croak, "Let me try to explain. Please?"

She finally turned to face him again, pinning him with a cold stare, while he held his breath in hope. Eventually, she shrugged. Then gave that awful, cheerless laugh again. "I don't think so, but hey, good try."

Chapter 33

JASE'S DISMAL FAILURE TO COMMUNICATE with Aisha was six days ago and he hadn't laid eyes on her since—something that was definitely not a coincidence.

Without her bright light in his every day, he'd moved dully through his week on auto pilot. Today was no different. He studied the list of repairs Callum wanted done, then checked the weather app on his phone. Seven days plus with nary a raindrop predicted. Decks it was. He'd scrape each deck in sequence and pressure wash each one. The first would be fully dry by the time he finished, and he'd paint in the same order he'd prepped. It would be a few days of mind-numbing labor. Exactly what he needed. To turn off his brain and lose himself in the rhythm of work.

Colton really had quit as promised and was headed for Vancouver. Without him around, and with everyone else busy prepping for Callum's mother's art show that was opening on the weekend, Jase worked in complete isolation. And he welcomed that too.

Only the pups, growing by noticeable leaps and bounds every day, so fast he'd actually called the vet to make sure they didn't have gigantism or something, elicited anything remotely like the happiness and peace he'd become acclimated to since coming to River's Sigh B & B. Yet even his amusement at their silly antics was diminished by his desire to share them with Aisha and Mo, to enjoy the puppy craziness and cuteness with his girls. Something in his chest clenched so tight at the realization that that's how he thought of them, as *his*, that he legit worried he might be having a heart attack. Aisha hated him now. Distrusted him. Thought he was—the very idea made him sick to his core—like Evan.

And he couldn't blame her. It was his fault. He'd known right from the beginning that he should respond to her openness in kind—but, numbskull that he was, he couldn't find the words. And then, Murphy's Law, the words had come, but not his, and Aisha had drawn logical conclusions. It was fair.

He pulled his hoodie up and got down to work. He'd let the hectic pre-art show hype settle down and give Aisha breathing room. Then he'd go to see her and ask once more for her to hear him out. If she wouldn't? Well, then he had some hard decisions to make. River's Sigh was her home, not his, no matter how much he wished differently. If she wouldn't hear him out, or couldn't forgive him once she did, he wasn't going to linger about and ruin the sanctity of her home, making her feel like she needed to hide away or move about in avoidance mode because he was there. Leaving would be his last gift to her.

Chapter 34

MO WAS HAPPILY ENSCONCED AT Katelyn and Brian's for the night, thrilled to be having a sleepover with Sawyer and Lacey and to be babysat by a "real" teenager. Aisha climbed into Sam's SUV, feeling half glad, half irritated—her go-to emotional state these days, so that was super fun, right?—to have a ride to Caren's show. The glad: it would be nice to have a glass of wine with everybody after she was done work, something she'd never do if she was driving herself. The irritation: Sam was too easy to talk to. She wanted to keep everything about Jase private, didn't she? Well, from the amount of her blather, apparently not.

"I just don't get *why,*" she moaned for the umpteenth time. Sam, to her credit, showed an unusual amount of patience and made yet another sympathetic sound. If their roles were reversed, Aisha wasn't sure she would be half as consoling. No, that was a lie. She already knew she'd be *nowhere near* as consoling. Snap out of it, she'd yell—and honestly if Sam did flip her lid, Aisha wouldn't hold it against her. Her whining was getting on her own nerves!

"Seriously, Sam. I'm asking you for answers."

Sam made a soft noise that sounded suspiciously like a laugh. "It never hurts to ask, but I'm sure you'll be disappointed in whatever I have to say."

Yes, Aisha suspected that was true. She watched the trees, reduced to featureless smears, as they sped by a good twenty kilometres over the posted highway speed, and resolved to stop repeating herself. Her resolution lasted until they were almost at the crossroads that fed into Greenridge.

"Why would he lie to me? I told him . . . so much. For him to hold back, to not tell me something so . . . big. That's what it was. A *lie*." Aisha wanted to sound angry, outraged, grievously *wronged*—but instead, her voice was full of tears.

Sam shifted in her seat, glanced in her rearview mirror, and then shoulder checked as well. Since there was no traffic to speak of, it was obviously a stalling tactic. She'd finally reached her limit and was trying to avoid further overt contact with Aisha's scattered emotions. Aisha didn't blame her. Only felt humiliated. Ashamed. Would she never learn? Above all things, she would've said Jase was honest. That he was integrity personified. She'd thought his quiet way of thinking before speaking showed a trustworthy character. She was a no-brain idiot! Really, he, like Evan, had just found the perfect oily method to slide around her defenses.

Waiting for the light to change and grant them passage on the single lane bridge that would take them over the river and into town, Aisha noticed Sam studying her with something Aisha could only call sorrow in her expression. Not what she was used to in the queen of poker faces. It pulled her out of her own misery for a moment. "What? I know I'm pathetic. You don't have to spare my feelings. Just say whatever you're going to say."

Sam shrugged and was uncharacteristically mute for a second—well, uncharacteristic for Sam when she was with other people. Aisha was well aware that Sam reined herself in around her, almost walking on egg-shells. Sitting there in her name brand yoga gear— she'd brought a dress to change into after she helped set out the food—with her sleek hair pulled back in a ponytail, she looked too impossibly young to be Aisha's mother, and Aisha was reminded again—as if she needed another stupid reminder!—of how young Sam had been when she had her, of how young she'd been when she'd had Mo, of the whole rotten circle of genetic-ineptitude.

A small white pickup bearing an orange and gray kayak zipped off the bridge, followed by a three-wheeled Harley motorbike. After a breath, the light turned green. Sam hit the gas and the action seemed to fuel her thoughts, not just the SUV's speed.

"Sometimes when people are really insecure, they lie, Aisha. It's not a justification or an excuse, just a fact. Do with it as you will."

"But that does sound like a justification! Everyone's insecure. Everyone has had hard times, or had bad things happen to them. Not everyone lies."

Sam shrugged again. "So what happened to you, like specifically?"

The question threw Aisha for a loop. As in what had her life been like? Or was Sam asking her directly about Evan again? Or . . .

"You've had hard times, for sure. Losing your mom . . . the circumstances around Mo's conception." Sam's voice was soft, yet also firm somehow. "But there are different kinds of hard times. Different types of insecurity and struggle."

Aisha snorted. "Thanks, Captain Obvious. It's still no excuse."

Sam's jaw tightened and her gaze was flinty as she darted a glance at Aisha's face, then refocused on the road again. "If you like this kid—or, given how hurt you are, maybe even love him—get over yourself. Yes, you've lost a lot, and, yes, you've experienced some hard things, but you had so much to begin with. It's not comparable to someone like Jase, who I'm guessing could only dream of having a pittance of everything you have—even after all you lost."

"What do you know about it? Giving someone up isn't the same as having them taken from you."

"Wow." Sam inhaled sharply, then raised an eyebrow. "You might be surprised," she said finally, without heat.

Shame soured Aisha's throat. She was being hideous to Sam. It was like she was trying to punish Sam for the very things she appreciated about her, that she was easy to talk to, that she was her mother, that she was *there*—but she didn't get a chance to apologize because Sam wasn't finished yet.

"Did I ever tell you that when Jo first called me and told me you'd shown up and wanted to see me, I was in Greenridge—and I left."

No, Sam had not told her that. No one had. "I thought it just took a while for Jo to track you down."

"Nope. I definitely bailed." Sam pressed her lips together for a moment, keeping her eyes firmly on the road. "It's not that I didn't want to meet you. That I wasn't curious or didn't hope that maybe, sometime . . . well, whatever. It's just that I was never like Jo." Sam shook her head wonderingly. "She always had this inextinguishable optimism and hope. Nothing could kill it. Like when she was a little girl, you could give her a stick to play with and she'd act like it was the best thing. I seriously did that—would go and gather sticks from the yard to entertain her with while I made dinner."

Sam was only a few years older than Jo, but when Jo was "a little girl," young enough that playing with sticks would entertain her, Sam had been in charge of feeding them. Aisha hung her head, remembering other bits and pieces of Sam and Jo's pasts that she'd heard, but didn't always think about because they seemed so removed from who they were now.

A faraway fond look softened Sam's features. "She really always has been such a weirdo. 'I have a happy tummy, Sammo!' she'd say about food, or if something good had happened that day—and her scale was pathetically low. 'A happy tummy!' What does that even mean?" Sam's face tightened again. "I had a gut full of rage for years. Anyway, after so carefully handpicking the parents—your parents—who'd raise you, when you showed up on the scene, I couldn't see what I possibly had to offer you, and I couldn't see anything happy, for anyone, coming from us meeting. Because when you've lived a certain way, that's how you see the world—like anything that sounds too good to be true, probably is. That if you hope for too much, you will be disappointed. That no matter how hard you work or try to better yourself, you're just one slip away from everyone knowing you're worthless."

Aisha couldn't speak. Sam turned onto the art gallery's street, driving slowly for once. "Anyway, I'm not saying Jase's omission was acceptable. My only point is that I almost sabotaged the single best thing in my life—knowing you and Mo—because of my own insecurities. Whatever his glitch is, it might be understandable. Then again, he might explain, and you may still feel he's untrustworthy and not for you. Either way, at least then you'll stop second guessing yourself and really know."

Aisha made a non-committal sound, her memory

replaying Jase's body language and the sadness that came over him when she refused to hear him out. Like he wasn't surprised at all. Like he'd expected it.

Sam came to a stop beside a navy minivan, darted a look over her shoulder, and speedily reversed the Mercedes into a spot Aisha would've thought was too small. "I'll drop you here and be back in a bit. I ordered a bouquet for Caren that I want to pick up."

Aisha nodded, blown away that they'd reached their destination already. She undid her seat belt, then turned to face Sam. "Your advice is fair, but I don't know if I want to let Jase explain himself. What if I do and he makes sense and I let him in again and he hurts me again?"

"Yep, that's the catch, all right. Do you let people in and risk getting hurt, or do you play it safe, keep closed off and protected, but rob yourself of potential joy and love in the process?"

Aisha raked her hair, which was back to its curly self, with her fingers. "When you put it like that, it sounds like it's supposed to be a no brainer."

Sam looked sad. "Not a no brainer. Not a no brain-er, at all. It's very hard to know what to do sometimes." She smoothed her ponytail as if subconsciously echoing Aisha's movement.

Aisha reached for the unlock button on the SUV's door, about to open it and climb out, but then she reached toward Sam instead and patted her arm. "Thank you . . . you really helped. And I'm sorry I'm such a jerk all the time."

Sam grinned. "Not all the time, and for the record, I find your personality quite winsome. Reminds me of . . . me."

Aisha rolled her eyes but smiled back. "Genetics are the worst."

When Aisha was safely on the sidewalk, Sam zipped out of her parking space and was gone. Aisha stared after her a moment, wondering, yet again, what her mother would've thought of her birth mom.

Chapter 35

As Aisha descended the stairs that led into the art gallery, Katelyn pounced on her like she was twenty minutes late instead of twenty minutes early. "Change of plans. Friends of Caren's are fundraising for a youth travel club and volunteered last minute to do the bar and all the serving for a very nominal fee, so unless you have your heart set on working, you're free to enjoy yourself."

"No chores? What will I do with myself?"

Katelyn laughed. "It'll be a shock to your system, I know—and no such luck for me. I'll catch you later?"

Aisha nodded and Katelyn bounced away.

Caren's friend Audrey, the gallery co-ordinator, took a mic, welcomed everyone and thanked them for coming, then said Caren wanted to say a few words. Aisha, like everyone else, paused to listen to Caren, but was distracted by lights strobing from the lower gallery. She wanted to get to the art.

While other people wandered and chatted in small groups, Aisha walked alone—and within minutes decided providence had given her the night off, not the fundraisers. She wouldn't have been able to concentrate on serving anyone. She would've poured wine into people's laps as she gawked over their shoulders. It was like Caren's incredibly personal show was somehow created just for her—and it was intense. By the time she'd taken in the last piece, it was like she'd been on a vigorous, almost spiritual, hike.

She would never say anything so trite or cliché to anyone else, but Caren's paintings had changed her. Or, at least, made her understand the world differently, more clearly or something. She always wanted things to be straight forward, black and white. Life and people . . . were not. They were layered and complex, and often, no matter how carefully you thought you looked, you only saw part of all that was there.

Of the many, many paintings that impacted her, two works were especially hard hitting.

The first: a massive landscape—similar at first glance to Caren's original style of painting, which had brought her some acclaim and sold well. As the light bar above the landscape cycled through red, yellow, green and blue, however, the terrain completely changed, to the point that if you weren't seeing the changes as they happened, you'd swear you'd viewed four entirely different pictures. The work was untitled, but a small white card said, "We see what we can see."

It was what was *not said,* but that Caren so cleverly revealed, that yelled at Aisha: all we see is never all there is to be seen.

The second: a trio of small, exquisitely detailed pencil sketches, hanging on a triangle-shaped pillar. Lit, yes, but only with a soft incandescent light—no layers or secrets to be revealed. One drawing showed a woman dressed to the nines, incongruously sitting on a log. She was smiling and staring soft-eyed at something just beyond the edge of the canvas. Her face bore such naked, huge and vulnerable love and yearning that you almost had to look away. The woman was Sam.

As Aisha stood staring at it, transfixed, she felt a gentle hand on her shoulder. She turned to see Caren.

"No light show," she said, "but check this out." She pulled Aisha around the corner of the pillar.

And Aisha inhaled with surprise to see two-year-old Mo, all chubby cheeked and baby-plump. She wore a strawberry print romper and was asleep amidst a pile of toys and books on a white blanket, spread out in the shade under a large tree. She had that crumpled, slightly sweaty look toddlers get when they drop to sleep mid-play out of complete exhaustion. Aisha longed to trace her daughter's sweet little face with a gentle finger. She'd been so small! She was still small, of course, but looking back always shocked Aisha with how much she'd grown.

Aisha moved to take in the third side of the pillar, certain of what she'd find. She was right. She stared at another meticulously rendered image—of herself, smiling down with an expression of love and affection that rivalled Sam's. As in the other drawings, the recipient of her beaming love was not in the frame—but it was obviously Mo. Aisha even remembered the afternoon now, though how Caren had managed to sketch her, Sam and Mo unaware for so long was beyond Aisha. She was touched by how Sam looked at Mo with the same love—wait. Something occurred to Aisha. She walked back to Sam's portrait. Then studied Mo's again. The angle of Sam's head was wrong. She went back to the picture of herself—and felt herself gape in surprise as it became clear what she was looking at. She had been smiling down at her daughter—and Sam had been looking, not at Mo, but at Aisha watching Mo.

A lump formed in Aisha's throat and she looked down at the small white card posted below the picture of her. A small line of text read, "Generations – NFS."

"Not the most original name for the series," Caren said from behind her, and Aisha jumped. She'd forgotten Caren was there.

"Jo snapped the photo and when I saw it on her iPad recently, I couldn't help drawing from it. I hope you don't mind."

Aisha could only shake her head.

"They're not for sale, of course. I made them for you—" Caren suddenly looked shy. "If you want them, that is."

"I—I would love them. Thank you."

Someone approached Caren and whisked her away

into conversation. Aisha studied the pictures once more, a sorrow-tinged gratitude welling up within her. The gratitude part was easy: she knew how much she was loved, always had—and Caren had merely portrayed tangible proof of it. The sorrow was more complex. Sam's words about Jase came back to her. From the little bits he'd told her here and there, he'd been shuffled about countless times, lived in a huge variety of houses, but none that were ever quite home. Had he ever had a parent look at him the way Sam looked at her, and she looked at Mo? Did he live with the idea that something he did or didn't do, or something he was or wasn't, made him unworthy of love, of happiness, because rejection was his most common experience?

She sighed heavily and considered the beautiful drawings again. In a few weeks, when Caren's show ended, Aisha would ask her a favor, see if she'd do another drawing in the same style, one of her mother Maureen from a photo Aisha loved. Then the series would be complete.

Walking back to the landscape, Aisha stood watching it change under the lights for several minutes and caught herself wishing Jase had come tonight, despite her anger with him. She would've liked to hear his thoughts on the various paintings.

Needing to be alone—wishing, actually, that she could go hide in the kitchen with her thoughts and do the washing up—Aisha spotted Callum in the crowd and made her way toward him.

She planned to tell him she was heading to a coffee shop and not to worry about a ride for her because Sam had volunteered.

Before she could say any of that, however, a brunette in stilettos that could compete with any of Sam's shoes, intercepted Callum. "Good grief," she said in dramatic stage whisper. "What gives with your parents? Are they together or not?"

Aisha understood why the woman asked the question. The whole extended family, most of their collective friends and associates, and no doubt the majority of Greenridge, thanks to the small-town rumor mill, had heard that Caren had asked her prominent lawyer husband for a divorce in the middle of their 35th wedding anniversary celebration. Yet, even to Aisha's mostly disinterested eyes, Caren and Duncan did seem closer than ever. He'd hung off every word of her mini speech, choked up when she thanked him for being a "rock of support," and visibly beamed with pride for her as he studied her work, as enamored as any other attendee. Most notable of all, however, was the fact that although even Aisha knew how much the big man loved to *be* the big man and hog the spotlight, he milled about quietly, letting Caren's show be her show.

"Nina," Callum said in a tone very similar to the one he used to announce "scat" whenever he came upon a pile of evidence that bears had been visiting River's Sigh. "I've given up trying to understand my parents, let alone explain them to other people."

He moved away, but the woman followed. "Jo!" Aisha heard him exclaim. "There you are!"

She chuckled at his blatant relief just as a low voice rumbled behind her, sending her heart crashing into her ribs. "I don't get the lady's question. It's all here."

Aisha turned to see Jase looking down at her, a hesitant smile creasing his face.

"What do you mean?" she asked, ignoring for the moment her real questions: *Why are you here? Why are you chatting so casually, like we're still friends, with nothing wrong between us?*

Jase shrugged. "To someone a few steps removed, this whole show is an explanation of who Caren is."

"Totally," Aisha agreed—then her mind flew to another changing-light painting that she'd admired, one of swirling, almost psychedelic shapes and images. "Wait . . . Union!"

Jase's smile flashed again. "Exactly."

The painting had been moving, literally and figuratively, and now that Aisha thought about it, it was also incredibly revealing. At first glance it appeared to be a kaleidoscope of interlocking shapes and spirals, but as you continued to look the silhouettes of a man and woman appeared. In one beam of colored light, they were completely entwined. Under another spectrum, they sat peacefully, close but not touching. Beneath the glare of two other colors, they were estranged: reaching out for each other, but not managing to connect, or standing as if alone, their backs turned. But the wildest part was that it was all *one* canvas. Each thing was true in a certain light—and one reality didn't cease to be just because the light changed to reveal something else. If you started to think any one position was dominant, the lights changed and the couple grew closer or moved further apart again.

Aisha thought for a moment. "How did you get here?"

"I borrowed Jo's truck—but don't worry. She knows. Volunteered it, in fact."

Aisha chuckled, then whipped out her phone and texted Sam: Have a different ride home. Thanks, though.

Her phone pinged back a thumbs up reply immediately. Aisha laced her fingers through Jase's and tugged his hand. "Come on. We've got to talk."

For an instant, his whole body was slack and unmovable with surprise, but then he looked into her face and nodded solemnly. He took charge, pulling her through the crowd to the exit, and she was the one who had to hurry to keep up. His speed made her wonder . . . Was he expecting bad news or good? Or maybe he was the one with news. Perhaps he'd shown up at the gallery to seek her out, and maybe his newfound ease was a form of resignation and meant he was about to tell her something she wasn't sure she wanted to hear. Maybe because she hadn't told him to stay, he was going to go. . . .

Chapter 36

AS HE AND AISHA BURST through the gallery doors, Jase was surprised by the light. He should be getting used to it by now, but then again, maybe he never would. Maybe he didn't want to. It was surreal: to live in a place where the "night" sky was bright as midday. The sun hanging low over the mountains in the west was still throwing heat and the huge full moon, visible in the east, glowed white as an egg against the baby blue sky. Beside him, Aisha's halo of curls shone just as brilliantly.

Her, Jase thought. Only ever *her.* He was in love. And he knew it. And when he realized it earlier that day, he'd also realized that loving was the point—not being loved. Would he like his feelings to be returned? Of course. But if that wasn't meant to be, it wasn't going to be because of his lame chicken ass.

"Look," he started as Aisha said, "So here's the thing."

He looked at her. She looked at him.

"Um, do you want to go for coffee?"

"No." Jase shook his head. "I couldn't handle being penned up right now."

"Yeah, I totally hear that." Aisha bounced in her red flats. "Gah! I wish we were chopping wood together or something. It would make this whole talking thing way easier."

Jase didn't care if this moment was easy or hard. He was falling into the shimmering jade pools of her eyes and couldn't help himself. He reached out and touched her face, first tracing her cheek, then resting his thumb on her curvy lower lip. She shivered.

His smile deepened. "And *I* wish we were lying on my big bed together and—"

Desire sparked and smouldered in her eyes. He wanted to pull her against him right then and there— but first. He swallowed hard. Forced himself to step back. He really did, *they* really did, have to talk.

As if intuiting his thoughts, she said, "Tree?" and inclined her head in the direction of a huge Maple.

"Tree," he agreed.

She dropped his hand as they walked but remained close by his side. When they reached the tree, Jase pulled off his dress shirt and stood in just his short sleeve tee.

"The grass," he replied to her questioning look. "It'll be itchy on your bare legs." He spread the big shirt on the ground at the base of the sturdy trunk.

"Why thank you, kind sir," Aisha said in an old English accent, and dropped to her makeshift seat, crossing her ankles primly and smoothing her short plaid skirt—which only made him all the more aware of her smooth, soft legs.

He sat down beside her.

"I need to apologize," she said.

He shook his head. "No, I do. Most everything you said was right, and I understand why you were angry."

"I wasn't just *angry*," Aisha said angrily. She plucked a blade of grass and drew it back and forth across her leg.

Jase smiled at the outburst but felt infinitely sad. "I know. You were hurt, you *are* hurt, and I'm so sorry."

She wouldn't meet his eye and didn't look convinced.

"But you were also wrong about one important thing."

Aisha dropped the grass and her eyes flashed. "Oh yeah? And what's that?"

"The reason why I . . . held back."

"So go on, what's this big oh-so-forgivable reason?"

Jase bowed his head. "It's just . . . you always looked at me like I was . . . someone worthy of respect or something. Like we were equals or whatever. I knew when you found out what I'm really like, who I really am, that would change. And I was right." He made himself meet her beautiful eyes. "I know it's not a good excuse, that it's juvenile even, but I . . . love you. I love you and I *like* you and I wanted, for as long as I could, to hang onto your good opinion of me."

Aisha reared back—because he'd shocked her or because the idea of him loving her was unacceptable?

"Not good enough," she said flatly. "I do like you, or, very clearly *did*—something I made abundantly clear in so many ways, including actually telling you point blank. And you responded by keeping something really big, something that could be a life changer, from me—and kept letting me blab every little detail of my life to you, making a complete fool of myself, over and over."

"No." Jase pulled his knees up against his chest and wrapped his arms around his shins. The hardness in her expression—a hardness against him—was too painful, so he stared at the mountains in the distance as he forced himself to do what he'd come to the art gallery for in the first place. To talk to her. Really talk. Then deal with the fallout, whatever it was.

"From the minute I first saw you, I was impressed—awed, even. You are totally hot, sure—but it was more than that, even at first. You were . . . self-possessed."

"Oh, yeah, sooo 'self-possessed.' I seem to remember slopping a whole bucket of disgusting mop water on myself."

Jase laughed. "Right! I totally forgot about that."

"Clearly."

He looked at her. She was smiling softly. The tight bunched up feeling that was choking him relaxed. This was Aisha he was talking to. Whom he should've talked to right from the very beginning.

"Anyway, sludgy water aside, though it was hilarious—"

"Oh, yeah, *hilarious*," Aisha echoed.

"The more I got to know you, then saw you with Mo, the kind of mom you were, you *are*, even though you had her so young, how you provide for her, how you're always there for her, so dependable, so loving, so . . . fun. How you've provided this amazing place for her to grow up and how you guys have this huge, close knit family—"

Jase took a deep breath. "I . . . well, I already knew, I've always known, I botched everything with Emily, but getting to know you highlighted it in neon or something. It showed me all too clearly that I was exactly the kind of father, the kind of *parent*, I'd never wanted to be. As in, no kind of father at all . . . and like I said, I couldn't bear to admit it. To see my failure through your eyes."

Aisha stretched out on her side on the ground, head propped on her folded arm so she could still watch him. "Emily," she said, as if testing the name for strength. Her eyes were as soft as the grassy park around them now, not hard like the jade stone their color matched; he loved them both ways. "Is that the mother, or your daughter?"

"My . . . daughter." The word sent awe and agony through him. Jase had hardly ever spoken about her to anybody.

He stretched out on the grass too, facing Aisha.

"Tell me everything."

So Jase did. He told her about the lonely kid without a dad, with a drug addled mother, who wasn't intentionally cruel or neglectful, just an addict—and with an addict, no matter how much they love you, you are always second—or last—to their addiction, and how at six he'd been removed and returned and removed and returned three or four times already. By eight, the removal was permanent.

"I was lucky," he said. "You hear horror stories about foster parents and foster families all the time, and Colton had some bad ones." He broke off for a moment, remembering the barely audible keening sound Colton made at night for months after he first arrived at Mike's, like he was crying . . . but not.

"But mine? Mine were all right." He nodded. "Some indifferent but not actively abusive or anything, some actually pretty nice and caring—those were almost harder because I'd always hope . . . Well, you know."

Aisha reached for his hand and squeezed it, and Jase knew she understood exactly what he'd hoped for that had never panned out.

"Yeah, so anyway, nothing terrible, just nothing ever . . . permanent. I told you a bit about Mike before, right?"

Aisha nodded.

"Well, his group home, where I met Colton, was

pretty great. He'd done a lot of traveling and told interesting stories, plus he taught us to work, not in a free child labor way—in a good way, like he thought we could make something of ourselves. He got sick though, emphysema." He went quiet again, longer this time. "But hey . . . I got a brother out of it, right?"

Aisha cleared her throat and nodded.

"It really wasn't terrible," he said again. "So fast forward to a new group home and me at fourteen. I've always been big. And dumb."

"You *aren't* dumb."

Jase shrugged. "Ask Colton."

Aisha gave a small laugh. "Oh yeah. He's a real poster child for *smart*."

"Okay, maybe not dumb, but definitely naïve. Colton always knew the score long before I did, but I looked older for my age and I craved any kind of belonging I could find. Bonnie was seventeen going on eighteen and she seemed to really like me."

"Oh Jase." Aisha's voice was different than he'd ever heard it, without a trace of mirth or teasing or stubborn crossness. "Of course, she did. You're very likeable. Very lovable."

He shrugged again, knowing that was just pity talking—pity for some kid she hadn't even known.

"Anyway, Colton and I would get weed or beer from the older kids in the house and sneak out to meet her and her friends every weekend and some weeknights too. I was blown away. This cool older chick liked me. I didn't know it at the time, but what she really liked was that dating 'some thug' drove her parents crazy."

Aisha glowered.

"She was on the pill, but something got messed up and she got pregnant. Her parents weren't thrilled to say the least. I wanted, I thought . . . " His voice failed him for a second, remembering his stupid, stupid hope, and his plans to quit high school and get a job, his vision of a family, mommy, daddy, baby—

"Anyway, she flipped on me faster than eggs on a griddle. Told her parents it was date rape to get them off her case—"

"Was it?"

"*No*. If anything she was the aggressive one. I was a virgin, completely inexperienced, and would've been totally happy to just fool around, but I wanted to make her happy."

"That's what you meant about sex being complicated when you're young."

"Yep."

They were still lying on their sides facing each other, and Aisha reached out, about to touch his shoulder—then hesitated and dropped her hand.

"So I don't get it," she said softly. "What are you ashamed about? It sounds like you were the one who got treated badly."

Jase shook his head. "I . . . did nothing. Acted like it had nothing to do with me after she dumped me, then hit the road the summer before high school to work, and just never stopped."

Aisha's brow creased. "That doesn't make sense."

"I know. I'm terrible."

"No, I mean what Colton said doesn't make sense. He said you've been taking care of your daughter since you were fifteen or so and that he doesn't know any men who are as responsible as you."

Jase laughed, but it was a bitter sound. "Colton and I just know the same kinds of men, that's all. The bar for what constitutes 'taking care of' is set pretty low. But yeah, I've been sending money—child support— for a long time, plus I have a savings account for her that Bonnie knows about."

"If you're helping out, why won't Bonnie let you see her?"

Jase hung his head. "Maybe she would, but what do I have to offer her? Bonnie's married now, has been for five years or so, to some teacher, who's apparently a good guy and who's 'one hundred percent Emily's dad.' They had twins, so Emily has two little brothers."

"But—"

"There's no but. I opted out of her life."

"You were fourteen!"

"That's not her fault and I'm not going to waltz into her life and mess everything up for her. She doesn't owe me anything."

"She doesn't, you're right. But she might want to know you. It doesn't matter how great her parents are, she's going to have questions about you. You're still her dad."

"I gave her mom a letter for her for when she turns like twelve or something."

"Will she actually do it?"

"I think so. I hope so. We rarely make contact. I send money by eTransfer, and once a year or so, she e-mails me a photo and a super brief recap of what Emily's doing, usually school-related, and that's that." They lapsed into silence and finally Jase couldn't bear not knowing a moment longer.

"So where does this leave us?" he asked. "Now that you know everything, I mean."

He kind of felt like he knew though. Aisha had shifted back slightly as they talked, so even though her position still mirrored his, a large distance separated them.

He wasn't wrong. She moved to sitting and wrapped her arms around herself. "I hardly think I know everything, and I think you're still painting some very dark times with too light a brush—but you're right, I do know enough. Maybe if you'd told me before it would've been different, but I . . . well, I don't even know that for sure."

Jase sat up too.

Aisha shrugged and looked pained. "I mean . . . you have a kid, Jase. A child you don't see—have you ever seen her?"

"Once. When she was new."

Aisha shook her head. "Minus the support money, which does speak highly for you, especially since it was voluntary, not court mandated—it was voluntary, right?"

Jase couldn't speak, but he managed to nod.

"Everything else . . . It's too much like my story. Evan bowed out so easily, so completely. He came sniffing around, saying he wanted me back, and if not that, then shared custody—but all Sam and my Dad had to do to get him to go away permanently was to say he wouldn't need to pay child support if he let me have full custody. He didn't even try to negotiate for visitation. He just disappeared, totally. Which is great—perfect, actually—as I don't want someone like him in my life or hers, but one day . . . " Aisha sighed. "Mo will learn about him, and it will be a blow. That he never even tried to know her."

"I am nothing like Evan." Jase knew he sounded furious, but for once he didn't care. It was true. He wasn't.

Aisha looked at him sadly. "No, you're not—but how will Emily ever know that? And that brings me to the real issue. You roam from job to job, one town to the next, living out of a backpack, never settling down, not because you're a free spirit or because the money's so much better in transient jobs—it's because you're punishing yourself."

"But—"

Aisha ignored him. "And Mo, who you're so good

with, so sweet with . . . she makes you sad. It's always confused me because you also seem to have fun with her, to *love her*, but now I get it. Whenever you see her, you see everything you lost, or didn't do or something. How would that ever work?"

What could Jase say? She was right.

"You need to sort out your life. I don't know how or what that will look like but until you do, you're not ready for a relationship."

Well, nothing else really needed to be said, did it?

Jase realized then that the light had finally left the sky. The night had darkened around them and he hadn't even noticed. He pressed his clenched fists into his eyes, holding them there, hard, for a moment. Then he got to his feet a little unsteadily.

Aisha stood too, rubbing her bare arms, and Jase became aware of a chill in the air that he hadn't felt until then. He scooped his shirt from the grass and held it out to Aisha.

She hesitated, then accepted it and slipped it on. It hung almost to her knees and she spent a minute rolling the sleeves.

"Thank you," she said softly. When neither of them made a move to leave, she added, "So where do we stand? Still friends, I hope. You're not angry?"

"Not angry, not at you, in the slightest. And yes, still friends. Always."

They started to walk and, though Jase could hardly believe it himself, he chuckled a little. "You're cute though, if you think that's the last of me."

Even in the shadows, he could make out her bewildered expression. "What does that mean?"

"Just what I said before. I'm nothing like Evan—"

"I shouldn't have said. I didn't mean—"

"Tut, tut, too late. And you're right. I do need to sort myself out—and I will. You'll see. Then I'll be back for you. For *us*."

Aisha laughed softly. "Is that so?"

"Yes, that's so."

They didn't hold hands on the way back to the truck—of course—but nonetheless, Jase felt something tangible between them as they walked silently through the quiet park, something that was almost as comforting as touch. She hadn't told him to go and stay gone. She made it seem like . . . he could hope.

Chapter 37

AISHA AND MO WALKED HAND-IN-HAND through River's Sigh's lush green grounds toward the picnic shelter with the barbeque pits and the outdoor stage. Mo was giddy with excitement and chattered away a mile a minute because Jo had said there'd be lawn games after dinner and maybe even Karaoke.

The small but ever-growing staff was already assembled, and from the sounds of the chitchat and laughter, Jo's idea to have a staff meal and fun night to kick off each new month was already a hit.

It was hard for Aisha to believe it was July already, and that as of tomorrow, River's Sigh B & B was booked to capacity for the next two months solid, and already more than half full for September and October. November looked quiet—but December and the first week of January were also full. What Jo and Callum had accomplished in just over four years, with help from Sam and herself—if it wasn't terrible to take a bit of credit—was astounding.

And the May and June they'd just finished, months Jo considered the low season, had seen numbers that not long ago would've been considered a very successful *high* season.

Jo was still firm about shutting down mid-Jan to mid-April, but Aisha wondered if that would always be the case. If business kept returning and expanding, it wouldn't make sense. They should discuss staying open year-round. Aisha could run things when Jo and Callum wanted holidays.

Even harder to believe was that Jase wouldn't be here to see them running full tilt. Wouldn't enjoy the rush, help with the work, and, most of all, take part in the family meals, evening fun—and her day off gallivants. At Callum and Jo's request when he gave notice, he'd stayed on through the end of June, but he wasn't even coming to tonight's picnic. He'd said he was packing and planning to catch the night bus.

Despite the affirmation that they were still friends, things had been strained between them since that night in the park. They worked together every day and hung out together most of their free moments, but they were both hyper aware that he'd be leaving—and that it was because Aisha had told him he had to.

He reiterated the promise he'd made in the park a couple of times, saying he'd be back, but Aisha didn't hold out a lot of hope. He would forget about her. He was a rolling stone and she was a cedar with deep roots *here*—but man, she was going to miss him. And always be grateful to him. For a brief time, she had felt what it was to be not only lusted over, but to be genuinely—and with affection—respected, appreciated, admired, liked, *seen*. She would never forget it—and she wouldn't fear romantic relationships as much in the future because now that she'd experienced what they could be, she'd never accept less.

Also, taking in River's Sigh through his eyes, had made Aisha see, really *see*, everything—*everyone*—she was so blessed to have: her huge blood and not-blood family. People whose bond was stronger because they chose it, hadn't merely been born into it.

She was smiling and her heart was full, but also heavy, as she approached Jo and Callum's Southern inspired spread. She helped herself and Mo to corn on the cob, dipping each piece of golden deliciousness in hot butter and salting it liberally. Then she added a heap of coleslaw to both plates and topped them with Jo's should-be-famous pulled pork. She couldn't believe Jase was missing this.

"Yum, mom!" Mo exclaimed, then giggled. "That rhymes!"

Aisha laughed. How had she gotten so lucky? It was like God or fate or whatever had known what she needed in order to heal. Her daughter. Heart of her heart.

Carefully carrying their laden plates, they walked toward the pretty tables decked out in yellow checked tablecloths.

Callum and Jo were already settled with their own plates, and just as Aisha came up behind them, Jo asked, "Do you think he'd reconsider and leave the dogs with us, at least? I'm really going to miss them."

The comment didn't slip past Mo either, and Aisha's heart lurched when Mo looked at her gravely. "Not just the dogs. I'm going to miss Jase very much."

Me too, munchkin. Me too, Aisha thought.

Callum shuffled over on the bench to make room for them.

As Aisha set her and Mo's plates down, he teased—though Aisha worried he was only half joking—"Why'd you have to chase off my best worker?"

Aisha's heart pounded erratically. Was that what she'd done? Chased Jase off? Regardless, she forced an equally jocular tone. "Pshaw—*I'm* your best worker."

Callum chuckled. "Okay, you have a point. Still, Jase is going to leave a big hole. He kinda felt like one of us, you know?"

Aisha did know. All around her, people were bantering, laughing, unloading about this slightly annoying guest, or that funny moment, and devouring the food, but she could only half enjoy it.

They were dividing into Bocce teams for an impromptu tournament when a water drop splatted Aisha's forehead. She looked skyward in surprise—and two more raindrops fat as tears hit her face. A bank of massive clouds, so dark they almost appeared black, were rolling in fast.

"Brr, Mom," Mo chattered beside her, and Aisha registered the temperature drop too—so noticeably colder in just minutes. And, of course, Aisha hadn't brought them sweaters or jackets or anything. Hadn't thought she'd needed to. The weather had been beautiful and balmy. She glanced up again, shocked by how quickly and completely the surprise storm had overtaken the sky, its serene blue now an ominous purple haze. A lion's rumble of thunder sounded in the distance—then pounced loud and close. Then louder and closer still.

The smattering of rain became a torrent. It pummelled with a vengeance, beating the earth in sheets. Aisha was already soaked. She had to get Mo in—

Lightning cracked and flashed in rapid succession. There was a collective shriek—the partiers' surprise mingling with a ferocious howling wind that kicked up suddenly. Aisha was vaguely aware of people yelling and trying to scoop up picnic leftovers that were being blown helter-skelter—then abandoning them and running for shelter. Tents Jo had installed for shade collapsed under its assault and one went flying. Chunks of bark, leaves and twigs whipped from the trees, peppering Aisha's bare arms and face painfully. A nearby tree flailed about, bending this way and that, like it was a sapling. A large branch tore free from somewhere and hurtled past. And somehow Mo had moved further away from Aisha, not closer.

"Mo!" Aisha's heart was in her throat. "Come—"

but another roaring crash of thunder obliterated her words. A fresh gale of wind hit, and she staggered under its force. It was like being shoved, hard, by another person.

"Mama!" Mo's wail cut through the storm and sliced Aisha's already raw nerves. Then she was at Mo's side, reaching for her—

Her hand closed on Mo's wrist, just as a mighty crack split the air, louder than the onslaught of rain, stronger, closer, more foreboding than the thunder that was booming almost ceaselessly—yet somehow familiar. What was it? Aisha's brain struggled to make sense of it, even as it was instantly followed by a splintering-swoosh.

She yanked Mo against herself, wrapping her arms around her and instinctively turning away from the noise. A crashing thud, so close the impact of it juddered through Aisha's body, shook the ground.

The wind died with the same abruptness it had started. And then—a frightening absence of sound. Just sensation. Icy needles of rain pounding down, pounding down, pounding down. Aisha struggled to comprehend what had happened.

A tree—a tree had fallen.

It seemed everyone else processed the event more quickly than she did. Within seconds, a frantic cacophony of voices and exclamations filled the air.

Callum called out, his voice shaking, "Is everyone okay? Was anyone hurt?"

A tree, thought Aisha numbly, a tree on the west side—one Jase had planned to fall soon, but never got a chance to and now never would.

Sam rushed through the streaming rain to Aisha and Mo. "Omigod, that was so close. Too close."

Charlie, on Sam's heels as ever, didn't say a word, just enfolded Aisha and Mo in a bone-crunching hug.

When Aisha pulled free, her brain battled to make sense of what her eyes clearly told her: a massive cottonwood, decades old, had been brought down by the wind. What shocked her most though—made her sick to her stomach, in fact—was a huge gaping wound in the dirt, a puncture where one of the tree's huge limbs speared the earth—less than two feet away from where she and Mo stood.

Staring at the deadly looking branch, protruding who knew how far into the ground, Aisha started to shake. If she, Mo, or Jase—or anyone else there tonight—had been in the path of that thing, they would've died. And that's how life was, people moved through it, death shadowing them constantly.

Suddenly, despite her terror and the near-vomiting state of her nerves, she knew something deep in her core. It wasn't worth it. Trying to be smart. Trying to figure out, plan for, mitigate all that could potentially go wrong. Trying to make sure your life was "sorted" before you let yourself live it. She couldn't bear to lose another person that she loved—but she also couldn't bear to be the fool who wasted precious time distancing herself from someone she already loved, when it could be over at any moment, for any of them.

Aisha closed her eyes against the thought, then opened them, resolve cresting through her. She was about to seek out Sam, to see if she would watch Mo for a few minutes, but Mo grabbed her hand and whispered urgently, "Mommy, we need to get Jase. He can't go."

Mo seemed on the verge of tears as Aisha scooped her up and started to run, praying she wasn't too late. "You're right, Mo-baby. You're so right!"

Chapter 38

THE WIND HAMMERED THE CABIN, rattling the windows and throwing the rain so hard it sounded like rocks pelting the tin roof. Jase scowled, rubbed his freshly shaved head, and pulled his raingear on over his clothes. Of course, a storm would roll in just when he'd changed his mind. He wasn't taking the bus out of town. As he crammed the last of his stuff into his pack, then tied his work boots to it, he wondered if he should let Aisha know—then decided against it. She might take it as evidence that he wasn't serious about getting his life on track and coming back to her. And really it was the reverse.

If he bussed, he had to leave Q.T. and Cedar behind. Jo said she was happy to adopt them, but that had been the word that decided him. She was obviously skeptical about whether he'd return as promised, and they were his dogs.

If he walked and hitched, he could take them. And if rides proved impossible and the walking got too much, he'd bite the bullet and buy a beater of some kind.

He was never going to desert someone he loved again, not out of fear, not because it was easier, not because he didn't know what else to do—and that included his dogs.

Leaving River's Sigh was different. Hard as it was, it was actually moving toward something—toward being the kind of man that could make a home with Aisha and Mo. If they'd still want him. He tried not to think about the other possibility, but it was almost impossible not to.

Not knowing how and if things would work out as he wanted felt like another loss already. He did one more cabin check to satisfy himself that he hadn't forgotten anything and that it was immaculate, then he swallowed hard.

Hefting his backpack, he opened the door and whistled for Cedar and Q.T. Rain came off the porch's tin roof in a solid sheet, obscuring his view. He stepped through it and moved down the stairs, grateful for his hood at least. It was going to be a long night. He whistled again.

Above the noise of the downpour came a crashing rustle from the rain-soaked bushes. Then Cedar and Q.T. bolted toward him at full speed—such good dogs! But wait, he'd praised them too soon. They stopped abruptly, then turned and galloped down the path into the shadows beyond the cabin's light. What the—

A giggle and shriek he'd recognize anywhere carried to him. "Cutie!"

He strode toward the sound.

All at once, Aisha was on the path in front of him, carrying Mo. They both looked like they'd been dunked in a lake fully clothed and their hair streamed water. Aisha set Mo down, where she fell into helpless giggles as Q.T. licked her face with manic delight. Jase thought dogs had it made; they could be as free with their emotions as they wanted and no one ever thought less of them.

Cedar, already as steady and reliable as her name, seemed equally pleased to see her girls, but had better restraint and manners than her brother. She stood there smiling and whipping her tail back and forth like a cheerful flag.

And Jase? Well, he felt as breathless and thrilled as Q.T. to get to see Aisha and Mo one more time before he left. He wanted to zip around with goofy happiness too, but alas, no matter how he wished he was different, he was closer matched to Cedar personality-wise. He settled for, "Hey, what's up?"

"A lot, actually," Aisha said.

Something in her voice shouted, "Good news," though Jase couldn't explain what exactly, just felt it. He smiled. Then he grinned. Maybe he had some Q.T. in him, after all.

"You decided not to take the bus!"

"Well, yes, but—"

"It's like you're reading my mind."

It was? If so, he'd obviously forgot what page he

was on.

"I thought you were going to kiss him and tell him not to go!" Mo said in a stern, reminding tone.

Aisha looked down at her daughter, then up at Jase. "Don't be bossy, Mo—but yes, that's exactly what I'm going to do."

She launched herself at Jase, and he caught her. He couldn't make sense of a single thing that was happening, but as she wrapped her legs around his torso, clasped his face in her hands and pressed her mouth to his, he didn't actually care.

"Ugh," griped Mo. "You kiss like Cutie!"

Aisha pulled away, laughing. "We do not!"

Still holding her, Jase smiled against her shoulder, then whispered, "I'm definitely not complaining, but I am confused."

Aisha pressed her forehead against his. "Don't go, Jase. I can't bear—I don't want to bear—losing you."

"You won't. I'll be back. I promise."

"Stay. We'll sort out our lives together."

Jase was silent. Maybe for a beat too long.

"I mean, if you want to." Aisha bit her lip, looking up at him.

Jase still couldn't speak. He just hugged her tightly.

"I, I . . . " he finally managed, speaking into her hair. "That's *all* I want."

Aisha leaned her head back so she could peer up at him. "Whatever happens, with Emily, with Bonnie, with anything else, going forward, I'm your home, Jase. Me and Mo. River's Sigh. You are home."

Only Aisha would know out of anything he could ever want to hear, how much that would be it.

Chapter 39

THE DOOR TO HER DAD'S study was ajar, and since they'd had a lifelong code—closed equalling do not disturb, open even slightly meaning he was fine with distractions—Aisha rapped lightly and slipped into the room.

Despite her knock, Charlie was startled to see her and jolted in his leather office chair, which made her laugh. He was always so deeply in his own world. Rolling his head to stretch his neck, he returned from wherever he'd been in his imagination.

"Hey, kiddo. What a nice surprise." He glanced past Aisha. "No Mo-bean today?"

"She's working in the garden with Jo and Jase."

Charlie's face creased with the half-frown Aisha had grown accustomed to seeing whenever Jase was mentioned. She sighed. "We need to talk."

"Whoa, sounds serious. Shoot."

"It is, actually."

Charlie's expression sobered and he leaned forward. "Is something wrong?"

Aisha fiddled with a bobblehead Charlie that Sam

had gotten him for Christmas. "I don't know. I hope not. It's about Jase."

"What's he done now?"

"Nothing." Aisha shook her head. "But that's what we have to discuss—exactly that. Your bizarre, over the top mistrust and dislike of Jase. I thought time and the things I've told you about him would take care of it, that you'd see he's a great person and get over whatever weird reservations you have, but apparently that's not happening, so what gives?"

Charlie's gaze shifted to his laptop and he clicked save, then closed it. He sighed. "My reservations as you call them aren't weird. They're perfectly normal parental concerns. You had a baby at seventeen under such unhappy circumstances that even now, four years later, you can hardly talk about it. You've rarely gone on so much as a coffee date since—and now you're . . . what? Tying yourself to some homeless, probable car thief, who has at least one kid out there and maybe a dozen for all we know. Am I supposed to jump for joy about it? What other secrets is he keeping? What happens the next time his feet get itchy? Callum told me in passing—seemed to think it was super cool—that the guy's lived in more than fifteen different cities and towns in *nine* years. That he's been on his own since he was fifteen-years-old!"

"And that should make you admire him! He has accomplished so much, can do so many things, and he's almost completely self-taught."

Charlie lifted an unimpressed eyebrow, and Aisha wanted to fly into a rage. For the billionth time since she'd pried the details of what had gone on prior to the truck's return the night she and Jase borrowed it, Aisha wished Jo had never let that stupid car story slip. It, along with the fact there'd been a girl somehow involved, seemed to have colored Charlie's opinion of Jase beyond repair, no matter how much evidence he heard to the contrary—or could witness with his own eyes if he'd spend even five minutes with Jase.

"You know he's not a thief—and we've talked about all this before. The stuff about his daughter was, *is*, complicated!" Her eyes streamed, infuriating her further. Why did her body always betray her? She hated it when she was flooded with fury and indignation—and what came out was wimpy, pathetic tears.

"Please don't cry." Charlie looked stricken. "I'm sorry. I just . . . want to protect you. We don't know anything about this guy, and I don't want you settling for him just because he's always around. You're my kid and you're amazing. I want the best for you."

Aisha had always known her dad's love was a constant. She'd grown up thinking it was a law, like gravity or something—and only understood as she got older that no, she was just really lucky. Not all her friends had a parent who was unflaggingly blind to their faults and who cheered unconditionally for them. She even understood and appreciated his overprotective streak. To point, anyway. Her tears dried.

"So here's the thing." She flattened her hands on his leather-topped Mahogany desk. "Saying 'we' don't know anything about Jase is totally false. *You* know nothing about him because you choose not to. *I* know everything about him, or everything that's important anyway. And yes, I'm your kid, but I'm not *a kid*. Haven't been for a decade or two, at least."

That line made him smile grudgingly, though his shoulders were still rigid.

"I know a thing or two about bad guys."

Charlie flinched.

"And Jase is a really, really good guy. You forget that I've had a good example. You. Plus, I'm not— despite all past, present or future evidence to the contrary—an idiot."

Charlie shook his head ruefully. "You're definitely not, but as you well know, it's not only 'idiots' who experience hard things or get hurt."

"So true." Aisha sighed heavily. "That's why I know Jase is the one."

"What do you mean?"

She bit her lip. "I mean if you think *you're* worried about me being in a relationship, you should've been stuck in my head the last few months."

"Yeah?"

"Yeah—and that's why I'm so sure about Jase. The only thing that scares me more than how hurt I'll be if something ever happens to him or to us is the idea of not taking the chance, of living some sad, scared half-life."

Charlie still looked less than convinced, but Aisha pressed on. "Do you remember when you and Sam first got together, and I was a less than thrilled jerk?"

"A *less than thrilled jerk* hardly begins to cover it."

"Yeah, well, takes one to know one."

Charlie laughed. "Fair point."

"Anyway, you basically told me to suck it up, though you put in proper Dad speech, of course. You said you really cared for Sam, blah, blah, blah, and while you realized it might make me unhappy or nervous, you were going to pursue a relationship and I'd just have to deal with it in a mature, self-controlled, supportive way. Now it's your turn to follow your own good advice."

In the silence that followed, Aisha started tapping the bobblehead again. After a long moment, Charlie put his hand over hers, stilling the motion. "You really love this kid?"

"He's also not a kid, but yeah." She smiled self-consciously, feeling the joy of it anew, the way she did every time she said it out loud. "I really do—and you will too as soon as you get over your grouchy avoidance stuff."

"Okay, you win. I'll try."

"Thank you. That makes me really happy." And it did—so happy, in fact, she couldn't resist one tiny tease. "I still don't understand why Jase's roaming ways were an issue, though. I've got plenty of money saved. We'll see some sights, do some hitchhiking, show Mo the country. . . . The open road appeals to me big time."

Charlie's mouth flew open—then closed. "Nope, not biting. Not this time."

Aisha laughed. "Sam has been good for you, old dad. Now when does it work best for you to extend an olive branch and meet Jase properly?"

"I don't know. Maybe this weekend?"

"Great, tonight it is. We'll be here for dinner at six. Sam already invited us."

"It's a conspiracy. You guys are ganging up on me," Charlie grumbled, but he was smiling.

"Absolutely," Aisha agreed. She was about to pop out of the room and leave Charlie to his work again, when he stopped her.

"I wasn't intentionally being an ass, you know. It's just you, him, an official relationship, being a . . . family. It's a big change."

Aisha returned to Charlie and hugged him. "It is, and it appears you and I aren't that great with change, but whatever. We have good reasons. We just have to remember, however, that not all changes are bad. In fact, some are better than we could ever imagine."

Charlie patted Aisha's back. "I love you, kiddo."

"I know. I love you too."

Chapter 40

IT WAS A BATTLE TO keep Sam moving forward through the lovely maze of The Second Chance Shop. All she wanted to do was stop and touch things.

"I can't believe this is a Greenridge store!"

"Um, thank you?" Madeline said from behind the counter, where she was busy with last minute details surrounding the upcoming opening.

"Yes, I meant it as a compliment. Totally."

"Okay, stop!" Aisha commanded. She and Mo each took one of Sam's hands. "Close your eyes and keep them closed!"

"Closed *tight*," Mo added.

She and Aisha carefully guided Sam to the arched entrance—then Aisha released her hand. "Three, two, one . . . Look!" Mo chimed.

Sam's eyes opened. Then widened. For a moment, she said nothing, then she spoke in a gush—and with such obvious pride—that Aisha felt herself blush.

"This is amazing, Aisha, absolutely amazing. *You* are amazing." She studied the weathered signpost that announced Aisha's brand in battered tin.

"Reclaimed," Sam murmured. "It's perfect."

She moved further into the room, stopping to touch Katelyn's creations hanging on a 50s style umbrella clothesline, complete with round-headed wooden clothespins.

She paused, smiling, by an assortment of hand-sewn, all original "scrap" monsters that grinned, one-eyed—or multi-eyed—and wonky-toothed from a massive work bench Aisha had salvaged from an old garage.

She stroked her hand along the satin top of a gleaming bow front buffet, vintage 60s all the way, with brass pulls and handles.

She oohed over a wingback chair that in another life had been a badly worn, particularly hideous example of 80s "modern," which Aisha had re-cushioned, then re-upholstered in a chocolate brown that featured a slight sheen and a subtle green dragon-fly print.

And the whole time Sam perused the tons of other finds, Aisha watched her body language carefully, with intensifying joy. Sam liked her stuff. She really liked it.

Finally, Sam turned to her, eyes shiny. "Your mom—" she began, but whatever she was going to say was cut off by Mo, who yanked her arm with great energy.

"You haven't seen the best part! C'mon."

Sam let herself be dragged away by Mo, and Aisha

EV BISHOP

followed along, curious about what Mo deemed "best." And when Mo paused and pointed, Aisha's breath caught hard in her throat.

"See it's us! You, me, Mom, and my other Grandma that I haven't met yet because she's dead."

Aisha let the "haven't met *yet*" comment fly as she took in Sam's face.

"I don't even know what to say, Aisha. Your whole collection and the way you've displayed it is just . . . " She shook her head. "And these drawings?" Her voice wavered. "They're . . . beautiful. So touching."

Aisha nodded, acknowledging the compliment and the complex layers beneath it that she had struggled with too. No matter how many times she saw them, she was still struck dumb whenever she looked at Generations.

The four pictures sat atop an antique writing desk, above drawers, shelves and cubbyholes carrying vintage stationary and ornate journals that Aisha had collected for a song over the years at various garage sales, plus an assortment of other paraphernalia that would appeal to writers and artists and gift givers. An ancient Remington held a sheet of crisp white paper that bore one line: strong roots.

"What were you going to say?" Aisha asked, suddenly remembering Mo had interrupted Sam's train of thought.

For a second, Sam looked mystified. Then she laughed self-consciously. "Oh—just that your mom

328

would be so proud of you."

"Yeah, both your moms!" Mo added.

A rush of saline filled Aisha's sinuses and she fiddled with the carriage return on the typewriter, looking down. "Thanks for saying that, Sam. I hope she is." Then she looked up and made contact with the jade eyes so like her own. "That you are, I mean."

Sam's eyes widened, then she blinked rapidly.

She looked as near to tears as Aisha felt, and the two of them having some big cry fest here in her new business opportunity was too lame. Aisha pushed on, aiming for a humorous tone. "And Sam?"

"Yeah?"

"On that whole topic. Mo calls you Grandma, you're married to my dad . . . and you are my biological mother. Would it be weird for you if I called you Mom?"

One of Sam's eyebrows arched. "Yes, totally weird. Super weird, in fact."

Aisha's feelings weren't hurt though. Sam's whole face was soft, and her eyes glowed.

"And nothing could make me happier . . . Or prouder."

"Okay, well, great. I mean, I probably won't do it all the time or anything, but you know—"

"Yeah, I get it. Totally."

They grinned at each other, and Aisha felt only peace and gratitude. It had taken four years, but she finally knew the answer to her concerns about her mom-Maureen and Sam: she didn't need to have any. Aisha loved Sam, appreciated her, found her hilarious—and the reverse definitely seemed true. Maureen would never have begrudged Aisha that. She would only be happy for her, the same way Aisha would be if something ever happened to her and someone else stepped up to be Mo's mother.

"Not Egbert!" Mo groaned dramatically from out of sight behind a painted privacy screen, lightening the mood. "You can't sell him. I love him."

Sam, normally even less touchy-feely than Aisha, reached out and squeezed Aisha's shoulder, then joined Mo who was clutching one of the monsters—a fuzzy purple creation with three eyes and a slightly worried expression.

"When The Second Chance Shop officially opens, you and I will be its first customers and we'll buy Egbert so he can be yours forever," Sam said.

Mo pumped her fist in a "Yes!" action she'd learned from Jase.

"No." Aisha shook her head. "I can't let you buy it. I'll just take it out of the inventory."

"You will *not*. Mo and I will purchase it on opening day—and you'd better get used to that, by the way, and get working. Your art is going to sell and sell. You're going to have your work cut out for you keeping up with demand."

"My . . . " Aisha's brain caught on the word. "*Art*?"

"Yes," Sam said softly, but pragmatically. "Art.

You create practical, functional things—to wear, to play with, to sit on, etc., and you have amazing technical skills. You can sew, paint, use tools I don't even want to know the names of—ugh. So much work!"

Aisha rolled her eyes but smiled.

"But you have a vision for each piece you collect or find, and you're trying to convey something with each new work. They're beautiful but they also have emotional power—like you're always exploring and expressing something with each item."

"You sound like you've been reading Wikipedia art definitions or something."

Sam laughed and shrugged. "Maybe when I realized you were never going to design things we could factory produce in China, I started doing some homework."

"Gag! I'm glad you figured out that's the opposite of what I'm aiming for."

"Also, I'm married to your dad, so you know . . . I've gotten an earful over the years."

Aisha laughed. Yes, everything Sam had spouted did sound exactly like her dad. "And what, pray tell, am I 'always' exploring or expressing?"

Sam looked genuinely taken aback. "You really don't know?"

Aisha shook her head, confused. She'd been joking. Other than naming her collection Reclaimed and the little bit she'd elaborated about to Madeline that first day they'd met, there wasn't some deep, unseen element to her recycling and upcycling. Was there?

"They're all about finding new homes for misplaced, discarded, or orphaned objects—showing the value in keeping things, re-fitting them, repurposing them. *Holding on to them.*"

Aisha fondled the tag on the monster closest to her, a tiny orange plaid cyclops with an endearingly hopeful expression. His tag read, as every monster's did, "Adopt me!"

"How embarrassingly transparent and obvious."

Aisha only realized she'd muttered out loud when Sam shook her head. "No," she corrected sternly. "How hopeful and inspiring—and true and wonderful."

Aisha was about to roll her eyes again to disguise her pleasure at Sam's praise—but was stopped by Sam's wink.

"And lest you think I'm losing my edge, how utterly *marketable.*"

Aisha laughed. "You're a terrible person."

Sam shrugged, glowing like Aisha had paid her the ultimate compliment. "I prefer to think of it as *practical,* dear daughter. *Practical.*"

Aisha moved to collect Mo, who'd wandered over to the brass bed in the corner and looked ready to jump into the soft array of homemade patchwork quilts, then paused mid-step and turned back to Sam once more.

"I love you, Sam. Thank you. Sincerely. For . . . everything."

"Oh shit," Sam said, then stammered, "Sorry. Sorry! I mean, I love you too. So much. Thank you—but also don't make me cry in public! I hate that!"

Chapter 41

BENEATH THE CANOPY OF MASSIVE cedar branches and golden sun, the whole world was full of verdant promise, green and glimmering. Jase surveyed the slowly filling rows of white chairs, pristine and sharp against the deep emerald lawn. There were fifty chairs all together, five rows of ten, framing an aisle of scattered rose petals.

"Yellow for friendship, pink for happiness, white for new beginnings and red for paaasssssssion," Aisha had chanted, giggling, when they decorated, flinging the petals about wildly and letting them lie wherever they happened to land, glowing like dreams.

He took a deep breath.

"Nervous, man?" Colton asked, shifting from foot to foot, clearly showing that he was, which was kind of funny since it wasn't his wedding.

"Not about marrying, Aisha. No."

"About all the eyes on you, shy boy?"

No doubt about it, infuriating or not, Colton knew him well. Jase, who'd been seriously overjoyed that Colton agreed to stand up for him and had actually showed up—especially since, let's face it, every other guest was Aisha's—was suddenly beyond grateful to him. No joke.

He jostled Colton a bit. "Thank you."

"Yeah, yeah."

"I'm serious. Except for when it comes to working together, you're always there for me."

"It's not my fault you're obsessed with pleasing the man." Colton grinned, then turned serious. "It—marriage, family, whatever—is not for me, but I'm happy for you, Jase. Legit. You're my brother. And I love you, man."

"Yeah, back at you—even though I suspect you'll use this moment to guilt me into providing bail some-day."

Colton gave an appreciative hoot, but if he made a smart comeback, Jase didn't hear him. It had started.

The low rumble of chatting guests instantly quieted.

Charlie—*Dad*, as Charlie had welcomed him to call him, having decided Jase was all right after all, to the point that he hotly debated the idea that he'd ever thought otherwise—caught Jase's eye. Then he winked and gave him two thumbs up. "You got this," the action said, and Jase stood a little straighter.

Emily and Mo appeared in matching cotton dresses, carrying baskets of more roses. When Emily saw Jase, she halted for a moment and raised her hand, then folded it in a shy wave. His daughter. Here to visit. To take part in this miraculous day. It was her first time here to River's Sigh, though he'd visited her home turf multiple times over the last couple months. He waved back, and the two girls, his *two daughters,* started down the aisle, grinning ear to ear.

And suddenly Aisha was there. She seemed to float as she moved toward him. Jase was oblivious to the oohing and ahhing guests. Could hardly register their presence. Ditto Mo and Emily—though they meant the world to him. *Were the* world to him. But Aisha? She was the universe. And watching her stride slowly and surely forward, he lost his breath. She was the most beautiful person, inside and out, that he'd ever known and she was . . . marrying him. Awe-mingled gratitude choked him.

Her dress was stunning too. What had she called it? Mermaid something? Whatever it was, it hugged her slight, muscular body and showed off every curve. But fancy though it appeared, it was made out of tough, everyday denim. Fancy and *blue jean*: perfect for his forest bride. He couldn't wait to pull it off her.

As if reading his mind, Aisha grinned at him, her eyes shining as brightly as any of the sun-kissed greenery around her. Looking at her, Jase thought if he died right then, he could honestly say he died happy and *loved.* It was a miracle and it didn't make sense, was wholly undeserved—but Aisha, this marvel, loved him. It radiated out from her. It made him want to weep. And she knew. He knew she knew.

"Hey," she said when she finally reached him, speaking so softly no one else heard.

"*Hey*," he replied, equally softly, taking her proffered hand.

As with the guests and witnesses, Jase couldn't really hear the pastor's words, encouragement or challenges—but it didn't matter. When he said, "I do," the vow that he was making to Aisha was bigger than the one put forth by the traditional speech, and he was making it to himself as well—and to Emily and little Mo. For life.

And suddenly Aisha was lifting her sweet face toward him, her eyes fluttering shut, and Jase realized it was time. Time to kiss the bride. Time to kiss his *wife* for the very first time!

Jo and Callum cheered. Sam whooped, then broke off, sounding on the verge of tears. He had a lot in common with his new mother-in-law. The rest of the crowd hooted and hurrahed.

As he and Aisha pulled apart, his flesh and heart already resisting even this slight separation, Aisha smiled up at him—then motioned at the cat-calling crowd and whispered, her eyes twinkling, "So I wanted to wait to rub it in, so you wouldn't have time to come to your senses and back out, but this is *your* huge, crazy family now. I hope you won't regret it."

Jase didn't bother even trying to joke. "Never. I promise."

Mo suddenly left the line up of attendants and

wrapped her arms around his and Aisha's legs. "We're so lucky, hey?"

Jase scooped Mo up, then turned to Emily. Her shy but hopeful expression mirrored his feelings and squeezed his heart. He lifted her too, making her laugh, and then both girls were sheltered between him and Aisha.

"The luckiest," Jase agreed. "The absolute luckiest."

Mo cheered, and Q.T. and Cedar, who'd been hanging around the perimeter of the service, could constrain themselves no longer. They galloped to the newlyweds' sides and danced about in glee.

Aisha laughed.

Jase was unaware of what the crowd did, whether they stayed or went, watched or not. He hugged his family close.

Epilogue

JEWEL-BRIGHT LEAVES COVERED THE LAWN and made a lovely crunch under Aisha and Jase's feet—something they could hear now that Mo and the dogs were "having a race" and had sprinted off. The sun, ripe and round, was slung low in the sky, and the soft clouds ringing the mountains were deep rosy pink, orange-gold, and purple against the twilight. Each cabin they passed as they walked hand-in-hand shone a warm, cozy welcome—and the huge half barrels of yellow and red nasturtiums they'd planted by every porch this year were still thriving, their brilliant green leaves the size of Aisha's palms. River's Sigh B & B, such a restorative, healing, joy-giving place to stay—or so she was often told—was *exactly so* as a place to live. It was all so beautiful that it took Aisha's breath away—similar to how she felt whenever her thoughts rested on the tiny secret she carried.

She pressed her free hand against her still-flat tummy and smiled. It was her favorite time of the day in her favorite time of the year, and she was filled with nostalgia and anticipation. It would be Thanksgiving soon and her heart brimmed with warm, mushy feelings of gratitude.

"Smell that," she whispered, filling her chest to bursting with the delicious crisp air, heady with notes of wood smoke, fish and river, rich earth and ancient forest.

Jase's fingers, laced through hers, squeezed lightly. "I know. It's like the smell of pure home, hey?"

Her eyes teared—nothing new there. She cried at everything these days, which was awesome. Not. But at least she couldn't blame PMS anymore.

And he was so right. And so . . . in tune with her. As always. Like they were two sides of the same coin. She hoped she never got used to it or stopped appreciating him.

It was impossible to believe that just over a year and a half ago, she'd considered leaving River's Sigh B & B—and now here she was, a part owner. A small part, admittedly, but hey . . . it was still amazing. Whenever she thought of the freshly signed papers, crisp and secure in a safety deposit box at her bank, she wanted to pinch herself.

Even harder to believe, and to accept the wonder of, were all the changes in her since then. As a place, River's Sigh was still her treasured refuge and hopefully always would be, but at the same time, she'd finally found—recognized, *reclaimed*—her true home, which wasn't a *place* at all. It was people. The people she loved who loved her, some blood, some not. And of those, especially, of course: Mo, as it had been all along, and Jase. And little Emily—who was every bit as sweet, kind, and reserved as her gentle dad.

Fresh thankfulness filled Aisha. She'd worried that Bonnie would be spiteful toward Jase, but instead she'd been genuinely happy that Jase wanted to build a relationship with his daughter, not just send money. She wanted Emily to know her biological father, to be connected to him. She even apologized for the way she had hurt him all those years ago.

"So when are you going to tell me what the surprise is?" Jase asked.

Aisha was ready to burst with it, but she had a special night in the works, so with great effort, restrained herself. "Soon," she said mysteriously. "Very soon."

Jase shook his head, grinning. "You're driving me crazy!"

"Excellent! All part of my devious plan, sir."

Jase shook his head again, still smiling, then, a moment later, asked softly, "What are you thinking about? It's like you're . . . shining."

What could Aisha say? That she'd found her forever home? Him, the rock that she'd always be able to rest on, regardless of whatever storm she found herself in? Yes, all that and more, but she settled for, "I'm just happy. Unbelievably, totally, completely *happy*."

Jase stopped walking. "Me too," he said softly. He pressed his mouth against hers in one of his trademark long sweet kisses that made every part of her body hum with love and desire. Tingling, dizzying joy and sureness welled up in her. River's Sigh B & B would witness countless stories and adventures as the future unfolded, but whatever those stories ended up being, or how much or little a part she played in them, she knew she was in exactly the place she—and her growing family—was supposed to be. It wasn't that she no longer had fears about the future or about potential loss, but rather that she realized there was no catch, no dark side, to loving or letting yourself be loved. Love was The Catch, the thing to seek. Loss and change were unavoidable parts of life, and it was only love, the memories of its old incarnations and the promise of new, that helped you survive. That gave you comfort. That made you strong. That filled you with crazy, unexplainable joy and optimism. And she was so unbelievably fortunate. Her whole life had been fuelled and shaped by love, even when she'd been unaware of it.

"We're having a baby," she blurted, unable to keep it to herself one second longer. The special night would still be special. *Beyond* special.

"What?"

"I'm pregnant."

Jase stared, as if waiting for a punchline. When one didn't come, he whooped, scooped her up, and swung her around in huge circles of wordless excitement. And even when Aisha's feet rested on the leaf-jewelled ground again, her love for him twirled on and on and on.

They walked past Jase's old cabin, now aptly named The Catch—Gee, how had she ever come up with that?—and then they were in front of *their* new place, hand-built by Jase and Colton. Its wraparound verandah had a bench swing piled high with blankets and four rocking chairs sat in a half circle near a big stone fireplace, so they could enjoy porch life all year round. Grapevines strung with tiny twinkling lights climbed the railings and beckoned them up the stairs and in for the night. Before they rounded up Mo and the dogs, however, they stopped and shared another kiss—this time in front of the cheery hand-carved cedar sign that set their cozy abode apart from the rest of the cabins at River's Sigh. "Home" was all it said.

Dear Reader,

Thank you so much for coming along with me on my many River's Sigh B & B jaunts. I hope you enjoyed Aisha's coming of age story (and adored Jase) as much I did and do. I have to admit writing *The Catch* was bittersweet for me. I can't believe the series is "officially" finished—and by that I just mean that all the main characters you met in Book 1, *Wedding Bands*, have had their own stories, along with several guests along the way. It's the end of an era! Thankfully though, endings in one aspect of life often mean new beginnings somewhere else . . . and happily, that is very true here.

Several early readers commented on The Second Chance Shop, saying how intrigued they were by it, that they wanted to visit it, and to know more . . . Well, how very convenient! I was hoping that would be the case because—insert drum roll!—The Second Chance Shop will be its own series, kicking off with Madeline's story. Look for it early 2021!

Want to connect? Yay! Please visit www.evbishop. com, where you can sign up for my newsletter, and/or find me on Facebook, follow my Twitter feed (Ev_Bishop), or drop me a line at evbishop@ evbishop.com. I'd love to hear from you! And on a similar note, reviews really help authors. If you'd be so kind as to leave a few words on Amazon, GoodReads, your blog, Facebook, or anywhere else you hang out when your nose isn't in a book, I'd be very grateful.

Thank you so much for reading!

Wishing you love, laughter and adventure—inside the pages and out,
☺ Ev

About the Author

Ev Bishop is an award-winning author, who lives and writes in a remote small town in wildly beautiful British Columbia, Canada, a place that inspires the settings for her cozy contemporary romances.

She is shocked (in the very best of ways) to have twelve published novels under her belt because writing stories for a living has been her fantasy job ever since she was a very little girl—like so young that she couldn't even print yet! Dreams do come true.

Ev is a weird (and delightful!) combination of complete, head-in-the-clouds, always dreaming romantic, and hard slogging, fish gutting, survivalist-pragmatist.

In addition to writing novels, Ev was a long-time newspaper columnist with the *Terrace Standard* and is a prolific scribbler of articles, essays, short stories and poems.

She hopes you enjoy her books immensely. She is, after all, writing them for you!